PENGUIN BOOKS

HOW TO HUNGER

Grace Chia is an author of over ten books of prose and poetry. She has been nominated for the Mslexia Novel Competition and Epigram Books Fiction Prize longlists and shortlisted for the Singapore Literature Prize (Poetry) and Singapore Book Awards, the latter for her Penguin Random House novel, *The Arches of Gerrard Street*. Her other novels are *The Wanderlusters* and *White Cloud Mountain*. Her poetry collections are *Mother of All Questions*, *Cordelia*, and *Womango*, from which her poems have been used in classroom teaching. In her free time, she enjoys baking or watching cat videos.

ADVANCE PRAISE FOR *HOW TO HUNGER*

'A magnificent collection, ravenous with longing, radiant with life . . . Chia's voice is unforgettable and her sympathies become, in these tales, their own superpower.'

Junot Díaz, author of Pulitzer Prize winner
The Brief Wondrous Life of Oscar Wao

'Grace Chia practices sorcery. Her masterful command of the language is a spell all storytellers aspire to cast. This mesmerising collection of short stories demands that all mobile devices be switched off and the bedroom door locked, for no interruptions must be tolerated.'

Sebastian Sim, author of Epigram Books Fiction
Prize winner *The Riot Act*

'Like the best of her poetry, Grace Chia's short stories cut to the quick of what matters: What makes the soul tick, itch and hunger? An incisive, insightful read.'

Felix Cheong, poet and graphic novelist
of *The Showgirl and the Minister*

How to Hunger

Grace Chia

PENGUIN BOOKS

An imprint of Penguin Random House

PENGUIN BOOKS

USA | Canada | UK | Ireland | Australia
New Zealand | India | South Africa | China | Southeast Asia

Penguin Books is part of the Penguin Random House group of companies
whose addresses can be found at global.penguinrandomhouse.com

Published by Penguin Random House SEA Pte. Ltd
9, Changi South Street 3, Level 08-01,
Singapore 486361

First published in Penguin Books by Penguin Random House SEA 2023

Copyright © Grace Chia 2023

ISBN 9789815127836

Typeset in Adobe Caslon Pro by MAP Systems, Bengaluru, India

www.penguin.sg

Contents

Chapter 1

The Cuckoo Conundrum

Standing at the topmost floor of Marina Bay Sands, my cousin, Raymond, asked me, So . . . do you miss home?

A sea of charcoal grey sketched in with a gleaming silhouette of uneven towering blocks, their windows squeegee clean, cars and roads blinking like crystals. All was aglow and kaleidoscopic. Streets so bright at night they had to be safe.

My panoramic eye captured this. A museum shaped like an open palm. An intestinal bridge incandescent like diamonds. A hotel with colonnades resembling a pipe organ. Minutiae Monopoly houses lined along the river's edge. A ring of blue fire. Twinned metallic eyes of a fly ogling at the night sky, indignant and proud.

I can't miss what I don't recognize, I said to Raymond frankly.

He smirked. It was hard to tell in the dark whether he was being ironic, in agreement or expressing disdain.

Somewhere, there was a corporate party. The throb of a staccato bass of some danceable tune synced with a gimmicky light show, its rotating lasers of blue-green-yellow cutting the dark like light sabres fighting the battle for the few, remaining stars on the yet unconquered sky.

This was what I saw. A vision of Gotham; a metropolis of wealth and urbanity above the ground.

This was what I imagined. An unseen, meandering underground of subterranean species scurrying beneath, living hand to mouth, dirt in their bellies, limbs moving faster than the mind, always hungry, always waiting to surface for air.

You've been away for too long, he replied in a tone I thought sounded reproachful. Maybe I was being paranoid.

I made a family, I said. My husband has a job that isn't here.

A lot has happened, you know, he said. We go on, unlike some people.

After, he took me to Race Course Road for fish head curry, and I pretended not to be offended by the tone and choice of words he left me puzzled over. Who were 'we'? What does it mean to 'go on'? What's the contrarian logic of that? Not to go on, to give up, quit? And who are the 'some people' he was referring to? Me? The segment of the population who had decided to live overseas? Regardless of reasons?

Does it boil down to this? The stayers versus the leavers? The fighters versus the quitters? The patriots versus the exiles?

Is it a testament of the largeness of one's love to the nation which option one chooses?

If you leave home, does it mean you love home less?

Even if you dream of home nightly? Even if each scoop of rice you swallow reminds you of the motherland? Even if every utterance of your country to someone foreign, whether they are white, black, beige or brown, is tinged with regret, nostalgia and pride?

When I left Raymond and headed back to my parent's house in the heartlands of my country to put my head down on the bed of my adolescence, in a three-metre cubed room where my child was sound asleep in a cot, the curry and ghee in my stomach wreaked havoc. I couldn't sleep. I was heartburnt.

* * *

The burping kept him awake. The pain, unabated even with antacids, was lodged somewhere along the path from his chest to his throat. When he had asked for extra hot, Raymond was trying to one-up his cousin. Toughen the girl up, he thought, all those years of living abroad and eating fish and chips and cold salads. He was convinced that what he had assumed was her predominant non-spicy Western diet must have softened her ability to consume fiery Southeast Asian cuisine.

It was true, in some aspect, except she had spent the last six years in Manchester, where South Asian curries were the norm rather than the exception; albeit a bastardized version marrying dual cultures.

Still, the signature fish head curry they had ordered decimated their guts and bowels.

The entire Sunday he spent recuperating on the toilet meant his wife had to manage the three kids, including an overactive baby girl. Their domestic helper was out for her weekly day off, and Mei Li was not amused by her husband's inconsiderately timed, hedonistic Saturday night spent gallivanting with god-knows-who.

Are you going to help out today or not? Mei Li grumbled loudly.

Raymond groaned. His stomach contracted again.

Yes, yes, later, okay?

It's three o'clock already! When later?

I don't feel good.

What did you do last night? You know I can't manage the kids all on my own!

Send them to your mother's then!

She is busy, okay? Why don't you ask your mother to help out?

She cannot! Her leg can't walk! Raymond tried his best to out-shout his wife despite his suffering. He meant, She can't walk or Her leg can't move, but diarrhoea and dehydration had the effect of butchering up his language syntax and logic. As long as he got the message across, Raymond didn't give a rat's ass.

Meanwhile, his eldest daughter, who was eight, was fighting with his six-year-old son. There was screeching and the sound of something breaking.

What are you two doing?!? Mei Li shrieked. Her larynx hurt.

The baby started crying, her sibling contribution to the assortment of sounds. Upstairs, a neighbour had decided Sunday was a good time to renovate their shelving. Drilling and hammering ensued.

When Mei Li had finished separating the two older kids, each now whimpering, the drilling had stopped just in time for someone's car alarm to go off in the multi-storey car park.

Later, Mei Li found her husband lying on the bed, pale-faced and immobile. She was too busy today to empathize with him.

Have you taken Po Chi Wan? Mei Li asked irritably, referring to the anti-diarrhoeal pills from Hong Kong.

I don't know . . . where is it? Raymond said weakly.

His wife produced it from the kitchen and threw it on the bed beside him. The baby resumed his wailing when the drilling upstairs restarted.

Alamak, Mei Li cursed and rushed to her baby, cajoling and patting her close to her bosom.

The phone rang. Her eldest picked up the phone.

Hello?

Hello! Who is this? The caller said.

Chun Yan.

Oh! This is Auntie Sandra. Where is your Daddy?

Daddy sleeping, I think.

Mei Li took the phone over from her daughter. Her baby kept silent, eavesdropping.

Hello? Mei Li said loudly.

This is Sandra. Is this Mei Li?

Yes? Mei Li grew suspicious. Was this the woman who had partied with her husband last night?

I'm Raymond's cousin. Sandra.

Oh! The one from London?

Not London. Manchester. How are you?

Oh . . . Sandra! Mei Li was relieved, glad there had been no horseplay after all. You're in Singapore now?

Yes. For a month. I was thinking if your family wants to meet up.

Sure! Mei Li replied, distracted by the baby as she tried to grab the phone receiver.

Great! Is Raymond around? I can arrange with him. I'm looking forward to seeing all of you.

Same here. Raymond!

Mei Li shouted for her husband. From the bedroom, she could hear him respond just as loud. What?!?

Phone! It's your cousin!

Raymond groaned, both from the bodily discomfort and the realization that he would have to pretend-play the heroic host again soon.

His body was not as strong as his mind had wanted it to be. What else could he do to outperform as tourist guide to a visiting countrywoman? How else could he show that he knew his Singapore more than she did?

For his own belly surrendered to the curry more than Sandra had—a fact she didn't tell him. Her life in a different environment had taught her to stomach a much stronger taste for life; and he would never want to embarrass himself by revealing his incapacitation at the hands of a curried local dish he had insisted on treating her to. He asked Sandra if she enjoyed the dinner last night, to which she exaggerated the merits of its worth; and he acquiesced just the same, even if he couldn't stand properly that afternoon with cramps worse than his wife's monthly blues.

Chilli crabs next time? Raymond offered brightly. The more expensive a dish, the more generous a host he would appear to his guest.

Maybe otah? I haven't had one for years.

You can get that anywhere!

Sometimes I miss the simple things, you know, Sandra admitted.

I'll buy you a dozen then.

How about if I come over to your house?

Not restaurant? Food is better there. My maid knows only how to make simple dishes. My wife can only boil water, Raymond said, chuckling.

Don't worry, anything is fine with me, Sandra said then added, I can cook!

You?!? Raymond snorted with a laugh. Last time when we were hostelites at Eusoff Hall, you burnt the chicken wings until they were black!

Hey, that was a long time ago. I've gotten better since.

It was true that Sandra had improved her culinary skills since she moved abroad eight years ago. It was the only way to save money on eating out and to satisfy her craving for Singaporean dishes. Britain wasn't like Singapore, where a few dollars at a kopitiam, food court or hawker centre could satisfy a tummy with a sizable carb-filled meal. After a few thrilling trips to the fish and chips takeaway shops in her neighbourhood, she loathed her limited choices of deep-fried cod and vinegar-doused greasy fries for meals.

Moreover, the takeaway Asian shops selling Chinese and Thai food were over-saturated with MSG; or were variations of something always wok fried with frozen-thawed chicken, rough cut onions, unplucked beansprouts and the gravy an indiscernible, cornstarchy concoction. Even the Indian takeaways tasted different from the ones she had in Singapore. Sometimes better, sometimes undecidedly foreign—even to an immigrant like Sandra who was from Asia, married to a Mancunian with a Scouser dad and a Geordie mum. From korma to vindaloo to balti to jalfrezi to tikka masala, all variations of curries made and customized in Britain that Sandra had to adjust her taste buds to. It took her years to get used to them. But her tongue needed the spice; it became her monthly fix, her 1,500-calorie dense lamb and pilau rice addiction to tide over her brunch hunger.

I can cook curry! Sandra offered to Raymond.

The kids don't eat curry. Just come over. We can *ta pau* from the *zi char*, Raymond said, implying they could do takeaways from the neighbourhood hawker stalls, adding, The maid can make fried rice. Steam fish? Anything lah.

Sure. 6 p.m.?

At dinnertime, Sandra arrived at a war zone. Raymond's eldest and second child were screaming at each other. The baby had upset a bowl of pumpkin puree on the floor and was crawling in an orange puddle, soiling her white Petit Bateau onesie. The maid was running from the kitchen with paper towels to clean up the mess while the wok in the kitchen was roaring at full flame; the exhaust hood hoarse and deafening with the fan at maximum speed. The television was cranked up too loud with *Phineas and Ferb* while Raymond hollered at Child One, Two and Three to behave, and a woman, presumably his wife, was noisily blow-drying her hair in the living room. The wall clock chimed six rounds of Cuckoo! Cuckoo! as an animated wooden bird popped in and out of a trap door merrily.

Sandra had her one-year-old strapped to her back in an Ergobaby carrier when Raymond opened the door. With a ten-kilo weight clutching onto her aching shoulders and her posture starting to sag, Sandra stood awkwardly in front of her cousin hoping she could enter his apartment immediately to offload her child. But he was blocking her way. She forced a smile, despite the discomfort.

SAY SORRY! Raymond turned his head towards the interior of his house and shouted to someone, presumably one of his kids before quickly recovering. He took stock of his cousin at the door—a petite woman with a baby too large to be piggybacked at this age. He moved aside to let them in, sweeping one arm with a grandiose gesture. Hello! Welcome!

Sandra closed the metal gate behind her. The legs of her child, Emily, swung briskly behind her; she gurgled.

Hello, excuse the mess! Mei Li yelled and put down the hair dryer on the side table, Come on in!

Long time no see, Sandra said and, with a sigh of relief, squatted down where she unbuckled the carrier and let loose her infant gingerly onto the floor.

Emily stood with an unsteady gait; her chubby feet eager to explore. Within seconds, she spotted a stuffed yellow and brown spotted giraffe in a corner and barrelled towards it. Raymond's baby, who was eight months old, looked wide-eyed as Emily grabbed her precious toy and she immediately started to cry.

Emily! Don't touch! Sandra called out. Her arms reached out to stop her daughter.

It's okay, Girl-Girl, share-share! Mei Li cajoled her own infant.

What ensued was a tug-of-war between two baby girls for a giraffe while both mothers tried various lies and distractions to cease the fight. Eventually, Mei Li's baby won by yanking the toy towards her so hard its tail tore from the stitch. Sandra gasped.

Girl-Girl! Oi! Mei Li cried out.

Off the infant went with a screeching wail, a giraffe with a broken tail, and a mother who wouldn't put up with a child's display of violence. Sandra watched the door to a room close, and much muffled chastising heard.

Time to eat! Raymond announced.

Child One came to the dining table willingly. She sat there like a queen while the maid cut up pieces of fried chicken to bite-sized morsels. I want ice! she ordered, and the maid swiftly dashed in and out of the kitchen procuring the ice. I want orange juice! Again, the mad dashing.

Sandra didn't know where to put her child. She had fed Emily mashed avocadoes and some milk before she came, so really, the infant only needed to be playing someplace safe. Raymond offered the play gym. Sandra agreed, and off Emily went on the fabric mat exploring the hanging toys, tugging and shaking the curved arches of the play gym till the music came on.

As Sandra took her seat, Mei Li came and joined her, pulling along Child Two to his usual seat. Child One was already guzzling down her meal while Child Two sat sulking, glaring at his father, not interested in the food in front of him.

Don't want to eat? No dessert for you later, Raymond warned his son. That elicited no response.

Hurry up, eat! Later will be cold! Mei Li chided. Sandra, come, help yourself!

Sandra took some chicken, fish and kailan. She stole a peek at Emily who was deliriously pleased with her new activity.

Where's your husband? Mei Li asked Sandra, in-between making dagger eyes at her defiant picky eater.

He's in the UK, Sandra replied. He has to work.

You came here by yourself? Mei Li asked, incredulous.

Yes.

You flew here with a baby by yourself?!?

Yes. It's not that bad. She sleeps a lot on the plane.

Mei Li declared, almost too loud, We haven't been overseas since Chun Yan was born! I can't imagine flying with kids. Oh my goodness! After that, I had Chun Rong and now, Chun Fang. Also, I work full-time. Seven years . . . haven't sat on a plane. I'm starting to have a seven-year itch!

Mei Li chortled at her own joke. Raymond laughed nervously. Sandra smiled wryly. She watched her child explore an alien environment, her infant arms as ivory pale as the off-white marble tiles of the living room floor.

The adults chitchatted as dinner progressed. The eldest child finished her food and drink and went to the sofa, where she lounged indolently watching cartoons. Raymond scolded her about not finishing her homework, reminding her about missing her violin practice. The picky eater was still chewing slowly, eyes plastered to the TV screen from where he was seated, half his uneaten dinner cold while being surrounded by fallen rice and vegetables strewn around him, both on the table and the floor. Raymond scolded him about the mess. The maid hurriedly cleaned up the spillage.

When the doorbell rang, it was a woman with a thick Putonghua accent there to give Chinese tuition to the two older kids. The picky eater gleefully got off the dining chair. The eldest managed a mournful expression. The three of them vanished into the kids' room.

Mei Li had fetched her baby and seated her on a highchair, spooning a fresh bowl of pumpkin puree into the baby's mouth. The child gobbled like a frog.

When the cuckoo clock chimed nine times, Sandra knew it was time to go. Emily was fussing from being sleepy and hungry. Sandra bade her farewells.

Thanks for dinner! Sandra said with as much sincerity as she could muster. For someone who had only one child, bearing witness to a family with three kids was quite revelatory, to say the least. She was exhausted just watching the shenanigans and shouting matches.

Come and visit us in Manchester, we have a guest room, Sandra continued. She realized a family of this size would need *rooms*, not *a room*.

Raymond's grateful face lit up with joy. Sure! Sure! he enthused at her gesture. He interrupted the tuition class, Girl-Girl, Boy-Boy, say bye-bye to Auntie Sandra!

Bye bye, Chun Yan said, appearing at the doorway and mustering some enthusiasm.

Bye bye, Chun Rong parroted, popping his head out of the room.

Bye bye! Mei Li called out, holding her baby's arm and waving it cheerfully.

Bye bye, the maid said by way of courtesy, appearing and disappearing into the kitchen again.

Sandra was glad to leave, in a way, for the everyday routine of the Singaporean family in the heartlands was something she had escaped. Tuition, music lessons, homework upon homework, the small apartments, the working parents, the maid issue. How could one cope in such a claustrophobic, pressure cooker?

* * *

Emily slept most of the way on the plane, snugly strapped into the baby bassinet in front of my seat, safely mummified in position. My thighs were squashed and trapped underneath. I knocked off and woke up repeatedly, neck aching from the awkward positioning of the seat.

Only a few weeks of acclimatizing to the tropical humidity had warmed my insides and defrosted my inner soul. I was glad to bring back a roasted tan to the thick of a January English winter. It was my badge of national pride. I had been back to my hood and had the skin tone to show it off. It might have been a borrowed summer; but having been infused with the herbs, spices and aromas of an earth from a different continent, I felt fortified, renewed and youthful, briefly forgetting what I had left behind in chilly climes.

A husband I hadn't missed in the weeks that I went home.

The reason he hadn't followed us to Singapore had nothing to do with work. He detested the heat. Loathed humidity even more. He had a thousand complaints about the country where I was born.

To be fair, he hadn't lived in Singapore before. Merely visited twice in five years. He'd read all about the inequalities, the governance, the inflating cost of living. He'd rejected every attempt of mine to live and work there.

We had a house in the suburbs of Burnage, two-storey high with three bedrooms and a guestroom, and four cats that roamed and shat in our backyard garden. He worked as a cartographer for the *Greater Manchester A-Z Street Atlas*.

How can I get a job in Singapore? he bemoaned each time I broached the subject.

I couldn't disagree. Still I insisted and badgered him, using my move to Europe as a sacrifice to guilt him into consent.

How can I afford housing? A million dollars for a flat? Where would I find that kind of money? he argued convincingly.

I couldn't deny the facts. Still, I used rhetoric to make a point about our daughter needing to know about her maternal culture: Emily with her large hazel-jade eyes and her alabaster complexion.

How can I leave my family now? My mother is sick. My dad is eighty. Who's going to care for them if I'm gone?

I shut up after that. I was thirty-four. Clifford was almost fifty, and his parents were much older geriatrics than mine. I had the moral obligation of filial piety to my in-laws as much as he did. That was my cultural ethos. As an ethnic Chinese, some vestigial Confucianism of my heritage bade me to put the needs of my immediate family above mine. As for him, a blue-eyed Westerner—and an only child to top it off—his egotistical right to pleasing himself was above the whims of someone else. Even to the woman he had married.

But somehow, despite all my grouses, I was drawn to England, to the man I had chosen to share my bed and fate with. Each time I left, it sucked me back in; so, this way, I flip-flopped my loyalties between two cities and nations with as much ferocious ambivalence as I possibly could. I had roots in both shores. I had spliced my heart and left two halves in two houses.

What was a good honest woman to do? Leave her progeny in the nest of another? Like the cuckoo conundrum? Both places were homes, and both were not. I belonged to both, and I did not. And the most depressing part of all, this which I could not control, was that I had inadvertently cursed my mixed-blood cross-cultural bi-continental child. She would feel the rootlessness far worse than I did.

It was then, in the dark of the flight cabin, as I heard the slightest baby snore from my infant, a pulsating muscle of mass I had given life to and nurtured, I decided I would try harder as a mother and wife.

I was homesick constantly, but home is where the heart is, wasn't it? I could try to rid my heart of this sickness, be at home in the present, this gap between there and here, wherever this shifting space might be, and try, try my darndest to make it work.

* * *

Raymond was sick of home, which was the reason he used work as an excuse to get away. When the secondment came up, he suggested to his boss he was the right man for the job no matter where it was—Sydney, New York, Tokyo, London or Vancouver. But not Timbuktu. That would be too far and too foreign for him.

They sent him to Cologne in Germany. It was a sizable city, so he could navigate the place even without speaking a word of German. That was for two months.

Next, they sent him to Marseilles, colourful, bustling and seafaring. He survived without speaking a word of French and put on ten kilos. That was for four months.

Finally, the company sent him to London. He thought he had struck gold. He imagined his side trips, the excursions, the touristic sightseeing he would pack it all in during his one-year work attachment. Wembley Stadium. Buckingham Palace. Madame Tussauds. Big Ben. Harrods. London Bridge. And being a diehard Arsenal fan, he would purchase all the red-white paraphernalia he could find.

Raymond imagined that he would be so busy with work and play he wouldn't have enough time to rest. Much to do. Much to take in. Like a paid holiday from his tedious routine and his everyday responsibilities in Singapore. Cheap beer and unlimited fish and chips. The stockpile of Twinings tea he would need to lug back for his colleagues. The Harrods merchandise his wife would expect. Everyone back in Singapore with their two cents' worth about what to buy and see and where he should visit when he gets to ol' Blighty.

He couldn't wait. Some remaining, misplaced colonial pride swells in his heart at the thought of spending time in the motherland of his native island.

What Raymond wasn't prepared for was how lonely he would get.

He didn't spell it out, but his cousin got the message. At first, when he had arrived to the UK, he emailed and texted Sandra sporadically once a week. He was considerate enough to know that she was manning a child and was solely in charge of domestic duties; while he, freed of parental responsibilities, was living largely in the style of a bachelor. Three months on, some unwavering depression seeped into Raymond's consciousness when initially he had thought it was homesickness that plagued him or existential angst about being a middle-aged salary serf. Sometimes he would call Sandra just to feel less alone.

Why don't you go for a short holiday? Sandra suggested, while her three-year old was squealing in the backdrop.

Hmph, Raymond grunted.

It's cheap. Fly budget. Cyprus or Spain. Or take the Eurostar and go for a daytrip. Have you been to Paris?

Don't feel like it.

Sandra wanted to suggest that Raymond ask his wife and family to accompany him, but they were continents away, and he didn't seem to mention them much lately. Each time she brought up their names, he would dismiss their existence with They're fine.

Come up to Manchester then. Just take the train, Sandra offered.

Really? Raymond brightened up at the idea.

So they made plans. Raymond was to pay Sandra's family a visit during the long bank holiday weekend in two weeks' time. She waited for him to call and say I'm here! but that never happened. I had overtime work, Raymond drawled.

They made plans for another visit a month later. Again, Raymond did a no-show. I had a bad migraine, he asserted.

Sandra started getting worried. He had stopped calling her.

Raymond, are you okay? Sandra called him on a day the weather plunged to seven degrees Celsius in spring.

Sure, her cousin mumbled back.

You don't sound okay. Are you sick? Sandra was trying to imply 'mentally' and hoped he got the message.

Just busy.

Look, I can come down to London and see you.

No need.

I haven't been to London for a few years. It will be nice for Emily. Her first visit.

Don't come.

And amidst some incoherent grumble, Raymond hung up. That strengthened Sandra's resolve to drop by and check on her cousin.

Now that Emily was three, travelling was easier and more predictable for Sandra. Her child still took naps and could be entertained with crayons and paper, sticker wads, plastic gadgets and could nibble at pint-sized portions of the adult food Sandra was eating. No more purees or mash or a special infant diet. In the last two years, the family had made weekend trips to the Lake District and Brighton beach, which gave Sandra the confidence to take her munchkin out of their suburban comfort zone, even without elaborate meal planning.

With Clifford down from his annual hay fever relapse, it would be a solo parenting trip for Sandra—not that she hasn't survived one, and yes, she was resourceful and capable enough—so, pumped up with adrenaline, she and her little girl trotted off to the British capital, both just as excited.

On the train, Sandra tried calling her cousin, but he didn't answer the phone. She tried to text him once, but her telco had a weak reception when the train went through the tunnel. After, Emily complained of hunger and that was that. Sandra had more pressing matters to attend to. She reminded herself to call him when the train pulled into Euston station. But she forgot, amidst the chiding of her child for making a mess of crumbs, taking her to wee in the stinking train toilet, and then mother-and-daughter taking a quick half-hour nap as the train trundled on the uneven and bumpy rail tracks. By the time they arrived at their destination, Sandra's start of her London daytrip was starting to feel like the end of a tiring, overstretched long weekend.

Sandra yawned as she dug for the Post-it that she had scribbled Raymond's address on. 3 Lordship Terrace. She hailed the first black cab that came along.

She rang the doorbell.

Who is this? A woman's voice piped.

Sandra's initial doubts about her sudden, intrusive trip dissipated. A busy mom like her had forgotten the correct civil behaviour between adults, and even though her intent for a surprise visit was to cheer up her cousin, she knew better than to drop by unannounced. But she needn't have worried. Raymond's wife was in town!

Hello Mei Li! This is Sandra!

Who?

The question baffled her.

Who is this? Raymond's voice came over the intercom.

Sandra. Is this Raymond?

Sandra?

Yes. I'm here with Emily. Can we come up?

There was a long pause, so long and silent went the intercom that Sandra heard the quarrel between two squirrels on the tree nearest to her. A large seed catapulted from the branch, bounced off the ground close to Emily and hit a stray weed. Emily was supremely excited. Mummy, kuirrel, look!

Then the door buzzed. Sandra pushed the heavy door and let her child in first. They walked up two flights of stairs to the first floor. Raymond stood standing in the open doorway with a barely concealed unhappy face. Sandra forced a big smile. That wasn't what she had expected.

Sorry I didn't call first, Sandra opened the conversation. I tried calling but couldn't get you.

So sudden, Sandra. Never mind.

Say hello to Uncle, Sandra prodded her daughter.

Hello Un-kle.

Wah, so big now! Raymond bent down and patted Emily's head. Come in, so cold outside.

Sandra stepped into the centrally heated one-bed apartment. It looked neat, with basic furnishings, khaki curtains, black furniture and white walls, and plenty of exposed connecting wires to electronic devices. Huge speakers on the floor flanked the TV screen. A desktop computer with a printer-scanner, hard drives, console, tablet. Two laptops connected to speakers and more peripherals. Architect lamp. Floor lamp. Lava lamp. A small fish tank lit up with blue LED lights and gurgling with popping bubbles. A digital photo frame tweening with pictures of his wife and kids.

You hungry? Raymond asked distractedly, not looking at Sandra.

A bit. Quite thirsty. Can we have warm water?

Sandra made her way to a two-seater sofa where a magazine was strewn carelessly on the seat cushion; she removed it and sank her bottom heavily into the chair. Raymond entered his tiny kitchenette. There were whispers and a few curt words her ears couldn't pick up. Emily went straight for the aquarium, leaving oily thumbprints on the glass tank.

Raymond emerged with two mugs of warm water and a young girl. She looked eighteen. Her pink metallic spectacles framed her squinty eyes.

Sandra, this is Cherrie. My . . . friend. Sandra's my cousin. She lives in Manchester, Raymond told the young lady.

Cherrie shifted awkwardly and smiled.

Hi, was all Sandra could say there and then.

It turned out that Cherrie was Singaporean and twenty-four, a PhD student at the University of Greenwich studying Computing and Mathematical Sciences. A meek and quiet exterior belies the brains beneath, Sandra thought.

Raymond's 'friend' was quick to avoid Sandra and turned her attentions to Emily, who was pleased to have a playmate. Cherrie let the child feed the fishes. Inside the tiny aquarium and the small rectangular water surface, the fish flakes Emily sprinkled were fought over vigorously by one hungry mouth and another. The bigger fishes elbowed out the smaller ones while the more aggressive ones finished the largest flakes. The two girls giggled. At the end, a thin dusty layer of leftover fish food blanketed the water surface and the littlest fishes cleaned up the scene, foraging through the soggy leftovers.

Have some muffins. Cherrie made them, Raymond said, offering a tray of blueberry muffins that looked tempting.

Emily took one and proceeded to gnaw away at her tea treat. Sandra took one too. It tasted amazing.

Your muffins are really good, Sandra said to Cherrie.

Thanks! Cherrie beamed gratefully.

Sandra wanted to ask Raymond about his situation but it wasn't the right timing. Social pleasantries needed to be performed first.

How long have you been in the UK? Sandra asked the student.

Three years. I did my master's here too.

All the time in London?

Yes.

Sandra wanted to ask about how and when she and Raymond had met, but she didn't know how to frame the questions without sounding rude.

We met a month ago, Raymond said, anticipating her curiosity.

Oh, Sandra replied, making it sound easy-breezy.

She's been . . . helpful. With my . . . research, Raymond added clumsily.

What research? Sandra persisted.

She's a computing specialist. My company has issues with the software engineering that I don't know what the problem is.

Oh. That's great. She works for your company now?

No. She's offering her services for free.

From where Sandra was sitting, she could see Cherrie cringe. Raymond's awkward response had its double entendre effect that all of them could infer.

Sandra stood up and explored the living room. On the window sill were three potted plants. Two of them had pink and yellow blooms. The third was a prickly cactus.

Pretty plants, Sandra said.

They are Cherrie's idea, she takes care of them, Raymond replied. The aquarium too.

You bought them? Sandra asked Cherrie.

Yes. To brighten the room. Not so lonely looking.

Sandra darted eyes at her cousin. He was gazing at his bespectacled friend with what looked like smiling eyes.

Finally, Sandra had to ask, How's your family, Raymond?

He looked at his dining table and responded, Fine, Good.

Sorry I came unannounced. I thought you were depressed, Sandra blurted out.

Cherrie swiftly popped into the kitchen. The kettle started to rumble and boil.

Raymond peered sadly at his cousin and sighed.

I was. Still am, he admitted.

What's going on? Sandra was annoyed and showed her displeasure.

Nothing.

Don't tell me nothing. I know it's something.

What are you trying to say, Sandra? Raymond looked at her with a deep sense of hurt.

Your friend? Seriously?

Yes. She's my friend.

You have a wife! Three kids! Sandra hissed, making sure only he could hear it.

She's a friend. Where's your husband? Raymond diverted the questioning.

He's not feeling well. He's, as far as I know, alone at home in bed.

The afternoon wore off in a kind of animated and hazy charade all three adults knew how to perform. Emily was the bright spark that glued them with a naivety that eased the tension. From the fish to the plants to YouTube videos of *Timmy Time*, Emily's attention span was spread over the different facets of Raymond's small and temporary apartment, a house he had to spend the duration of one year before his sojourn was complete and he had to head back to Singapore.

Three hours later of reminiscing over Singaporean food the adults had missed, it was close to six in the evening. Almost dinnertime.

Are you staying for dinner? Raymond asked Sandra, his mood having settled by then.

We need to head back.

But you need to eat, Cherrie said. I have chicken thighs and bak choi in the fridge. I can cook fast.

Sandra didn't know what to say to that. It was true. Emily needed dinner. Her train was at 8 p.m. anyway. It was sensible to eat then leave. A mother's instinct.

That means I'll have eaten at your place twice, Sandra said to Raymond. You have to come to my place once. I'll make you nasi lemak with sambal belacan chilli.

Cherrie can make that too, Raymond laughed mildly, sounding almost proud.

After dinner, as Cherrie was loading the dishwasher, Sandra packed her belongings to go. It had been a tiring day. Time to catch the train back.

It was good seeing you, cousin, Raymond said. I'm glad you came.

Same here. I was worried for you.

I was in a bad place, you know.

Was?

Now, much better, Raymond said sheepishly.

Raymond . . . , Sandra had to broach the inevitable, deliberating over her word choices. Please. Be careful.

Can you do me a favour? Raymond pleaded.

What?

Don't tell Mei Li.

About what? Sandra pretended not to understand her cousin.

About . . .

I don't know what this is. Is this something to be concerned about?

No. No. Forget it.

But Sandra couldn't forget it. Not on the way to Manchester to her house. Not when she lay down to sleep on the bed next to her wheezing husband. Not a week later when she made her own homemade muffins that were unequal to what a twenty-something had concocted. Not a month later when she got Emily her first goldfish that lasted three months and died floating face up, googly-eyed and bloated. Not nine months later when she realized that Raymond would have completed his work stint and gone back to Singapore.

She never talked to him again. He never called or texted or emailed. A cousin forgotten and blotted out by time, geography and purposeful erasure on both sides of the globe. Wistfully, Sandra assumed Raymond had gone back to the place of his origin, having swapped one maternal figure for another, raising children instead of fishes and plants and electronica; while she herself pondered on and off how England was treating her, and whether she liked it or not.

Her answers invariably depended on the weather. Most days she wished she was in someplace hotter, where she wouldn't have to pile on three layers before she dashed off round the corner for milk and bread, the basic necessities to sate her hunger. Other days, she was content, not minding the chilly placidity, the vast green swathes of fields, the uncrowded sidewalks, the mellow traffic, the variable seasons. Where she raised her offspring became a factor towards how Sandra viewed her environment. Like Emily, they were both outsiders and insiders of two countries. She had to teach her daughter how to cope and adapt her temperament to the differences of cultures without losing a sense of her own person.

One day, flash forward, Sandra would have to ask her daughter the same question when Emily grew up and moved miles or cities or oceans away. So . . . do you miss home?

Chapter 2

Galaxies

I suppose now we have to speak in code. The lazy fox jumped over the quick brown dog, he whispered.

What? Wait a minute, I said, doing a double take.

He smiled broadly, showing zero teeth.

Isn't it supposed to be . . . ?

Have you boiled the chicken head yet? he asked cagily.

The WHAT???

The snow will fall soon. Come in and take the clocks out.

Okaaaay . . . I get that you are speaking in code. But this is gibberish. How on earth will I know what is code for what? I protested.

The spider has caught a bug. Let the impregnation begin.

Alright, enough. Can you be serious for one minute. Stop this charade.

My galaxy is bigger than your galaxy. I could destroy yours with a sneeze, he continued, eyes dancing.

You've got an iPhone. I've got this.

At that, I whipped out my Samsung Galaxy smartphone, parading it in front of him. It was bigger, glitzier, had more icons. I still got lost trying to navigate between pages, finding files saved an hour ago, for it was, after all, a galaxy.

Jump on the solar system, sucker. Our systems don't match, I said, with aplomb.

No, we don't. Thank god. We were the forerunners; we started it all. Yours is just a copycat. Size doesn't matter when you don't have the muscle to back it up, he answered then swelled his chest out.

He was right. In the history of mobile telecommunications, the hippies started the trend of smartphones. But it took the dorks a very short time to reinvent the rules to make the gadgets better, bigger, faster. In the modern computerized world, it was always about who was fastest, whose reflexes were better and who could cut through liquid air like a torpedo. Today, we are in an age of code speak, of abbreviated language and indeterminate identities; from text messaging shorthand, chat acronyms, emoji, teen speak and cyberslang to social media personas that have become hard to distinguish fact from fiction.

Still, even if Apple had invented the iProducts, in this day and age, being a pioneer has no merit. Androids rule over dinosaurs. And humans like their sparkly minted toys.

Get real, we've superseded you, I sputtered without thinking. Psychedelic acid-tripping ho-hum can only serve you so well, for the last few decades, maybe. This is the new age of techno zombies. My gadget is waterproof, dustproof, virus-free, hands-free, with the camera lens capacity of an SLR camera. I hear they're going bulletproof, and soon, it will even be transparent, see-through. The text will float in the air. There will be a function to teleport, time travel, clone anyone with the click of an app. I could vaporize your galaxy with a single swipe of my kryptonite screen, then put it back together again, Mr Dumpty.

This is how you speak in code, he responded with a smile. Good job, Jedi.

Touché, I replied and ran my finger gently over his arm, knowing the little hairs were tingling against my touch.

* * *

I always have a hunch about people, even before I hear them speak. Sixth sense is intuitive hogwash. What I have is a calculated observation of body language. Analysis of their nervous tics;

suppressed rage, desire, sadness. The way I know a man is by the way he pretends not to look at me.

He pretends not to look at me because I smell. There is a certain whiff of the pheromone I carry, I suspect, that makes men turn their heads when I walk past. Used to think that I smelled bad, or just odd. Can't be. They don't walk away, get further into the train cabin, make a look of disgust. They penetrate with stares, undressing me to my bones. Which makes women look at me, to see what it is that makes their men ogle; and soon, everyone is staring, so I learn to walk fast, I sprint, I can't slow down.

This was how he came to smell me, to look at me, to see me return the gaze, to see him bat his eyelids quickly for being caught in the act. His eyes are startling, blue-green-brown, specks of ivory stars; twinned orbs of galaxies.

This was how trouble began. How his nose fell for me, and then his groin, where everything coalesced and detached at the same time.

He was introduced to me as 'the man of my dreams'. He, a stranger, was introduced to me by a stranger. They were ordinary looking with sun-kissed fair skin; both were stocky, possessed jet-black hair and were desperately hip. The club itself was poorly lit so I could have been mistaken. In daylight though, I verified that this was absolutely true. Two short, dark and unhandsome men.

The Liquid Room was one of those trendy clubs at the edge of Clarke Quay no one would accidentally end up in by mistake. Along the Singapore riverside quay were plenty of bars and restaurants, chockfull of twenty-something old souls and forever-young-at-heart middle-agers: some were weekend dance machines; others only wanted to get laid. Seasoned partygoers knew the best clubs through word-of-mouth, and The Liquid Room had cemented its reputation through unknown grapevines as a 'hunting ground' for fresh meat.

It was clear that I was introduced as that weekend's lay. A random event, really. About to take a wee, I was rubbing body against body through the sea of sweaty human drunken boars when a hand tugged at my elbow, hard enough for me to stop and glare. It was his friend's face that greeted me first.

Hallo, his friend grinned.

What? I snapped.

What is your name, madam? his friend asked.

None of your business, I replied, turning to go.

His friend yanked me back.

WHAT? I half-yelled.

A pretty girl like you must have a pretty name, his friend goaded.

Isabella, I lied.

Ah, I was right. Isabella, meet the man of your dreams, his friend said to me by way of introducing him.

Hi, my name is _____.

He uttered his first sentence, leaned in towards me to take a closer look and inhaled, his pupils dilating. I was unimpressed with his face, and he knew it. For lack of an eventful Saturday or to cure boredom, I went along with what followed next.

His first kiss was dry, insipid, tentative. I was a cold fish, about to swim away. Peeing was on my mind. He tried again. This time, enveloping my entire head with his arms—which were ridiculously muscled—he swallowed my breath with an urgency that triggered a hunger in me. I wrapped my lips around one of his biceps and bit down with my teeth, feeling the muscle harden, his grip on me tightening so our bodies were meshed closer. The bass on the dance floor thumped louder, though muffled by the cocoon he had us in. Someone bumped into me, so I drew myself closer to him, feeling hot and hungry and swooning. I tried sucking at his bicep, trying to leave a hickie but it was rock solid, a turgid muscle that he flexed the more I pretended vampirism. We knew we were hooked, both of us. We knew we were in trouble, even if it was the good type.

Now, I could say his name, but it wasn't his real name anyway. Like how I introduced a fake name to him that very day.

I'll call him Ah, since that was how he was introduced to me, in a way, for he was a type of surprise, an abbreviated person.

I never knew where Ah was from. He told me, but it wasn't the truth, and his weird accent just gave me no clue.

I'm American, Ah said after we had left the club, on the way to our first rendezvous. We were within walking distance of his hotel, the Furama RiverFront.

Ha! No really, where are you from?

From Los Angeles. Really, he pleaded.

I have a friend from LA. Where exactly?

Sherman Oaks.

You liar. You sound nothing like an American.

Okay. You're right. But I have cousins in Sherman Oaks.

Where are you from exactly?

Johannesburg, he offered, beaming sweetly.

I narrowed my eyes suspiciously.

South Africa? I said with uncertainty, for I had no idea how their accent sounded.

Well, trust me. This is what we sound like.

Which part of Johannesburg? My colleague is South African, I lied boldly.

Uh . . . Harare? he said.

That's the capital of Zimbabwe! I blurted loudly, glad to catch him in the act. Years of nerding out over Trivial Pursuit hadn't been a waste.

Alright, you got me again, he smiled sheepishly.

Really. I can't go to bed with a stranger if I don't know where they are from. I'm not gambling my life on a potential psychopath, I haggled, one act for one piece of information.

Does it matter?

We had stopped at the traffic lights. There were no vehicles, strangely. He checked his watch, and I watched a tiny frown crease his forehead.

What time is it? I asked.

Almost two, he said, reaching for my hand and holding it while we crossed the street at the red light.

I peered curiously at him, at his gesture. His palm was warm and soft, cushiony.

You know you are jaywalking? I said to him.

What's that? he answered, hurrying his footsteps.

When we reached the other side of the road, he turned to me, wrapped his arms around my face and kissed me, hot, breathy, with a slight grunt that told me he wanted me. I almost fell backwards. He caught me, our bodies curved like shrimps, limbs moving in tiny circular movements, caressing heads and hair and back and butts, right there, under the glowing light of a streetlamp past midnight, where a few cars flashed past us; in the half-dark shadows of our made-up lies, we made out for a while, smelled and tasted our salty skins. The Furama was seven minutes away but it felt like seventy, as we half-dragged our intoxicated bodies to the hotel, hands and lips hungry for the new meat we had both discovered.

I'm not even sure how we found our way to his room on the twelfth floor, the fifth room following two right turns and one left turn after exiting the lift. Days later, I recognized the flower vases and the wall paintings, and of course the room number. But that weekend of lust was a hazy shade of good trouble with a man I didn't know the name of, from a place I had no clue of.

What I did know—and this was a fact—was that he was a spy. This was the truth I had put together from the puzzle of lies he tried to sell me.

Which, of course, turned me on even more.

* * *

He was an expat whose assignment was for two years. That was the first big lie I would never forgive him for. He was working for a marketing company called Asia Market Research. That was the second lie I could forgive for it sounded so absurdly banal and unoriginal I knew it had to be fake. I was special to him. That was the third lie I heard him say and reminded myself to think of it as a lie, for it had to be, even if my heart protested, and the words came from his lips; there was no truth to such sweet words.

It had to be a lie. It sounded like poker's bluff.

I lied to myself that it wasn't, he was telling the truth. That was where bad trouble came in.

You're nuts. You're special. I like you. He said to me on three separate occasions.

I remembered them as a single paragraph, taking the sentences out of context. It had a nice ring to it. Like a proposition. What he probably meant was:

You're nuts. Why are you laughing like a hyena? I wasn't trying to be funny. Does everything I say make you laugh? You're not cuckoo, are you? He said during lunch when I couldn't stop the giggles. If my scent tickled his nose buds, his presence tickled my funny bone.

You're special. You say these things I've never heard any girl say before. How did you guess that I made up the name of the company, Asia Market Research? It's quite a believable name, no? You're right. I'm not a marketing person, he said after lunch when we took a stroll down the promenade to digest the hearty carbs.

I like you. Why are you looking at me this way? It's true, he said when we were lying naked on the bed pre- and post-coital, declarations uttered twice. The gravity of its meaning was weighed down by the almost juvenile simplicity and sincerity of the choice of words towards a woman he had been bedding.

It had only been two weeks. I was having too much fun. I was in way over my head. I would never say I like you to someone who made me lose track of time, who made me laugh over nothing and everything, who made me quiver in my underpants at the sound of his voice.

That was bad trouble for me.

The truth. He was working in the embassy of his country. He clocked very early hours, so he had to be at work before the sun broke, meaning late nights were out, hence, his annoyance at our sweaty sessions going into the early hours of the morning. He spoke Arabic. But he wasn't Arab. He didn't like to speak the language. But he could. I didn't understand the contradiction until I realized he was a reluctant translator. He had been through war. He would stand in the shower, unmoving, letting the water run over his head nonstop, thinking, reminiscing or cleansing his conscience.

He had most certainly killed someone before. He wouldn't say so, didn't deny it. Whatever he did or didn't do certainly made him a sort of heroic figure that plucked him out of his local suburban home into consular work all over the globe.

That was how we met, on the dance floor in a swanky club of Singapore, this man of enigma who had since then travelled many continents, meeting exotic women, tasting new meat.

So what are you then? No longer a soldier, definitely not a marketer. You don't dress formal enough to work in a corporate office. Are you a spy? I asked him, watching him get ready for work in his polo shirt and his khaki slacks. With the blanket snaking between my thighs, I seduced him with nude shoulders, licked by the length of sleek black hair.

He looked at me, unfeelingly and continued his motions. He didn't want to be late. A purposeful man. A punctual man. A responsible man. I liked that.

You're not going to up and leave next week, are you? You're not going to leave me suddenly without saying goodbye? Mister James Bond.

He looked at me for a few seconds too long. Something passed over his face. I couldn't tell what it was. Our eyes tried to communicate but there was a shadow over his face from the low light in the room. We had different things on our minds. Different priorities. There was sadness in his eyes. Mine held eagerness.

I like you, you know that, right? he whispered, when the spell was broken.

You've said that before, I reminded him.

Remember when I said my contract here is for two years? Well, it's not exactly going to be that long, he mumbled and cleared his throat.

How long then?

Shorter. Much shorter.

Why did you lie? So you could make me think you were going to hang around and be my boyfriend? I teased him, though something hurt behind my ribs.

I adjusted my torso, feeling an ache, and the blanket slid down to my navel. I was nude as a worm, all mocha tan and goosebumps from the air-conditioning. He stared. I blushed, pulling the fabric over me. He sat down on the bed, looking intently at my lips, my eyes, the skin between my shoulders turning ruddy. His hands roved under the blanket.

Exactly how long are you going to be around? I'd like to know, in case you become special to me too, I asked again. I was heating up under the blanket.

I don't know, he lied again.

A cold blast of air came towards my direction. I shuddered, pushed him away, then put on a brave smile, telling myself, it doesn't matter, he's nobody, this is all fun and games, don't be stupid.

I have to go. Can't be late. Let yourself out, will you? he said, stood up and left me in his hotel room.

In the next hour or so, I went through his luggage, his things, and found nothing that informed me where he was from. No passport, no luggage tag, no journals, no postcards. Just clothes, toiletries and a pulp novel that looked brand new and unread. A decoy, possibly.

The more I didn't know about him, the more I was intrigued. He had to be a spy, I told myself. Such a wonderful lie it would be.

We both liked each other, in the same measure, at the same time. This was just a passing phase, a summer fuck, an antidote for boredom. Such a wonderful lie it would have been.

* * *

In essence, when you meet a stranger without a true name and a place of origin, treat them as an alien. Bestow respect, emotional distance, curiosity and trepidation for someone, or something, you know nothing about but have, in fact, ingested parts of their entity as a host does for a foreign body. He had been inside me. I had been inside him. We were whole for multiple moments. Then we separated, dislodged our organs, breathed and pumped blood on our own. When hunger returned, we came together again, ravaging each other as animals do in the heat of the mating season.

There is danger and thrill. And the unknowable. The narcissist in all lovers forgets the other party has as much to fear of you as you have to fear of them. I could have borrowed a fake identity myself. I could have been diseased. I could cannibalize my mate after copulation, as black widows do.

If he had been a spy, what kind of life would he have led? Forget about spy movies with super heroic fighting skills, bullet-dodging unassailable villains. How would you recognize a real-life spy? Wouldn't he attempt to be a fly on the wall or an average Joe as much as possible? That would be part of the profile, wouldn't it? He, or she, would walk among us, be our friend, family, fraternity, foe. An invisible unknown alien who behaved like a law-abiding, morally conscious, socially pleasant person with no obvious kinks, where underneath the scratched skin lies a reptilian creature, cold-hearted, perhaps, veins pulsing from repressed energies, dying to live like a normal human being with nothing to hide?

Ah!

He was right. About our systems not matching. About being from a different galaxy. A man living in the open yet hidden under the floorboards. So much falsity the entire time we were together. It was an adventure: a boy and a girl playing pirates-and-gypsies. We wanted to see who would walk the plank, jump off the ship, test the fool's courage.

The game was romance. He was a gamer. I tried to outgame him.

Thing was, he was skilled in the espionage of manipulation. It was subtlety he had always been using as bait. I stood no chance.

When I slapped him, it was all over. He didn't mind the slap. I had never done it before in my life. Never had violence been a part of my physical makeup except that day, when he was grinding his groin on the dance floor with a hussy he had just picked up in my absence.

It was all over for me. Watching him as he bent his knees to her knees, legs arched, their groins rubbing against each other, the music too fast a rhythm for their movement, my head about to explode, bad trouble surging blood lust to each cell in my cerebrum, my teeth hungry for revenge.

He didn't see me. Didn't know I would be there. He was baiting for fresh catch. I was spying on him. Sure enough, I caught the would-be spy in the heat of a lambada, aiming his genitals at a new female host. I had never felt more dead and alive at the same time.

I went up to them, two dancing spiders in a copulating frenzy. I pulled the hair of the woman. She screeched. I pulled it so hard

I peeled her body away from her mate. They disentangled. The disco strobe lights rained down on me. I looked cut up, polka-dotted, alien. In the dark, my white blouse was luminescent. My eye whites and gnarled teeth glowed.

What the . . . ?!? the woman yelled, though her words were interrupted by mine.

Shut up skank!

Who the . . . ?!? the woman lunged at me, and my words drowned hers, for I was stirred by a kind of hunger which her shallow protestation stood no chance against.

Get outta my face!

Excuse me? Are you insane? the woman continued but someone had pulled her away. It was her female friend—who had seen that I was about to start war—saving her.

I was with you only last night! I turned to Ah and hollered with a surging rage like a beastly alien tearing me from within.

Mind you, I was half his size. Ah didn't immediately recognize me. I had turned into an alien, ravenous, murderous, grotesque in every ugly sense. When passion takes over, consciousness is lamb to the slaughter. Ah was still bent on his knees in the short interlude of my dramatic hair-pulling of his dance partner. The music was feverish, pumping shots of metallic snares my sharp ears had now picked up. Some bad vocalist was howling like a wolf. Sampled melodies of tribal chants and the breakbeats of DJ Shadow filtered through the spasmodic gurgles of a lugubrious chorus. I looked around me, saw predatory gleaming eyes encircling me. My heart was inside my eardrums, telling me to slow down, slow down, calm down, calm down.

Then he saw me. His face could not lie. I caught a glimpse of regret and compassion before I sent my hand flying into his cheek. It was a great force. For someone much smaller and slender, with hands that had never been calloused by labour, the slapping of Ah was a phenomenal event. The palm of my hand hit his cheek, his flesh wobbled, the meeting of our skins burned like hot stones, his jawbone hard against the bones of my right hand, yet his face turned to the motion of my wrist, my arm, my shoulder, my torso, my posterior and spine that supported the entirety of my upper body.

His head turned against its will sideways then to the back, forcing him to face the opposite side from where he had been.

I'm very sorry. Ah said, when he recovered, looking at me with sadness.

Everything inside me that had pretended the fling was a lie had come to a catharsis with one slap. Everything evaporated. He was, and probably wasn't, a spy. He did, and probably never did, find me special. Nothing mattered. Chemistry between two rotating, diverging galaxies strong enough to pull them together was not rational enough a cause for the devastating effect of heartbreak. He hadn't felt it, I told myself, again and again. My passion had exposed me. He knew, he felt it, he regretted it. It was in his eyes, and the warmth of his arms as he tried awkwardly to hold onto me, this black widow, despite my assault. A plea for me to eat him alive.

I'm truly sorry, I didn't know, he said, trying to embrace me back into what we had but it was gone.

I'm sorry, I didn't know either, I answered and pushed him away, disentangling my arms and legs. I had to get away. Everyone was looking. I had to scuttle away, let my mate go.

We were both sorry about different matters. In truth, we both didn't know about many things. He didn't know I was going to be present, or he wouldn't have hurt me. My passion had alarmed me and revealed too much to both of us.

Perhaps, sometimes a mate eats another because he tastes too good, borne of the same hunger that inspired the sex. In consuming the mate, it's simply a way of saying you make me feel so good inside you I just want to keep you inside me forever.

Violence and sex. Two flipsides of the coin of passion. No lies can disguise its very simple truth.

Ah had always been my continuum of orgasm. I never want to learn his real name or know where he was from or where he was going. He remains a desiccated memory anchored in nothing but a fleeting moment of extreme and intense hunger. For each time my appetite is summoned, I salivate, feel the shivers and the quake rumbling from a deep well inside this alien I sometimes forget is my inner beast looking for a mate such as him.

Chapter 3

Berries and Weeds

When he said I'm gonna kill you I prayed to my agnostic god those berries we had picked earlier that I had eaten off his palm weren't poisonous. I had nowhere to go. Six degrees Celsius out there after dark, me not knowing anyone else but him, my only roof here, courtesy of him; I'm vulnerable, a potential victim.

I had never learned to lie well, a handicap I blame on my guileless mother. Being good and honest is an overrated virtue at a time like this. *Lie!* My imploding brain implored. *Save yourself or you'll soon be a corpse in this frickin' godforsaken Canadian cold!*

Nineteen is the age when a boy is legally old enough to drink, drive and die for his country. Wayne was nineteen, dressed like sixteen, and brooded like a twenty-nine-year-old. He knew if I died no one would find out. Maybe my parents would, weeks later, my body not found till months or years later. I imagined in a split second of a heartbeat how he would kill me or dispose of me. Kitchen knife manslaughter? A twist of my neck? Suffocation from a pillow, or from his large wide palm? Dumped in the woods? Shackled in the basement? Thrown into the river?

I fell for Wayne at twenty-one, the age when I was supposedly far more mature than him, considering that girls mature faster than boys. To die at twenty-two would break my poor mother's heart. And over what? A minor quibble over words?

We stared at each other, shipwrecked on either side of the dining table, brains trying to outthink the other. I searched for the right words to save myself; they were my bag of tricks, turning water to wine at the scratch of a ballpoint pen. But away from paper, my oral skills failed me. Tongue-tied, my reaction was delayed by fear.

Words were not a weapon to this fine arts undergrad. Wayne used words like Jackson Pollock, splashing random letters and colours motivated by feeling, agency hurled out the window for the postmodern conceptualist in him. The sophist in me knew my language was airy and light. His was dense, destructive, fuelled by his explosive temper. I had never seen him lose it so badly. Today was my first. When he completely blew up, it made me tremble, despite my false face of fearlessness.

Take it back, he growled in a voice low and combative.

What did it mean to 'take it back', I wondered, almost aloud, but saved myself by biting my tongue. What's out there was spoken. The only way to retract words was to say sorry or lie that they had never been uttered. I was terrible at both options. Especially since it was the truth, and I was *not* sorry that I said I didn't love him anymore. At that age—of early twenties—love is a source of adrenaline that bobs and stops and weaves and dives and when the ride's up, what's left are empty disposable boxes once filled with sparkly chocolate hearts and saccharine candy bars. At twenty-two, I was capricious. What did he expect of me?

I can't, I blurted rashly.

You can't or you won't? He threatened convincingly.

I cowered behind a tissue box, It's not working out. You know that just as well as I do.

In my mind, my strategy was to push the blame back to Wayne—never underestimate a creative mind.

If you don't love me anymore, you can't stay here. In my house.

Where would I go?

I panicked, realizing I was foolish to try this trick when I was stranded in a foreign place. It wasn't as if I could take a bus or a cab and say Adios! I'm going home now! The responsibility for my safety had shifted from my parents to my boyfriend. Had I forgotten that in my recklessness?

That's not my problem, he said.

I looked at Wayne. He had won by a long stretch. Technically, the apartment where we were staying belonged to his parents. His Mom was a Hong Konger and Dad was Indonesian; both had bought the two-bedroom apartment as a real estate investment, a home through which he could then legally apply for permanent residency in Canada. I knew they had disapproved of my coming here to bunk with their only child, seeing me as the bad influence who would ruin his future. Still, he had the right, the absolute power to throw me out.

But . . . I'm a girl. It's night-time! Things could happen to me out there.

Wayne's apartment was half an hour from downtown Victoria, fifteen minutes' walking distance to UVic and ten minutes behind the thick of a British Columbia rainforest. In the three weeks over which I had flown from Singapore to spend my college summer vacation with him, we had strolled through the woods every day, dwarfed by the titans of red cedars, spruce, oak and fir trees. Nothing was green in this weather. Only grey and white with the brown of bark peeking out in patches. In pictures, they looked romantic to someone who had lived in the tropics, used to being bitten by colonies of mosquitoes hiding in the underbrush of designer landscaped parks. Here, up close, the weather turned nature dismal, from trees to bush to weeds, all manner of frostbitten foliage deadened by the inescapable cold. I didn't even have the right coat on, thinking I would be blessed daily by temperature highs rather than lows. But all I got every goddamn day was the lowest of the lows.

Well . . . Wayne drawled his words out slowly. You should have thought of that. I can't live with someone who is breaking up with me.

Newsflash! Did I say I want to break up with him? I had said to Wayne that I didn't love him anymore. Can I recant, reinterpret, re-justify? I try anyway.

I'm talking about love philosophically, I said, Just because the feeling isn't here anymore doesn't mean it cannot be resuscitated. We have a problem. We need to fix it. Don't you think?

Wayne knew this was my way of begging. He gloated.

Go on, he said.

Look. We spent a year writing to each other. Our love grew between the pages of our letters, our words. For six months, I worked in a café serving sandwiches and cleaning tables, just to save enough for this trip. If that is not love, then what is that?

I saved my pennies too. I was eating leftover lunches from other people, Wayne said softly.

I balked at the thought that I had slept with a guy who was behaving like a hobo, pilfering the remains of food from cafeteria trays. This was what he said and I believed him. It was disgusting. *He* was disgusting.

Right. We both sacrificed a lot. This is my first trip overseas. Everything is too much. Too intense. And different. Forgive me if I'm weirded out by everything around me. Even you. You behave differently.

How? I don't think so.

You were so affectionate before this. You came to Singapore to see me, that one trip four months ago, and I was crazy in love with you.

I paused, then for dramatic effect knew just the right words to push his soft button, It made me realize you were *the one*.

Wayne stirred. The harshness of his eyes mellowed. His chest heaved and sank with a sigh.

I thought you were the one too.

I know. So, what happened in this month?

I don't know.

Me neither. That's why I said what I said.

To dump me? In my own home?

I never said that. I was expressing my thoughts, trying to work things out, Wayne. What we have is special, don't think it isn't.

Wayne stopped talking. I waited. He didn't speak again, stood up, took his empty plate to the kitchen and went to the living room where he turned on the TV, ignoring me completely. I sat in the dining room for as long as I could stand it. The silence was a cloud that took over the air, building into a storm that never happened. The minutes crawled by. An hour later, my cramped legs creaked painfully as I stood up. I went to the sink in the kitchen and washed the dirty dishes, thinking about the almost-incident between a man-boy who had my life in his hands, and how I argued my way out to survive another day. Maybe I could be a lawyer, I thought and sighed weakly.

Wayne switched off the TV and went to his bedroom, closing the door shut. He locked it. That meant I had to use the sofa in the living room. I wouldn't freeze to a hypothermic death alone on a deserted treeless street on foreign soil. Not tonight.

I waited until daybreak before I picked up the phone and dialled Rose's number. She was the manager of the community theatre I was interning for the month I was in Victoria, the arrangement made possible by my Theatre Studies' professor in Singapore. I explained in detail my situation, and could you help me please, where can I stay at such short notice, the sooner the better, I fear for my life.

Come over right now, she urged. Leave his place and seek refuge in my house.

And so I did.

* * *

Overnight, snow had fallen. Little wonder I had shivered while I tried to sleep, despite having covered myself with a cotton throw, curled like a cooked prawn on the sofa. Wayne never used the heater while sleeping, preferring to use thicker blankets or pile on more clothes. The double glazing of the windows fought off the chill as much as it could, but once temperatures dropped to zero and below, the claws of winter crept into the small apartment. To insulate myself further, I had taken all manner of cushions and pillows and built a nest on top of me while I hid my bony frame under the mountain of cotton oblongs.

Whoever said necessity was the mother of invention was a genius. No shit.

Wayne had left for school at eight, an early class perhaps or maybe to avoid me. I emerged from the cushions and the blanket, an animal in hiding, and scavenged for breakfast. It was either cold cereal or oatmeal porridge that I had to cook. I ate the latter then packed my luggage, dialled for a cab and headed for the theatre where Rose worked. We had agreed I would turn up for my internship work as per normal and go back to her house at the end of the day.

Llewellyn Playhouse was staging Tom Stoppard's *Arcadia* in two days' time. Tomorrow was premiere night. My misadventure should not interrupt the flow of events; box office sell-out was the priority. I manned the ticketing with two other girls, and in between, assisted with the making of the props.

Rose didn't mention our conversation over the phone when she saw me. I was to see Mr Plishka, the props maker, who had a job for me.

Find another vase for these flowers, Mr Plishka instructed. It needs to match the one we have here. Go to the back where the props room is.

I took the vase in search of another. I switched on a hanging light bulb that flickered; the props room was tiny, dusty, filled with props from previous shows. Something caught my eye among the pile of plastics and fabric. It was green and brown and purplish red.

A crown of twirled twigs with fabric leaves entwined with berries. It reminded me of the movie *Dead Poets Society* when Neil, played by Robert Sean Leonard, put a similar crown on his head in homage to Puck, the character he was playing in his school's staging of *A Midsummer Night's Dream*. In the scene where Neil killed himself, he had disrobed completely, a naked figure in a room blasting with the wintry cold, windows wide open, his body shivering as he crowned himself, fervent in his belief he was a martyr dying for his conviction.

At fifteen, I believed in the possibility of a Puck or a Neil or how ideas were above the pragmatic. You drove yourself insane with love. You drove yourself insane without love. Or passion. Or desire. Or hate. Or depression.

Or ennui. Everything during one's teenage years was so intense one could die of boredom. Whatever combination of an excessive emotion was to adolescence and young adulthood, the mostest a human being could ever endure. Often, it was unendurable.

There was to be no compromise or reflection. That was reserved for dull adults who didn't understand, themselves inching foot by foot into old age. Anything beyond the mid-twenties was an escalating descent into the Big Three Zero. Many a woman would set their biological clocks at thirty as the max. If babies pop out from her foo foo before that, she might very well clap herself on the back for, in giving birth, the woman would grow simultaneously with her infant, each reaching one milestone after another. Beyond thirty was worse—a mad dash to the finishing line, each year ticking by dangerously till the Grim Reaper drops by for a chat.

This was what Faith—my oldest friend in the world—said to me. Find the right man, don't settle for less, but don't waste too much time searching either.

Faith should know. She was already engaged to her sweetheart from junior college. Family planning, she called it—a mission to fulfil the nation's call for breeding babies from healthy, youthful genes. Faith had already planned the registration of her marriage before graduating from university, to be wed in the first eight months of her first job and to have a baby within the first two years of becoming a Mrs. Ideally, she should manage the production of the second child with quarterly gynaecological updates to ensure a well-timed two-year difference from the first child. She had worked out the KPIs of her family planning to best maximize the government's maternity benefits and subsidies. In fact, she had a regularly updated Excel sheet with multicoloured columns and itemized rows to record the nitty-gritty details of what and how much parenthood means to her.

Faith was explaining her foolproof strategy to me the day I had finished cleaning the tables and was taking my lunch break in the students' union café I was working at, as I gobbled down big bites of my free egg mayo sandwich. I nodded as she yapped away. This was not the first time she had prodded me along on my family planning strategy; I hadn't even graduated.

I didn't have one. I was—I thought I was—in love with my long-distance beau to whom I had written long form, sending ten pages of text handwritten with speed and passion about our futures together, about what I was doing in the present, and what my past was like. I had picked up a demo tape of homemade lo-fi songs from an indie music shop at Sembawang that Wayne had recorded on a six-track with his guitar and, as a dedicated groupie to him, had written copiously to him about music and art and films and literature, all of which he was immensely interested in. Somehow, the Nirvana fan in me, who also loved Tori Amos and Carly Simon and Rickie Lee Jones, found some strange common ground to connect with Wayne's world of The Grateful Dead, King Crimson and Frank Zappa. We were different; we were alternative. We clicked.

The superficial reasons for our union, of course, were a tenuous fabric and facade that tore wide open just as easily as it had stitched into place.

That day when I left Wayne's house and came to hide in someone's home, I grew up. I chucked away some of the ideas that had formed in infancy or adolescence, from films or music or art or books.

We fought for what we believed in. Nothing else mattered, no matter what anyone had said—not even the disapproval of parents or the institution of schools. We grew up believing that meritocracy would one day lead us to our dream paths. In the case of Faith, it was the institution of marriage and the state that had been a pillar of values for what she should strive for.

I was a sceptic. I didn't see myself as a lamb.

In my hands, Puck's crown was both lamb and leader. In the moment, I was so moved by the feeling of reenacting a scene from the beloved movie in which Robin Williams had incited a class to *Seize the Day! Carpe diem!*—the mottos I had held to heart. For an agnostic; they were my secular prayer, but no less powerful.

No mirror around but I knew how I would look. I put the circle of berries and weeds on the top of my head. Mr Plishka was behind me.

Looking good, Robin Goodfellow.

What?

I swerved around too fast. The crown flew off my head, crashed onto the floor and blended into the dusty shadows. I couldn't see it without searching for it.

Have you found the vase yet?

I'm so sorry. It was too dark. Couldn't find it. Will do now.

Think you broke it. My pride and joy.

Mr Plishka picked up the crown. A few berries had dropped off. One side of the circle was crooked. I was mortified.

I'll fix it! I cried out loud.

This is artisan work. Only I can do it. It's not supposed to be here anyway.

Mr Plishka placed the broken crown on the top shelf against one side of the wall.

Go on. Get going now. We've work to do.

But the vase?

Rose will find it. She knows where everything is. No more mischief today, young lady.

I hung my head low. Playacting had gotten me into trouble. I wanted to make amends.

I'll pay for it, Mr Plishka.

No. You get back to box office. Besides, another six months before the next run of *Midsummer Night's Dream*.

So, it really is for that? I exclaimed, pleasantly surprised.

It's a crowd favourite during summer. We do it outdoors. Reenact the scene from the movie.

Mr Plishka winked at me. He understood my fangirl moment earlier. Pop culture had appropriated from Shakespeare and given impressionable youths from the twentieth century a modern myth so close to our hearts we inserted darkness into a light-hearted Elizabethan comedy.

Heard something happened to you. You alright? Mr Plishka asked, his face gentle as a sheep.

I'm alright now. I hope so. I don't know what I did or what I'll do from now.

That night, I returned to Rose's house, had dinner with her and her husband, slept over and went back to the Playhouse the next day. On the third day, Wayne called, filled with regrets. He urged me to come back, let's try again, work things out.

I did. We didn't talk about that night. The air had changed. Winter had settled firmly in place, layering every windowpane with a thick cushion of white. The ground was white, slippery for me who wore the wrong shoes, who didn't know how to walk on snow. The treetops were wrapped in powdered snowflakes, their twigs having stopped breathing for the season.

The last night before I left Victoria for Vancouver, where I would stay with an aunt for a week before flying back to Singapore, Wayne lit up a reefer as he slouched on the sofa, manspreading wide across the faux leather two-seater. He smoked occasionally, only because he couldn't afford it regularly.

The apartment filled with a smell I didn't recognize, sweet and smoky, light on the nostrils, pervading my clothes, hair and skin. My pores sucked in this new scent mixed with the burning of tobacco.

Want some? Wayne offered.

I shook my head. I didn't smoke. My reflex to smoking was to gag violently.

What does it do? I asked

Relaxes you. It's considered medicinal in Canada, you know. They're petitioning for it to be legalized.

I've never heard of something like that.

Wayne giggled, either from the effect of the smoking or he was laughing at my ignorance. His opinion mattered little to me right now. I just wanted to get away from here, from him. The feeling of an end. It might be mutual. I couldn't be sure.

I'll be in Singapore over the summer, Wayne announced.

Why?

He peered at me curiously. My starkly brusque question surprised him. I knew he knew his trip wouldn't revolve around my presence. Not anymore, not this time.

My parents expect me to be there every year. I can see you too.

Oh.

You know they live in Singapore. They work there. I'm just here for college, Wayne paused then added, To get away from them.

I always knew that about him and his family, about how dysfunctional his emotionally unstable mother was, the control freak he painted her out to be, the workaholic distant father who paid more attention to his bank account and golfing trips than to his only son. All the backstory to this man-boy that I had skilfully filleted out of the bones and then kept the best meat of him as the reason for my passionate long-distance love. Much hogwash I fed myself—as women groomed on romance often did.

Something had to give. Some sacrifices had to be made for this trip. If only for closure's sake.

Let's go to the bedroom, I said with a tinge of weariness. I could see Wayne dart a funny look sideways. We hadn't been intimate since my return from Rose's house. We hadn't attempted. The desire had deflated from both our hearts. The only air left in Wayne's apartment was rank from the leftover plates we forgot to wash and now, the overpowering smell of his smoked weed.

We held hands limply and marched to his bedroom. The bed was a mess, Wayne having become too slothful to bother smoothening out the sheets which were a dark blue so filthy they looked ash black.

The two of us tried our best to have our last union. The sounds we made, the movements we shared, they were a mimicry of something pure that had bonded us before. Now, it was the paired rhythm of two people who had lost each other and found themselves separately— some birthed version of an adulthood emerging from our young and impressionable shells. I was leaving. He had left. The loss of our love imagined from strings of declared sentences bled in print and uttered in person was heartbreaking. I think I saw him cry a little. Even I couldn't resist a tear or two.

The climax we shared was good in its pain. He dug as deep as he could to my inner core, trying to fish out the remains of me, the centre of my universe. I pulled him closer to me, the last bit of skin contact I would have with this person who had taught me to grow up despite myself. When we collapsed in bed, we were both expended and frustrated at the same time. I slept the rest of the night as far away as I could from his naked body.

When I came home to Singapore, jet lagged and in a foul mood, I squirreled myself in my room. It was midnight and I was wide awake, hungry for supper with a stomach looking for breakfast. I turned the TV on. *Dead Poets Society* again.

I turned the screen off and picked up a cross-stitch frame I had been working on months ago and neglected, continuing where I had left off. I would pass another day before I indulged in movie magic. Lest I got my hopes up that life was as magical and absurd as the stories and songs we inhabit.

Chapter 4

Gold Water

In forty seconds, this water will turn gold, said the man in the soya-hued, Mandarin-collared linen tunic, his movements graceful and languid, a face of creaseless serenity, even though he must be at least fifty. Highly popular with the locals and tourists, this we call *jin xuan* or Golden Lily, he added.

As if on cue, the steaming tea that poured out of the earthen teapot turned golden, so luminescent the trickle reflected beads of liquid-like crystals from the morning sun. On the tray were five teeny-weeny earthen cups, terracotta red, small enough for a child's make-believe tea party. I looked sideways at Ai Ning, we suppressed our delight; imagined that she was Hello Kitty, I was Pooh Bear, and our master of tea ceremony was the Mad Hatter garbed in tai chi pants.

Ai Ning was still holding the sniffing cup. It had been passed around earlier from tea master to me, then to her. As part of the ritual, we had taken a whiff of the milky fragrance permeating from the oolong tea we were about to enjoy. It was one of my favourites. For Ai Ning, it was her first. She had always been a coffee drinker, a caffeine addict with no desire to discern the delicate aromas of tea. From cappuccino to macchiato to frappu-mocha-whatever, her regular choice of beverage was always in fifty shades of brown. Ironically, as a Taiwanese, she had never been interested in the local, famous teas her country of origin produced.

Why's that? I asked her.

Don't like tea, never did. Tastes like boiled water to me, she answered nonchalantly.

No, it doesn't. There are layers upon layers of tastes you can detect from tea, from the first infusion to the next.

You like your tea, I like my coffee. We are different, that's all. What's the fuss?

Curious, that's all. It's everywhere in Taipei, isn't it? Teahouses and bubble tea stalls?

Do you have many coffee houses in Singapore?

Plenty. You can have cheap kopi in a local coffee shop or designer coffee in a café. I don't know much about coffee. It makes me sick.

Sick? Do you cough or sneeze?

No! I get tummy ache. Nauseous. My hands shake.

Well, tea does nothing to me. Zero effect. The last person who made me a cup was my ex-boyfriend.

He didn't make you a good cup?

So-so. More like not a good match. Left a bad taste in my mouth.

You associate tea with a bad relationship. I get it. Trauma spoils the appetite.

Excuse me?

Never mind. Let's drink tea. *wo men lai he cha.*

* * *

Ai Ning was the best friend I'd ever had, a friendship so undemanding we'd met maybe two dozen times in the last decade, yet each time we met, the spontaneity of our laughter and joy was undiminished. A cross-cultural, intercontinental friendship had blossomed out of mutual curiosity about our differences and similarities, with an instant and mutual chemistry that was hard to find in women nearing the age of thirty. She had lived in various cities, and so had I, though our first meeting had occurred in London in a seminar room for graduate studies in English Literature over Derrida, Lacan and Giles and Deleuze, or some esoteric theorist and philosopher whose phrases, sentences and chapters one could spend hours nitpicking. She had pored over much material in translation, and it was the English version she struggled with the most. Despite the difficulties, she couldn't give it up, for she had a thesis to produce and a dissertation to complete—her postgrad education sponsored by her middle-class family back in Taiwan. Why she got herself into such an uphill challenge, I've never understood. Still, the unspoken rule of agreement in our friendship was this: she never asked me about my private affairs; and I avoided probing into hers.

The first time I met her, she was late for class. As she tucked her body into her seat beneath a bookshelf, she banged her head hard against the wooden plank with a loud thud and an *Oh!* that made me notice her: this curious, pale-complexioned Taiwanese of indeterminate age with her rebonded tresses and her hippy attire of baggy hemp or linen slacks, which I now understood to be Zen style rather than hallucinogenic inspired.

Over time, I found out she was strictly religious, a vegetarian Buddhist who was extremely frugal yet efficient with managing her limited finances and fanatical about recycling and waste disposal. That last characteristic might have something to do with the waste disposal culture in Taiwan, where excess garbage would be charged by weight, and its residents had gotten used to managing waste to reduce the need for more landfills. Something of the holistic karmic Confucian doctrine of humans and the universe being interconnected seemed to have seeped into the consciousness of the Taiwanese— and into Ai Ning.

In the Chinese language, *ren* is human, *tien* is sky. *ren* is under the auspices of *tien*, that is sky or heaven; humans are not above or independent of it, rather, tucked under, with the weight of two *heng* strokes on its shoulder and head. To be humbled by the universe, to share the treasures of the world; the codependency of people, earth and its creatures, big and small, is a simple philosophy, an ecopoetics inspired by nature. The idea of a classless, benevolent reverence for everything, living or nonliving in everyday practice, is a kind of antidote to the egocentric, existential materialism of modern times.

She had noticed me too, that day in class; my tanned tropical limbs, intense eyes and my frenetic energy that spilled over during the graduate seminar. I was one of those in the class who couldn't, and wouldn't, shut up—the five-foot, petite Asian intellectual with the obligatory black-rimmed glasses and a chip on the shoulder, who took the seminar students hostage and forced anyone within earshot to listen to her opinionated barrage of everything she'd read and not read. It occurred to me she had never seen a Singaporean at close range. I had never met a Taiwanese person before her. Our discovery of each other was a revelation, as if the bubbles we had been living in had finally popped upon contact. We shared a diaspora. We hailed from the East.

The year was 1999. We were at Goldsmiths College. I was a master's student in English and she was doing her PhD in Cultural Studies. Everything about me was infused with the Western, from theory to narratives to brassy cockiness.

That sleepy afternoon, a middle-aged British male student, Jones, referred to Chinese characters as ideograms, and further called the Chinese culture 'inscrutable'. I hadn't quite realized that the pride of my culture, and hers was at stake. Only when minutes had passed, when the seminar had progressed, when a bulb lit up in my head, did I realize he was referring to me—to us—not some unknowable Other in an anthropological textbook. My blood boiled. I spoke up.

Wait a minute! I protested.

The entire seminar class looked at me, all seven students, including Ai Ning. The professor, white, British and Jewish, scrutinized me. He knew I was ready to spar.

I was not white. I was not them. I spoke and wrote and read the same, damn it, but I felt I was being made reference to like natives of some savage tribe, foraging through bamboo forests, eating raw roots with fingers, chewing insects for snacks, or worse, grilling long pig.

The Chinese language is NOT made of ideograms. It uses characters, not pictures! I barked.

They are symbols, aren't they? Jones questioned.

In what manner of symbols do you mean? Random symbols? Each Chinese character is a composite of smaller words to make up a bigger, more complex word.

That's like an ideogram. A word transmitting an idea without sound or meaning. Like pictures that children draw. If you must know, I think they're exquisite.

Just because you don't read Chinese characters doesn't mean they are meaningless. Or they have no sound. They are phonetic characters. Not pretty little pictures. They are bloody words! Like the English language, or any other language, for that matter.

Well, they do look vastly different from the Roman alphabet, Jones added.

Tell me, does Arabic look like squiggles to you? Does it also remind you of early cave paintings? What about Japanese? Tamil? Cyrillic? Hebrew?

Jones fell silent. It was near impossible to convince someone who had no access to a culture and language so complex, his only source of information was likely through pictorial encyclopaedias. What the Occidental doesn't know about the Other falls quickly into a basket of culturally reductive semantics, like things oriental or chinoiserie.

I can't tell. They all look inscrutable to me. And I don't mean it in a bad way, Jones replied.

What do you mean 'inscrutable'? I bristled.

Across the room, Jones returned my glare blankly. I glanced quickly at Ai Ning, who was of 'my kind'. Everyone shifted uncomfortably. The professor tucked his glasses higher on the bridge of his nose, glanced from me to Jones and back again. We were a game of ping-pong no one dared interfere.

Lévi-Strauss in his books referred to the Chinese ideogram as inscrutable. I was merely making reference to his term. Is that wrong? Jones said.

Do you even know what the word means? I asked bitingly, unable to repeat the detestable word.

Does it mean unclear? Difficult to comprehend? Complex? Mystique? Jones valiantly offered an explanation.

But what is it trying to IN-SI-NU-ATE? I badger, visibly annoyed.

What do you want me to say? I'm not insinuating anything here! Jones cried out.

Oh! But there is a lot of meaning in your definition.

Such as?

SUCH AS? Are you kidding me? The history of colonization? Yellow Peril? The inscrutable oriental Chinese with pigtails and chinky eyes and kungfu up their sleeves?

Jones squirmed uncomfortably in his plastic chair. No one defended him and no one backed me up. All the other students kept their heads low except the Northern Irish girl who had a wicked glint in her eyes, the professor who was cupping his bearded cheek in his palm, trying to psychoanalyse our conversation, and Ai Ning, whose eyes had widened with awe.

What do you think? I turned to her abruptly, forcing her to take a position.

Now, Ai Ning, who had finished her Masters in Cultural Studies at the University of York, and was now pursuing her PhD, was good enough in English to know what had traversed. But no matter, her lips were pursed. Fear and embarrassment at her inadequacy with a foreign tongue prevented her from speaking English in the country that had invented the language.

She knew what the fight was about. She understood what was going on. But she couldn't fight in a borrowed language, so it had to be me: the woman warrior bearing the flag and burden of all Chineseness in my blanketed appropriation. I, who knew my Shakespeare more than my Li Bai, who had read Dickens, Austen, Hardy, was raised on Enid Blyton and Agatha Christie, but couldn't fathom a single page of *Dream of the Red Chamber*. Couldn't get the insinuation of a single Chinese poem on a calligraphic scroll.

It was hard times, then, learning to navigate my sandwiched body, my cross-cultural chasm of Asianness and Westernness those years in London. Ai Ning became a friend, a godsister. She offered friendship on the condition that I spoke to her in Mandarin, and I translated for her the eccentricities of English, nay, Western customs, or any traces of insinuations she didn't fully get when in contact with that 'other' society she found herself in.

It compelled me, with my passable grade in Chinese at A Levels, to become quickly fluent in Mandarin. She became, at the same time, slowly proficient in book theories written in English, where on more than one occasion, I sat down and tried to argue my case for certain writers, whether I understood their insinuations or not. We were both the blind leading the blind. It was a great, fruitful time, learning to navigate the murky wet roads of the English capital, a bustling cacophonic city during the years we had decided to burrow our noses in our adopted temporary home, for whatever reasons she and I both had. Perhaps we were trying to change ourselves. Turn ourselves into something else, something improved.

Ten years on, we found ourselves staring at golden water in a teahouse on a corner of Taipei's zigzagging streets. I was teaching her again, this time in her territory, unsure whether she and I were in or out of our comfort zones.

* * *

The first brew is often forty seconds for a high-grade oolong tea, increasing ten seconds for subsequent infusions. *jin xuan* was a specially concocted breed produced by Taiwanese tea farmers. The signature trademark of this tea is its milky aroma or *nai wei*, a whiff the nose picks up easily from the steeped tea either in the sniffing cup or teacup. The scent can also be sniffed from the dried curled leaves, directly from the packet or canister or, in more genteel fashion, offered as an aromatic sampled specimen on a bamboo or wooden scoop in the teahouse by the seller.

As exotic as this tea may seem, the exact timing of its infusion is almost a precise science; while the ceremony of serving oolong tea is often a hushed ritual performed by both the tea maker and his guests.

Around the table, which is often marbled or porcelain, the guests sit and make small talk. The tea master arrives with his equipment on a large rectangular tray. On it are earthen cups, a sniffing cup, teapot, pitcher, a tea scoop for scooping up dry tea leaves from the bag or canister, wooden tongs to pick up the scorching teacups, a saucer for the teapot, a container to hold the utensils and an absorbent small square towel, while a kettle with water boils on hot charcoal beside him.

The tea preparation is necessarily elaborate. It is, after all, a kind of soul food to nourish weary spirits. To start, the water has to be boiling hot before he proceeds. Then he warms and rinses the crockery, pouring hot water from the kettle into the teapot, covering it for a minute as he explains to his guests the type of tea leaves which he has chosen that day. Much oohing and aahing happens in the interim, with questions asked and pithy answers given, perhaps a joke or two, to the glee of the guests. The atmosphere is relaxed, receptive.

In the meantime, he opens the tea bag, takes the leaves out with the scoop and places it on the tray. Next, he pours away hot water from the teapot into the pitcher to warm it, after which he distributes the water from the pitcher into the teacups to warm them. Once warmed, the teacups are emptied as he uses the tongs to pick the cups up individually, pouring away the water on the saucer or in a bowl he has brought along.

Into the warmed teapot, the tea master inserts the scooped leaves. The amount varies from a rounded teaspoon to a tablespoon, depending on the size of the teapot, number of drinkers and strength of the beverage required. He then pours hot water from the kettle into the teapot, covers the lid while the tea leaves inside unfurl and steep.

Often, the first brew is discarded, as it is a cleansing process to remove dirt or grit. Hot water is then poured again in the teapot to steep the tea. Next, the entire contents of the teapot are poured into the pitcher, with a small portion poured into the sniffing cup which is passed around from guest to guest to savour its aroma, while the rest of the steeped tea is distributed into individual cups. The tea master then invites his guests to enjoy their tea.

The quality of the tea depends on the temperature of the water, amount of steeping time and quantity of the leaves. Left any longer in the teapot, even for a minute more, the taste of the tea is altered, becoming more bitter or robust, with increased tannin easily detected by tea connoisseurs. That is why there is a pitcher—to prevent prolonged steeping, the tea maker can pour the entire contents of the teapot while conversation and snacking takes place and tea is consumed; and more steeping is done for second, third or even fourth infusions till hours have passed, discussions have simmered down and the sun has perhaps, unnoticeably, set.

The day when Ai Ning and I met at Heavenly Earth teahouse, we hadn't seen each other for two years. She looked the same, save for more wisdom lines framing her eyes. It was her town, her city but she had never tried a teahouse such as this.

Why not? I asked her, after our bear hug to break the ice.

You know me. Also, they're pricey.

That was true. The tea we were about to have at Heavenly Earth cost ten US dollars for a portion of tea leaves enough for three brews and a few hours of hearty conversation. Double that price and it could fetch a 50-gram bag of tea leaves from the retail shop.

We were seated in lush surroundings of bamboo shoots, maple leaves, lotus pond, pebbled ground and a meandering gurgling brook with several idling koi. The garden itself was littered with a selection of haphazardly displayed potted plants from pomegranate to pomelo. The architecture of the Chinese courtyard and the interior of the café, resembling a traditional inn in ancient, rustic China brought us imaginatively to a more peaceful, alternate world in the midst of urban Taipei. It was an exquisite tableau vivant. An oasis.

The wind chimes tingled in the breeze; its hollowed tubes swayed while a paper talisman twirled. Soon, we were served confectionery to accompany the tea: homemade *mochi mochi* with red bean paste, peanut and sesame; two tea-infused hard-boiled eggs or *cha ye dan*; and a dainty plate of mixed nuts with raisins. The man at the table behind me was thick in the middle of a Chinese novel, thumbing it from back to front. An elderly couple in the corner were picking with their chopsticks at several small-plated tofu and vegetable dishes— marvelling at the aestheticism of their meal that had added to their feasting pleasure.

This was Ai Ning's turf—Taipei. She had searched through internet forums for a teahouse located in Yong Kang Jie, a famed culinary street. She had emailed me with specific directions, mapped from my hotel to the subway to crisscrossing multiple streets to several building landmarks. After settling ourselves at a table, she was suddenly quite shy, like a fish out of water. Here, in a teahouse, Ai Ning was tourist to the tea culture I had goaded her into trying.

This place is lovely, she gushed.

I agreed. We were both so pleased with the venue she had picked. It was at the top of the list of must-try culinary places in Taipei.

Are you hungry? I asked.

Quite. Haven't had my breakfast today. Was rushing to meet you.

Do you want lunch here or somewhere else? I asked

We both examined the menu in detail. The prices were much more higher than what she would normally pay for her lunch; I knew, seeing her intense expression.

Hmm, she murmured.

Yes or no? I prodded.

We'll go somewhere else for lunch later, after this tea. I think all this snacking will tide me over for a while.

Curious about her living quarters, I was wondering if she was going to invite me to her home for lunch. I'd known her all those years in London, and it was only in the later part of our friendship that she hesitantly invited me to her flat, where she and I would both cook our meals.

It was a learning curve for me, as an omnivore, to know what dishes she could eat—a Buddhist vegetarian able to consume eggs and dairy. The criterion was this: all vegetables except onions, garlic and chilli, for the that reason they were ingredients that would excite the flesh, according to her theology.

Ai Ning didn't do things in half measure. As a Buddhist, accountable to her own conscience, she wasn't interested in merely going through the motions. At the heart of human folly, as deterrent to enlightenment, is desire. This was something she was willing to control via her diet and lifestyle, through daily meditation, the practice of tai chi and renunciation in ways she was able to, as creatively an ascetic intellectual could manage. She was, by far, the most austere semi-celibate non-nun I had ever known.

And therein began my education in a different sort of culture, through the lens of someone I respected who showed me much affection and kindred kindness in London, when we were both far away from home. Though it was tea that brought me closer to her culture, it was tea that threw her the curveball.

The thing about Ai Ning was, she was not a pedant even as she strived to be a purist. After the teahouse, I was disappointed when she didn't mention a visit to her home. Instead, she took me to a restaurant famed for a much-loved local dish, *lu rou fan*, which was rice in a bowl topped by soy braised pork belly and pickled vegetables.

I was a guest in Ai Ning's country. She wanted to be a hospitable host even if it meant seeing a meat-eater operate at close range. It was often the case, even in London, that Ai Ning would watch me ravish roast duck breasts, curried fish head, grilled lamb chops or baked chicken thighs right in front of her while she tucked into her flaky mock goose, crushed tempeh, sliced soya spam, chopped cabbage and stinky tofu.

I always only ate meat when I was a child, she admitted, when our lunch was served and she picked up her vermicelli with her chopsticks at the same time as my teeth sank into soy-doused juicy flesh.

Really? You ate meat?

Always. It's easier to be a meat-eater in any culture, even in Taiwan. My parents didn't raise me vegetarian.

This was new news to me. I asked, What happened then?

I ate so much meat in my lifetime to kill thousands of animals that didn't need to die for me to live. My desire to consume flesh has been expelled out of my system. I just stopped. It's been ten years. I'm the only one in the family who is vegetarian.

Oh.

I pondered over her altruism, an idea so strikingly simple yet acted upon with great effort. The things she would have to give up. The aromas she would have to resist. The strength she had in exerting a philosophy to permeate all facets of life. I popped a piece of belly fat in my mouth.

And the meditation? Tai chi? When did you start all that? I questioned as I bit down on the meat and savoured the sweet grease in my mouth.

Tai chi is on and off. Last five years or so. I've been meditating for a long time though. Even before I became vegetarian. It centres me. Keeps my focus.

Why? How do you find the discipline to do this? Don't you get distracted? Don't you get tempted to watch TV? The movies? Read inane magazines? I said, while a piece of pork fell off my chopsticks and landed on the table. I watched it, caught indecisively between picking it up and popping it in my mouth, or letting it remain there with the existing germs from the table.

Ai Ning watched me curiously.

Not going to die, I thought, and promptly picked up the piece and ate it. She smiled, recognizing the glutton that I was.

It's always hard. Nothing comes easy just because you think you want it. I had false starts. Failures. Went straight back to eating more meat after two months of vegetarianism. Redid the cycle again. Happened twice. Then Guanyin spoke to me.

I was perplexed—I didn't know the Goddess of Mercy spoke to mortals.

It was the talisman from the temple, Ai Ning said. Before I gave up on Taoist practices. The message I received was: 'All that we are, is the result of what we have thought. If a man speaks or acts with an evil thought, pain follows him. If a man speaks or acts with a pure thought, happiness follows him, like a shadow that never leaves him.'

You're a believer. Would never work for agnostics like me.

Never say never. I changed my life. The divine guided me. Here I am today. I'm content, you know?

Not happy?

The pursuit of happiness is futile. Inner contentment is a power that comes from within. No one can take it away. Happiness depends too much on factors beyond your control. I've made peace with the fact that I can't control the world or people, the senseless slaughter of animals, cruelty against nature, greed of mankind, the madness of politics. I don't need to fight against the tide. What for? Struggle is a kind of pain, a daily dying of the spirit. Just so we can win a small battle, achieve temporary happiness?

That sounds pessimistic to me, I said, rather dejectedly.

Renunciation is a way of life. It's not about not caring. It's about giving up desire, giving away the ego of the self. We can never own the cosmos and the earth no matter how much we try. Everything that rises must converge. Someone said that.

It's a book title, I pointed out.

It is? Too much research. Everything gets jumbled up, Ai Ning shrugged.

Flannery O' Connor. She wrote the book.

Ah.

I thought deeply about what Ai Ning said. It sounded logical to my inner rationalist. Appealing in its platonic idealism, there was, however, one incongruity I disputed.

What about your coffee? Do Buddhist monks drink coffee?

Ai Ning looked at me squarely. Without blinking, she replied, That's my fuel for book reading. Besides, I'm not a monk.

Nor a nun, I reminded her, beaming.

No. That's the last thing I'll have to give up for nirvana.

Is that your aim?

What do you think? Ai Ning said, her face lighting up with mirth as she noisily slurped a spoonful of soup speckled with seaweed and *enoki* mushrooms.

I never found out that day. Ten years later, I was enlightened.

* * *

It was true to our strange, forgiving friendship for one of us to drop a random email out of the blue a decade later. Most times it was me for she needed the world less than I did. Her reply came from London. She had gone from there and returned, time and again, an exile flitting between cities. Great timing it was, for I was headed to London for a conference in a fortnight.

When we met, it was in a café in Chinatown off Gerrard Street. She was plumper, matronly, greying hair in a loose bun, still donning loose slacks, this time in hemp. My hair has been chopped to a chin bob, the only marked difference in my physical appearance while both our faces had grown a rivulet of laugh lines.

So, we both said at the same time, after we sat down and got over the delight of our reunion.

You first, she said.

Well, believe it or not, I teach at the local university in Singapore.

Really?

Yes. Got my PhD and started teaching two years ago. I specialize in postcolonial theory, I said sheepishly. That's my update. And you?

I'm married.

You're what?!?

I have a daughter.

You have a child?!?

I'm running this business.

Ai Ning gestured around her. It was a bubble tea café. There were students clustered around some tables, three middle-aged men arguing in the corner about current affairs and an old man with a scraggly beard seated next to the window reading a Chinese language newspaper.

Bubble tea? Since when do you know about tea?

It's a franchise. Not much to learn except following instructions. It's easy.

Do you still drink coffee? Or have you switched sides?

I drink both. Of course I have a preference. But I'm not that particular these days.

What do you mean you're married? Who did you marry?

I had always assumed in the years I'd known Ai Ning that she would have dropped a hint of a boyfriend; but since she didn't, it was implied she didn't need one. She didn't need a lot in her life for she controlled her desire and lived with the bare minimum. How did a man come into the picture?

I met him in Taiwan. He's a BBC. It felt right, you know, so we moved back here.

A what?

British-born Chinese.

Oh.

He's an accountant. Suggested I start this business since I was looking for something to do.

You have a daughter?

She's four.

Wow.

And you? Are you married? Ai Ning asked, shifting her seat closer.

No. Disillusioned with men, and love, I answered without irony.

Don't be. It will happen when it happens.

Are you happy?

This was the obvious question. How did she take a different path and end up on the route that, at first glance, was what I should be taking? Was the aphorism she said years ago accurate? Should it actually be: Everything that rises must diverge?

I'm content. That's all it matters, she uttered wistfully.

You've always wanted contentment.

Comes in various forms. How it appears is beyond our control.

And your PhD? What happened to that? Did you finish it?

Ai Ning diverted her eyes away. She looked at the old man. He looked back at her while she cast her eyes down. The meeting of the eyes of exiles.

No. I gave that up.

I see.

The language problem was too big. Besides . . .

Ai Ning pulled a waiter aside, murmured something then turned her attention back to me.

What is the point?

I wanted to argue against that. But it was a hard point to argue against the domestic bliss she had found herself in. I didn't know that world. She had opened a door to a revelation that enlightened her, the kind of contentment that had eluded me. I grappled with words on a daily basis, a battle in which I tried to find conscripts among my students, winning and losing sides among my academic peers; hair greying, facial lines deepening, brain imploding with ideas, ideas and more ideas. Sure, a part of me was satisfied, though it was cerebral gluttony I fed myself—glutted on theory, expanding the scope of humanities research that bordered on preaching to the converted. What was—or is—the point?

So, your PhD . . . all that is gone?

Life is my research, she said with a smile. For instance, this tea business, no one can teach you how to do this. You just have to find a way to believe it will turn out well. I can't control the outcome. But I'm content with the way it has turned out. The way my daughter, my marriage, my life has turned out. Can't ask for anything more than that, can you?

The waiter brought us our beverages. Mine had ruby sago pearls swimming in a sea of green tea, cubes of black jelly and glaciers of crushed ice submerging everything else of rainbow colours. The syrup was too sweet for my liking. The ice too cold. The jelly ungraspable with my teeth. As a whole, the concoction was bliss in the sudden heat wave that had plagued London that week. Summer had arrived. And so, the seasons ebb and flow in temperate countries, while unseasonal Singapore was predictably hot and humid. Nothing changed in the tropical climate. Some found it dull. I found it consistent. My demands of my environment had become less compelling as the years rolled by.

I stopped sipping, nodded sagaciously as I spoke.

Well, as they say, forty is the new thirty.

Like the first brew. When the water turns gold, when the golden lilies open with the fragrance of their youth, Ai Ning said.

Youth? I laughed.

All the good karma I've gained from not eating animals surely has earned me some extra years of feeling young. Yes, youth.

Still vegetarian? I asked, wondering if that had changed.

Yes I am. That is a diet I can control in my family.

Namaste.

Namaste, old friend. *A mi tuo fo.*

I studied my drink hesitantly, the kind of tea I had no urge to explore. This was oolong tea served cold, colourful and bubbling over with youthful effervescence. I thanked Ai Ning for her hospitality and chatted more about the past which we no longer remembered the same way, and probably never did.

Two hours later, I took my leave, departing step by step away from Ai Ning and our years of idealism. Some shops closed their shutters for the evening. The heat had plummeted to a stinging chill. Even in summer, London's weather oscillated between extremes, temperature being a fickle but constant variable. I stood on the pavement, waited for the stream of crowd to pass by and hunched my shoulders, avoiding contact with anyone. When an elbow bumped into mine, my temper rose; the words of an expletive hung on the edge of my tongue. I stopped myself. *Namaste.* I had just gifted the salutation of the divine. In the twilight of my life, I should start telling myself to let it go, let it be, let it alone. The moment passed; my heart calmed.

Water and gold, both elements melt, solidify. Both alchemize. Though water, more malleable, evaporates, turns to steam, migrates everywhere, rising to the clouds of the sublime.

Was Ai Ning water or gold? Which was I? Did her former idealism float with the wind? Or were my intellectual ideas, the ones I preached for a living, merely hot air? It was here, there, nowhere. Based on nothing solid, nothing of value?

We had both come so far in learning about each other; and in the end, it was about not knowing who we were, trying to uncover our own mysteries and coming back home to our exiled selves that mattered the most. We mirror ourselves through the friendships we make. We outgrow friendships. Sometimes, we outgrow ourselves. There is no permanence in our likes and dislikes, or our needs and our wants. All is immaterial. Immeasurable.

May Buddha protect you, as the wise would say. *A mi tuo fo.*

Chapter 5

Every Moving Thing That Lives
Shall Be Food

The other side of Huey's bed had been stretched tight and smoothened at eight-thirty in the morning when she opened one sleepy eye. The pillow, undented, had been fluffed and positioned neatly. This only meant her boyfriend was up, but with the room being so small, her peripheral vision took in all three walls from the door to the toilet to the curtains on her side of the bed—she knew he was out and about.

Jonathan's buffet breakfast. Huey imagined this was what he would have: a smorgasbord of muesli, rustic grains, unsalted nuts and seeds, tricoloured berries, cubed mangoes, dried guava, fat free Greek yoghurt with some brie or camembert to go along with a fresh, crusty baguette. Ingredients that Jonathan would loathe to pay top dollar for outside his complimentary hotel breakfast. In Singapore, his usual breakfast mélange cost twice as much as what he would pay in Oregon. So, he made the most of the opportunity, Huey knew he would, since her father had already paid for the rest of their ten days' stay in the Four Seasons on Orchard Boulevard.

She rolled over to her side table, fumbling for her phone. She knew where he was, but just in case, for Jonathan could sometimes get lost even in familiar environs. *Where r u?* she texted, then smothered her face in her pillow while she waited for his reply.

On the other side of her bed, another phone, on silent mode, trembled vigorously. She groaned. Obviously, Huey thought, he's left without taking it.

The minor irritation of the situation woke Huey up completely. She sat up, darted an accusatory glance at Jonathan's phone on his bedside table, then parted the curtains. The sun flooded into the room, bounced against the faded Victorian roses on the wallpaper and back on her bed, illuminating it where the whiteness of her duvet and bedsheet glowed even whiter. A baptism in hotel room number 724.

It had only been three days. She still hadn't gotten used to the tropical weather. The damp on her nose made her Emporio Armani silver-plated spectacles slippery and uncomfortable, the damp on her neck left her skin clinging to her collar while the hair at the end of her bob poked her bare flesh, but mostly, it was the damp under her armpits that reminded her she definitely hadn't gotten rid of her body odour all those years living in a cold, temperate climate. Huey had acclimatized to her adopted country. No longer did she have the patience for the oppressive heat and humidity of the tropics in which she was born.

Morning! Jonathan said as he swung the door open. His flannel jacket was bulging at the sides where his pockets were. He grinned at Huey. Room service!

What did you get me this time? Huey yawned widely.

Multigrain bread, croissant, raspberry jam, butter, yoghurt, cheddar and soya ham.

All that in your pockets? Ham? Cheddar?

I've got Ziploc bags.

Nice. Very enterprising. No wonder you wanted to buy the bags yesterday.

It's not all for you, by the way.

Jonathan emptied the contents of his pockets on the writing desk. Huey could never eat that much, not in the morning especially. But at least he was thoughtful, she mused, feeling grateful.

You couldn't get me real salami, could you? Champagne ham? Chorizo or prosciutto? That's the costly stuff here, you know.

They don't have them, ham perhaps, but I thought you could detox today, after that binge you had last night. Boy, how many crabs were killed for your dinner?

Yeah, poor crabbies. I'll save a prayer for them next time I go to mass.

Huey didn't have the heart to tell him her dinner crabs had died a painful death, first as they were chopped alive in pieces by the sous chef, their limbs, eyes and heart still moving as they were doused by scorching hot oil in the wok and flambéed while the chef poured stinging chillies and slimy egg on them as they breathed their last, each part of their pulsating flesh slowly soaking in the ingredients, becoming no longer a living thing but hardened under the extreme suffering of being cooked alive. One moment, they were pinching warriors; the next moment, they were food in her belly.

What do you want to do today? Huey asked as she reached for a slice of soya ham, stuffing it in her mouth.

I was thinking, enough of malls, let's go somewhere . . . ethnic . . . traditional.

Chinatown? We were there on the first day. And Dad wants to take us to Little India and Kampong Glam this weekend.

Temples. How about that?

Alright. Any idea which one? We've got plenty. I don't know much about temples. There's one called Bright Mountain or Bright Hill, something like that.

I've been doing some research. There are two temples in this place . . . Bugis? A Hindu and a Buddhist temple. And there's a building nearby with vegetarian and organic cafés. I could eat my soul food and get my soul blessed, all in the same place. Sounds good?

You're already having withdrawal symptoms? Huey asked.

Jonathan had been a vegetarian most of his life, went the organic route in the last decade, and became a rabid Whole Foods convert in the last five. Huey had dated him for fourteen months and knew his eating habits. He was as religiously anti-meat-eating as she was carnivorous. Coming to Singapore with her on his first trip to Asia had upset his routine. He didn't know where to find organic restaurants; and Huey and her family and friends were not vegetarians. Their feasts were strange and spicy and full of animal body parts. Who on earth would eat intestines and livers and hearts and brains and skin and trotters and feet of chicken? Jonathan balked each time he saw them on the table, so he opted simply for rice and noodles with vegetables or tofu. For the most part, he was okay with it.

Of course, there were vegetarian organic cafés in Singapore, but they were scattered far and wide and were too logistically cumbersome for him to ferret out while Huey or her family chaperoned him on their sightseeing excursions. Today was their day without family interference. Finally, Jonathan could be true to himself and be the meatless hippy his heart truly desired.

Alright. I must warn you. Temples and incense give me a headache. It's not like your one stick of patchouli puffing away in the corner while your world music CD loops on didgeridoo and rain sticks. This is the gritty, messy, stinky real deal.

Huey was chewing on her cheddar; crumbs of cheese fell on the bed. Jonathan started to pack his map into his satchel, along with a tourist guide and bottled water.

It's fine, you underestimate me. I'm vegetarian, not a wilting plant that can't handle a bit of heat. Do I look that weak and useless?

I'm not saying you are. Just warning you. There's no air-conditioning in temples.

Speak for yourself, princess. You're the one who's been complaining since we've arrived.

Well, then, Mister Nice Guy, it's going to be a hot and sweaty affair.

We'll see about that.

* * *

He wanted to explore the temples first, but Huey would not have it. Food then tourism then back to food again, was Huey's itinerary. Jonathan had had to grapple with his new understanding of his girlfriend in the last couple of days. Before the trip, she was a modest snacker and ate three petite-sized meals; Weetabix every morning with raisins and cold milk, one slice of dry buttered toast with chamomile honeyed tea every night before she slept. It was as if her Singaporean genes, having lain dormant during her stay in the US, suddenly resprouted overnight the minute she touched down on her turf. No cold cereal or cold cut meats for breakfasts—no! It would have to be something so steaming hot or spicy, it would wake her up like a slap to her senses. Her breakfasts in Singapore thus far—congee, fish ball noodles, bak chor mee, laksa, nasi lemak, mee siam, mee soto, masala thosai, roti prata. Followed by a caffeine overload of sickly sweet kopi and Huey was ready steady, buzzing like a mad bee that made him wonder if she had consumed all that on purpose just to be on edge. At night, she would make him sit next to her while she wolfed down hor fun close to midnight, and even better—as she proclaimed—was char kway teow at two in the morning when they were both jet-lagged and insomniacs.

In her feeding frenzy, Huey sometimes forgot Jonathan was vegetarian, egging him to try the meat dishes she herself was devouring. So voracious was Huey that she seemed to be starving all the time, her nose following the trail scent of anything resembling herb or spice.

It was this altered version of Huey who demanded that her boyfriend take her for an early lunch the minute their taxi landed on Middle Road.

WHERE TO?

The hound that was Huey barked at her hapless companion.

Fortune Centre, Jonathan read from his guidebook.

This place? Looks tired, could use a makeover.

They both stared at the building. It did look like a place stuck in a time warp, unlike the glitzy malls they had seen since their arrival. Where their hotel was, Orchard Boulevard led right to Orchard Road, steps away from Wheelock Place leading into ION, Wisma Atria and the entire stretch of a pulsing heart of a shopping paradise Jonathan was initially overwhelmed by, before becoming quickly bored. Too plastic, too capitalist, too trendy, he had said to Huey. Give me something organic, something real, something of soul, to which Huey would roll her eyes and respond, You want soul? Sure, die right here and presto, you've got a soul!

Jonathan was checking the notes he had scribbled that morning when Huey asked impatiently, Where's the restaurant?

On the fourth floor. New Pasture Café, he replied.

After you. Ladies first, Huey chuckled.

Jonathan glared at her. And you have the name of a man—Huey Lewis.

Stuff it now, it's not even a fair fight. You know I shortened my name because you white people can't pronounce my actual name. Say it. Say H-W-A-Y, H-W-A-Y.

H-U-E-W-A-Y. H-U-E-W-A-Y.

That's not even close!

Sounds the same to me.

Do you know my name means flower-flower? Twinned flowers. Huey Huey. I'm the original hippy chick. You're just a wannabe.

Yup, flowers that eat a lot of meat. Haven't seen one till I met you.

Fortune Centre was an unusual building, for which time seemed to have stopped still, even in Singapore's madcap and continual reconstruction. There was no design aesthetic or ambience. Everything that was there was perfunctory. On the ground floor were plenty of small retail shops peddling Buddhist paraphernalia and vegetarian grocery shops that sold vegan and organic produce, and a plethora of hole-in-the-wall eateries—Chinese, Japanese, Indian, Malay Muslim—that sold typical local dishes, reinterpreted with vegetarian ingredients.

The second and third floors were full of makeshift tables and chairs or plastic stools where a busy lunch crowd was tucking into, again, more vegetarian or organic fare. Among those shops were shipping companies or distributors selling god-knows-what, and a smattering of beauty related shops, TCM clinics, skincare retailers, beauticians and massage parlours. On the fourth floor, it was more of the same—beauticians, massage parlours, and then the place they had come for: New Pasture Café.

Huey and Jonathan found a table outside the restaurant. The ones inside were taken.

You go first. You're the hungry sow, Jonathan said.

Huey went inside and stood near the cashier. The menu was plastered on the wall; large photographs of a variety of dishes. She mulled over her options then ordered a cold soba noodle since the lady behind the counter told her that was their signature dish. Comes with free hot soup, the cashier said. Huey retrieved her wallet to pay the cashier, took her own utensils as it was a self-service café, ladled her complimentary broth with melons and grains and returned to her table.

What are you looking at? Huey asked Jonathan, whose eyes were focused on the shops opposite where they were sitting.

Inside Fortune Centre—which was built in the eighties— shops were lined alongside the rectangular walls where an up- down escalator connected the different levels so the middle section was empty space. It was a straightforward, functional design. The building itself wasn't big so the shops running parallel to each other were about forty feet away. Staring at someone on the opposite side meant the other person would definitely notice. Unless they were blind or were pretending to be.

Huey followed Jonathan's gaze. On the opposite side of New Pasture Café were the shop fronts of a few dodgy looking signage advertising massage services. Beauty Jasmine. Spa De La Salon.

Nothing, Jonathan mumbled, stood up abruptly and walked away from their table to order his food.

Huey's eyes followed her boyfriend, returning to the curious shops that had piqued his interest. Each had a door open. Each doorway framed a curvaceous woman in a tight skimpy dress, cleavage popping out of its push-up bras, severely high hemlines, dyed bronzed flowing silken tresses gracing their backs. They each gave Huey a stony look. Huey blinked but continued to stare. One of them, disliking the length of time Huey's eyes were fixed on her, thrust her chin out aggressively, her eyes widened as if taunting Huey: See what, bitch? Huey was taken aback. Was she being challenged to some kind of a girl fight?

Jonathan returned, his soup spilling out of the brim of the bowl, scalding his fingers. Ouch! he yelped, quickly landing his soup as incident-free as possible on the table, then stuffing his injured fingers into his mouth, sucking them with a grimace. Huey felt his pain, winced in empathy and took out a tissue to dab Jonathan's hand dry.

One of the girls across—the less aggressive one—started to giggle audibly. The aggressive one laughed along with her. Out of the corner of her eyes, Huey could detect the girls waving. She turned her head. They were gesturing to Jonathan, accosting him. She saw him trying hard to fight back a grin, his eyes sparkling wide, darting across at them and back to her.

Huey fumed, hissing at her boyfriend, They are hookers, you idiot! Why are you encouraging them?

No, c'mon. They're masseuses.

Masseuses dress like that?

I don't know. I've never been to a massage.

Are your eyes blinding you or is your dick making you dumb?

They're human, Huey. Get over yourself. Don't be judgemental. I'm not!

The waitress appeared with their food. Jonathan's vegetarian curry and Huey's soba noodles. No meat in sight except mock chicken made of reconstituted soy. Jonathan tucked in without a further word.

I can't believe you are flattered by the attention of whores.

Jonathan kept silent and continued his meal, eyes downcast.

That says a lot about you, Jon. For all your Zen beliefs and philosophy, you don't think it's hypocritical to condone sin?

Huey looked back at the massage parlours. Right next to them was a retail shop selling Buddhist books and paraphernalia—statues, amulets, mala prayer beads and pendants. She let out a derisive grunt in view of the juxtaposed contradictions.

Jonathan ignored her. He was halfway through his lunch. She hadn't touched hers, merely mixing the noodles and salad with the sauce using her chopsticks.

I'm disappointed in you, frankly. Thought I knew who you were, but yeah, come to Asia and all the exotic junk goes to your head.

Jonathan glared at her but said nothing. He resumed eating with contained ferocity.

So predictable of you. Of course, I'm Porky Pig compared to those lotus flowers with their bamboo legs and Wonderbras. Guess

I was good enough for you when there was no competition but now I can't even fight with *that*?

Jonathan scratched his plate with his fork. It squeaked high-pitched angrily.

I wonder what my dad will say if I tell . . .

You done? Jonathan slammed his spoon down on the table. His soup spilled, forming a wet circle around it.

I'm going to the toilet, Jonathan spat the words out, stood up abruptly and walked off.

Huey called out, B-b-but you haven't finished!

Huey picked on her food, fuming and sulking while she swallowed bite after bite in an agonized state till the minutes crawled past slowly, she felt her temper cool down gradually. In her mind, she was crafting lines of scathing retorts for her boyfriend, each to be unleashed one by one when he reappeared. She waited and waited. By the time Huey finished her food, she had lost her will to fight. Jonathan was back. His food had turned cold. Feeling contrite, she apologized. I was a bitch, sorry.

I'm not feeling so good. The toilets here are filthy. I'm going to find a cleaner one. I'll call you when I'm done, okay?

What's the matter? Diarrhoea?

Maybe, don't know. Maybe it's breakfast. I might be long. You can check out the area first.

Jonathan picked up his satchel, his phone and started to go.

Jon! Why don't we go back to the hotel? Huey shouted after him.

Jonathan turned to her and in a resigned tone, said, I'll be fine. You go ahead and I'll catch up. Maybe I'll go across to the arts school. Or use a hotel nearby. Won't be long.

All alone, Huey pondered her options. Was she supposed to sit there and order more food while waiting for him to return? Or was she supposed to check out the temples first? The area? Find more delectable morsels to snack on?

The girls at the massage parlours were chatting between themselves. A third girl had appeared, more youthful, her face like a twenty-year-old student's, dressed almost the same as the rest though her minidress was black, making her appear more chic than tart. The girl gazed at Huey with pensive eyes. Across the divide, between the creaking escalator separating them groaning loudly, both women briefly wondered what the other person's life was like. The Singaporean undergraduate from Portland State University who had lived abroad for six years starting from middle school wondered what the Asian girl of indeterminate nationality—Vietnamese? Thai? Mainland Chinese?—was doing in her country working in this field. What drives an attractive young girl to become a masseuse with add-on services? Is she really a prostitute? Does massage lead to fornication? Question after question Huey could not answer. She wondered if the girl masseuse was asking similar questions about her. Who is this bespectacled girl in linen shorts and a polo shirt with the white dude? What kind of life does she lead that I can never have? Why is her life better than mine? Even for someone so unadorned and plain looking?

After a while, the girl masseuse pulled her gaze away. She retreated into the parlour, into the darkness, receding from view inside the doorway while the older woman, the one who had suggested aggression to Huey, stood proudly like a human shield, checking out any man who passed by, coyly flirting and advertising whatever service it was they were selling.

The carbs inside Huey filled her with a stupor she couldn't resist. Her eyelids weighed heavy; her brain dulled with post-lunch drowsiness. Fighting off sleep, Huey made herself walk to get some sunshine. She took the escalator down, one last curious peek at the dubious women who had no interest in her before descending to the ground floor and outside the building where the overpowering afternoon heat whipped her wide awake.

Hot, hot, Huey grumbled then checked her phone.

It was fifteen minutes past the time Jonathan had left her and he hadn't called yet. She walked several steps and saw the temples, smelling the incense. She decided she would call him later; or he would call her when he was ready.

Huey headed for the temple with the signage of the Goddess of Mercy. She knew her boyfriend would be more interested in the Hindu temple so she reckoned she should explore the one he was less interested in.

A huge cast iron incense burner stood sentinel nearest to the entrance of the temple. Worshippers were praying then planting sticks after sticks of incense into it. With both hands, they held the incense upright, moving them downwards swiftly then moving them back up again repeatedly. Huey saw a large square red mat on the floor before the statues of the gods and goddesses. Guanyin's statue was the biggest, her multiple arms each frozen with a gesture. On her left and right were other statues; all of them coloured gold. God of Fortune. God of Judgement, Huey guessed, completely clueless about Buddhist deities but remembering the social studies group project on religion she had been involved with in secondary school. The entire altar and its architecture, including the pillars around her, were garishly bright, predominantly gold. Huey wondered if the gold was real or artificial.

On the red mat, men and women were on their knees; everyone was praying fervently. Some were holding wooden containers filled with wooden sticks of amulets that they shook vigorously. Only one stick was meant to drop out, Huey noticed. The worshippers returned the containers with the stick that had dropped out to a table counter where an elderly man and an even more elderly woman manned the station. Sticks were exchanged for pink slips of paper; the messages answered their prayers with words written poetically or cryptically, depending on the skill of translation.

Huey, the observer, was fascinated. It was all very alien to her; the lapsed Catholic whose faith had been thrust upon her at birth, when catechism classes proved to be many years of painful obedience to spiritual teachers she mentally revolted against, and weekly masses during her school-going years was an obligation she dreaded but couldn't refuse. It was ironic that Huey rejoiced whenever tests or examinations came round the corner for they were reasons that allowed her to excuse herself from mass. The intellectual in Huey regarded her textbooks as religion as long as she could avoid pledging complete allegiance to the Old Testament. She couldn't—she simply wouldn't—allow herself to stop questioning systems and gods she didn't understand. One ritual for another, what's the difference? Huey often thought.

When she got bored of her mini exotic trip into the Taoist faith, Huey wandered outside the temple. The square was filled with a crowd—people, more Buddhist paraphernalia, pigeons. A tree some feet away from both temples had branches populated with dozens of pigeons. They seemed to fly in a horde, swooping en masse from the tree to Fortune Centre, going back and forth. They flew at such a low height that Huey found herself bending to avoid pigeons crashing into her face.

Whoa! Huey hollered, as one pigeon she hadn't seen almost crashed into her, missing her hair by an inch. She could hear the swoosh of wings past her head. Filthy buggers, Huey grumbled, preening her hair, trying to sweep away whatever she had imagined landing on her head. Vermin, she muttered with disgust.

The humidity was getting to her. She was sticky from perspiring. Huey was losing patience. She took out her phone and texted Jonathan: *Are you done? I'm outside the temples.* For five minutes, she didn't hear from him. Huey went to one of the shops and looked at jade bracelets, rings, pendants and necklaces. She was almost tempted to buy something. Another five minutes passed. Huey started to worry. It had been over fifty minutes. Was her boyfriend sick? Passed out from over-excrement?

She texted him again: *Where are you? Shall I come and find you?*

Three minutes later, Jonathan replied: *I'm fine. Was horrible. You don't want to know. See you in five.*

When Jonathan finally turned up, Huey sidled up to him affectionately. She missed him in the time he had temporarily disappeared. She tucked her arms around him. His shirt was slightly damp.

You are messed up. You're all sweaty. Better now?

Much better.

Need a doctor? What did you eat?

I'll be fine. Maybe it's the yoghurt from morning, Jonathan said and pushed Huey away. I stink. Don't get so close. In case I'm sick.

Oh, Jon. I'm so sorry. Welcome to your first tropical germs. Look at you, you're all flushed. Drink some water.

It's quite an experience, I must say.

Huey chortled loudly. She grabbed her boyfriend's arm, his muscles against her fingertips making her feel girly—she squeezed, enjoying his flesh against her flesh.

Come on, let me give you another experience. Which temple are you ready for? Which gods do you want to be blessed by first?

God of Eros, Jonathan said, smiling with one side of his dimpled cheek.

Sexy beast, you.

* * *

For the rest of her vacation, Huey spent her time increasingly with her folks and friends from her childhood. Since his tummy troubles, Jonathan avoided all tourist jaunts, preferring to lounge in the hotel while Huey pigged out in her former haunts with her former BFFs. There was a Jennifer, a Rachel, a Hui Ling, a Wei Wei, a Shanti, a Roseanne, a Merlinda, an Athene and so on and so forth. Jonathan barely remembered half of their names. Sometimes, he butchered their names—Jessica, Rachelle, Wei Ling, Hui Hui, Sandi, Rosie, Melissa, Andi. Each day, Huey would repeat the same names in the same order, and each time, Jonathan would forget.

When their vacation came to a close, Jonathan looked well rested. In fact, he had recovered so well, he was positively radiant. Almost buff. Rather handsome. Glowing with a bronzed tan.

Wanna make out? Huey said, getting into bed with her boyfriend. It was eleven at night. Their flight was due next morning at nine.

I'm tired. Need sleep for our long flight, Jonathan muttered, turning his back to her.

A quickie? Come on. We haven't done it since the first day we arrived.

I don't want to pass you any germs.

Jonathan tucked the duvet under his legs, cocooning himself away from her. Huey looked at the leftover length of duvet she had on her body. She slipped her hand under her boyfriend's shirt, fingertips barely touching him, hoping her tickling would change his mind. He shifted his body closer to the edge of the bed.

Hmph, Jonathan snorted.

Huey leaned her breasts on his back, pressing herself to him. Her thighs rubbed against the back of his legs. One of her hands squeezed his butt.

Stop. I want to sleep, Jonathan commanded her in a voice that was absolute.

Huey would not be stopped. She planted her face on his neck, kissing him warmly, wetly and insistent.

Hmmm.

I said stop!

Jonathan leapt out of bed. He stormed into the toilet and closed the door. There was the sound of water running. A few dry coughs. Huey heard him brushing his teeth. Didn't he brush his teeth earlier?

The tap ran for a long time. Huey must have waited for more than half an hour while she turned the TV on and watched a rerun of *Titanic* disinterestedly as her annoyance at being rebuffed rose and waned. Jonathan was still locked inside the toilet. Her eyelids fluttering heavily, she finally shut them and fell asleep. When her boyfriend reappeared and took the side of the bed next to hers, Huey had no idea. Her guileless mind drifted into dream after dream, crossing continents of images from Singapore to Portland and back again, pulling scenes of nondescript locations that could be universally anywhere: a bedroom, a café, a mall, a church, a clinic, a massage parlour. No wait, they couldn't be universal, Huey's subconscious reminded her. Some things were homogenous. Some things not. Some things were infused with alternate meanings that she would never be able to comprehend.

And comprehend she couldn't, Huey realized, when Jonathan broke up with her soon after they returned to the US. The swiftness of his action astounded her. What happened? Huey demanded to know.

You're a snob, Jonathan accused her.

I'm not! That's not even a good enough reason to break up with a person.

You're not vegetarian. It will never work out in the end.

You didn't have that problem for one year! What changed?

It's not you. It's me. Okay?

Of course it's you. But why?

I don't know. Maybe some couples shouldn't travel together. Brings out the worst in them.

Tell that to my father who paid for your accommodation.

I didn't ask him to.

You certainly didn't complain.

We can do this the amicable way. Stay friends, shall we?

Huey was aghast. He was dumping her and he wanted to remain friends? Was he an imbecile? Or should she be one and agree for the sake of agreeing?

Fuck you, Jon.

Jonathan smiled slyly. He shrugged indifferently.

Well, I tried.

We shouldn't have gone to Singapore. We shouldn't have.

They were in their favourite organic café. Both of them had finished their veggie burgers. Huey was halfway through her mango lassi. Jonathan had finished his wheatgrass pineapple juice.

Do you mind if I go to the toilet? he asked.

Suits you.

Be nice. We were friends before we dated. Let's be civil. Wait five minutes.

Huey watched her boyfriend—no, ex-boyfriend—leave the table, going behind the chintzy tassels separating the dining area from the corridor to the washrooms. She clenched her fists, feeling like she should punch his face. She wanted to; she knew she wouldn't. But she wanted to, badly.

His phone was on the table. It trembled vigorously with a fresh text. What the hell, who was texting the jerk now? She picked up his phone to read the message.

Darling, call me back. I miss you. See you every day now you fly back USA. When you come back and kiss me? I think of you and pusy so wet. Love you long time! You miss my massage? I miss your cork. So big and long. Call me, I miss you! XXX Dolly

Oh. My. Lord. Huey's hands froze. When she recovered from her shock, she looked up and saw Jonathan staring at her. His mouth opened; no words emerged. He closed his lips, face pale as the whitewashed wall.

And I'm the hypocritical one. And I'm the snob. And I'm the meat eater who takes the life of animals. Who's the animal here now? Huey spat at him.

Jonathan's phone rang. Huey saw it was the masseuse calling him. His hands reached out for his phone. Huey swung her arms backwards and, with a graceful swing and a calculated arc of a radius that would be just right, flung his phone across the café where it smashed into pieces on the hardwood floor. The ringing of the phone stopped. Huey beamed widely.

Chapter 6

Ice Flower

One day I'm going to retrace my colonial roots, Peter declared.

It was our third official date; lunch on a student budget, street food, hawker style so Peter could go native. Official I suppose, since the previous four times we met we were with a pack of five other college slackers; out of that, twice we had fooled around, once in the bathroom, another time in the cinema, giggling while our fingers played with static in the dark.

I gave him the blank, disinterested look the way I always do when he's trying hard to bait me. Noodlehead, I muttered the words under my breath, then stabbed the chopsticks into the bowl, lifting my wonton noodles; the long-yellowed strands rose with a curtain of hot air. A cloud of steam dissipated, smudging the shape of his face. He ducked his head to see me better. I glared back.

I'm sure your father, your father's father, your father's father's father's father's father, will be very proud of you, I sniggered. Oh wait, did I miss out one father?

Peter tried again, You can be my second wife. No, first wife . . . no, second wife . . . you can be all my wives, how about that?

How about I don't ever marry you? The words flashed in my head.

I kept mum. Peter was looking for a reaction. I didn't want to give it to him. I was never a match for his sharp tongue. His comeback would always be deadlier than whatever I served him. Guys like that—they were flames to my moth brain. It's a paradox of attraction, I know; a part of me liked being the bait.

But Peter had gone too far. On usual days, his wit, I would say, was humorous though off-kilter, goofy yet cutthroat. Today, he was spewing garbage. A white Briton talking about colonization in Singapore as if the imbalance of human relations in our recent history was a blip that didn't matter. He didn't need to be politically correct, but he didn't need to be crude either.

I wanted to go. He was as funny as the bone marrow inside my rib cage about to leak from contained implosion. I had a case of what the Chinese would refer to as *nei shan*—to suffer from internal injuries. He had touched a raw nerve. My organs were wilting.

God, how I truly hated dating. Problem was, his brown Bambi eyes sucked me into his vortex of evil seduction. Peer close enough, and you could probably detect broken amber pieces floating inside a rimmed golden halo.

His soul was angelic. His mouth was the devil's advocate.

I was only glad he was an exchange student here for a semester, and I would never, hopefully, ever see him again. Against better judgment, I was pawing all over him two weeks ago at the billiards clubhouse, drunk on two beers and a margarita, which was 300 per cent over my tolerance threshold for alcohol. I felt like celebrating, having gotten an A minus for an almost botched, almost late essay assignment on Ethics 101—Socrates and me, we talked apples and kiwi, though I tried, I tried so hard to get behind the fuzz in his logic.

And Peter, well, he had been trailing me like a terrier. He chose to sit next to me during class every week. He followed me to the canteen for lunch each time, never mind the other exchange students he repeatedly ignored. All it took was one intoxicated kiss on the dance floor, a pulsating headache to the hammering bass of some forgettable and insistent house track, sweaty limbs and hungry lips and he had me returning his slobbering kisses. What a mistake. Twenty, horny and reckless. It was somewhat premeditated on my part. I knew he was leaving Singapore in a fortnight so, in a way, I thought I could slut it out, have my cake and eat it, and my debauchery would not return to taunt me. Well, I forgot he could be annoying as heck.

Your place or mine? Peter said, half-jokingly, half-seriously.
I caught the twinkle in his eyes, but he had ruined my lunch. An
unsatiated stomach doesn't have the capacity to forgive.

It had started raining, in typical Singapore style. I would describe
it as a sudden mini monsoon, a whiplashing tropical thunderstorm.
The kind that would start without warning and end like a miracle,
clouds parting, sun rays piercing through, leaving thick moisture
to humidify everything. It was like God had a tantrum and all
was forgiven.

When it rained, the cabs went into hiding. I had no intention of
going with Peter to his place or mine, but I had to get back to the
hostel. Sharing a cab was the logical solution. What could I do?

Look, Peter, I said, with feigned exhaustion. I'm tired, I just
want to go home and call it a day. Can you order a cab?

Peter sighed; a sigh so soft it meant he was genuinely disappointed.
It took him half an hour before he was matched to a cab—one that
had to drop a passenger off and was ten minutes away. Peter muttered
a machine-gun barrage of expletives under his breath.

There was nothing else to do but wait. We could only sit tight
and wait for our ride and pray for the torrential downpour to subside.
We were trapped at Newton Circus, which wasn't really a circus but
a hawker centre. The only thing remotely 'circus' about this place was
the freaks—us, for instance—who didn't mind paying double for the
same fare you could get in another hawker centre, only without the
pretentious name.

It was Peter's idea that we come here. He wanted to have local
food in a place that was highly recommended, and on the tourist
map he had, the review was four thumbs up out of five. I warned him
he would be disappointed. It was overpriced and overhyped. Still, it
was highly popular with the expatriate crowd—the *new* expats, that
is—having been sold on the idea this is as local as it gets, save for the
hijacked prices.

Ten minutes later, our ride arrived. Once inside, the cab driver,
who looked about seventy-plus with a full head of white hair and
age-spotted hands showed Peter how right he was about his colonial
heritage.

Good afternoon, Sir! You going to NTU, Sir? The driver asked the twenty-something British undergrad in a cringingly obsequious tone.

Yes. Nanyang Heights, Peter said.

Peter's hand magically appeared on my knee. The hand found its way to my thigh. I shifted my bodyweight and moved my thigh quickly to let his hand fall on the seat. I peered outside the window. I could feel his eyes on me. I pretended not to notice, breathing on the glass window.

The cab driver started chatting with Peter.

Where you from, Sir?

I'm from Britain.

Ah! London, is it, Sir? London?

No, not London. I'm from Bristol.

Oh, not London? You here working?

No, I'm an exchange student. I'm only here for a few months.

Few months only? Then you must visit Night Safari. Must go! Singapore Night Safari very good, very famous one. You sure won't regret. I tell all the tourists it's the best attraction in Singapore. Zoo also. Can see giraffe, lion, tiger, elephant, can spend whole day there. Mandai Zoo, you heard of, Sir?

Sentosa, what about that? Do you recommend it? Peter asked.

Best. Must go morning and stay overnight, watch sunrise. Universal Studio also lah. Plenty to see. They make the place look like movie set. You been to Lau Pa Sat? Anything you want to eat also have. You like clubbing? Zouk? Been there yet, Sir? How about Chinatown? Mount Faber? Can take cable car, Sir.

I thought if the cab driver said one more 'Sir' I was going to vomit. In the confined space of his vehicle, I was subject to the sad display of ingratiating colonial legacy Peter had dredged somehow out of the poor man's memory. Was this all for a big tip? Or did he really think it was alright to call a man 'Sir' just because of his ethnicity?

For the duration of the trip, I zoned out. Even when Peter was trying to engage me in the conversation, I would shut him out and look out the window, check my phone, rummage through my bag. I had lost interest in the forced exchange between the two, and most certainly in my date.

We finally reached our hostel. The rain had almost stopped.

We're here, Sir. $24.20, Sir.

I slipped out of the taxi and stood on the pavement while Peter paid the driver. I was fuming mad. From inside the taxi, the cab driver thanked Peter effusively with a few more 'Sirs' that grated on my ear.

As Peter sidled out of his seat, I couldn't resist breaking my silence. I had been quiet throughout the journey watching the charade, thinking I had been transported back to the 1950s when the Empire meant something, and Singapore was a mere fishing port waving the Union Jack.

Peter stood beside me on the pavement, and before he closed the door to the car, I stuck my head inside the cab and raised my voice.

Uncle! Can you stop calling him 'Sir'? We're in the twenty-first century now. Singapore has been independent since 1965. We're not under the British anymore, Uncle. Have some self-respect.

The cab driver looked at me through the rearview mirror with a disgusted look and said nothing. I slammed the door and the taxi sped off. Peter stretched himself and yawned. I was ready to have a fight.

Why did you let that Uncle call you 'Sir' all the way?

I didn't ask him to do so. He chose to. It is weird to me too but that's his problem. Don't get mad about everything. You're much too serious. Besides, I'm not really this wanker you think I am. I'm just trying to loosen you up. Can't take a joke, can you?

How's any of that funny? I snapped, irritated.

Sorry if it annoys you. Just taking the piss, you know.

Don't aim your piss at me.

Don't be so uptight.

Are you calling me a square? I retorted, face reddening.

I'm not calling you anything! And no, I would never think of you as a square. If you were a shape, you'd be a star. A flashing, neon Christmassy star shining the living daylights out of my eyes in this goddamned tropical heat!

I didn't buy his charm; I wouldn't let him schmooze me with a cheap trick. I wanted to have the last word.

If I'm a star, then I must be talking to Uranus, I blurted.

We looked at each other, and despite my best effort to keep a straight face, we burst out laughing. Peter drew me close. His breath was on my cheeks, warm against my coolness. Whenever he did that, I melted a little, never mind my no-nonsense tough-as-nails runaway mouth. I pulled away a little.

Peter continued, Look. Will it make you happy if I opened the doors for you, bought you roses, serenaded you? Would it please you if I behaved with old-fashioned gallantry towards you? Because I can do that. I can fake the gentleman.

Oh please, I dismissed him flippantly, though I couldn't look him in the eye as I uttered the words.

I love Singapore, he turned my cheek to face him. I love how everything works, except the things I don't understand.

Such as?

Such as why it's impossible to find a cab when it rains. Or why is it when you hail a cab and it stops but if the driver doesn't agree with where you're going, he can choose not to take you. This doesn't happen anywhere else in the world; it's thug behaviour, Peter said.

I don't know. I do agree it's infuriating that cabs can choose their customers instead of customers choosing their cabs.

Exactly. There's another thing I don't understand.

What's that?

Why everyone is called Uncle or Auntie. They're not *my* uncles or aunties. How do you know when to use that term? Or when it becomes an insult? I called a saleslady Auntie the other day and she was terribly offended. Why? I don't get it.

Uncle and Auntie are generic terms. Usually you use them on people much older than you, like on middle-aged men or women. How old was she?

Late twenties, perhaps? I don't know. Asians tend to look young.

Well, then, you basically referred to her as a middle-aged person. You should be glad she didn't punch your lights out.

And you know what I don't understand most of all in this country? Peter asked, his eyes opening wide as he leaned towards me.

No. What's that? That the rich get richer and the rest don't? That we like to stay in air-conditioned rooms and freeze our toes in eighteen degrees Celsius when the sun is out there waiting to be basked in? That we take our year-round summer for granted when Northerners like you would kill to get out of the winter? What is it? Which part of this strange land don't you understand most? I demanded.

Quite simply. You.

* * *

When Peter left in November, I wasn't sure if I was relieved that he had gone, or sad I wouldn't see him ever again. In January, Peter flew to Munich for the New Year holidays. He sent me an email with an attachment of a picture. It appeared to be snowflakes on a window in a sea of grey-mauve blur, pixilation that created a dreamy effect where the cold from the outside touched a warm surface on the inside. The snowflakes resembled feathers crystallized by ice; they were individual silvery-frosted sculptures that were so petite, so delicate and yet so unsymmetrically perfect. Each diamante crystal bloom was one-of-a-kind. My chilled heart thawed a little.

This is what they call an Eisblume here in Germany. Literal translation, ice-flower. Pretty little thing, isn't it? Peter had written, adding at the end, *Just like you.*

I was about to cringe but the sentimental in me made me fall for his glibness. I typed back a reply.

Thanks for the picture. It's beautiful. But not as beautiful as the tropical sun you left behind. Stay warm.

My classes were about to start in an hour and a half. After Peter had left Singapore, I moved back home from my hostel. Money was tight at home after Father's IT company had downsized and they were looking for people to fire. He took a 15 per cent pay cut to keep his job so I decided to do the prudent thing—give up on-campus accommodation. He was, after all, still paying my school fees. If I hadn't done so, it would have cost Father a few thousand dollars for my dorm experience that year, which essentially revolved around me goofing off, partying late, sleeping late, studying late and waking up late. My wanton lifestyle was surely bad karma if I didn't balance it with the good. I knew, by giving up the hostel, I had to put up with a ninety-minute commute each way by train and bus to get to school. It was a small sacrifice, but still a painful decision, nevertheless.

So I moved back home, shuttling back and forth from my home in Yio Chu Kang, in the northern part of Singapore, to the university which was tucked away in a corner of the island so far west and distant students called it Pulau NTU—'pulau' meaning island. Some days, getting there did feel like travelling to an island off Singapore. You almost needed a passport to get there.

Today, the air was heavy, damp and sticky. Suffocating and windless. I knew that meant rain was coming. It would summon gusts of whiplashing heaven's water brought in by waves of ocean breeze to lift the parched and dense dusty air off the hot earth. Everything that was before would be washed away, new things would grow in its place; a baptism of faith and ideas that had seemed so relevant before a storm would become irrelevant, lose their importance.

With classes due to start, and the sky growing dark as my temper, I knew I would have a problem soon. I had already missed the window of time to catch the bus and connect to the MRT. Cabs were a luxury to me. One journey would cost me three days of my student allowance. But I had no choice; I had been so engrossed in writing an essay assignment I had miscalculated the time.

The minute I stepped out of my HDB building, the rain poured its heart out. I had no umbrella. I ran back to the ground floor shelter but my hair was already drenched. I looked at my watch—an hour left to my class. If I catch a cab now, it would be a half-hour journey at top speed. That meant I was left with thirty minutes to find a cab, somehow, in rainy weather.

Ten minutes later, the rain had eased somewhat. It was drizzling, no longer a storm. This was the tropics—tempestuous weather as unpredictable as the spiciness of your curry. Still, I had no luck ordering a cab—none were available in my area; one eventually matched but cancelled on me within minutes. Frustrated, I stepped

out into the light rain and hailed for any cab whizzing past. Lo and
behold, three cabs stopped in the span of fifteen minutes. The first
was empty, with green signage flashing the telephone number of its
company. I've won the lottery, I thought and rejoiced.

Where you going? The cab driver asked.

NTU. Boon Lay, I shouted. I couldn't hear myself very well.
Water was in my ears.

He waved to dismiss me and stepped on his accelerator, splashing
a puddle of water on my canvas shoes. I cursed. I shouted after him:
Idiot! Times like these made me want to draw the edge of a metal
key on the side of a car.

The next cab driver was nicer. Atop his yellow vehicle, his
signage was green but had the letters S-H-I-F-T. This meant if my
destination was on the way to wherever he was going, he would take
me. Desperate, I waved to stop the cab.

Miss, I'm going to Hougang. Where you want to go? The cab
driver sang the words melodiously.

NTU? I asked without confidence, knowing he wouldn't take
me. Hougang was in the opposite direction from NTU.

Sorry ah. I change shift, later go home. Must pick up my daughter
lah. Sorry, Miss, the cab driver apologized. He had a daughter; he
felt sorry for a girl like me, getting drenched, trying to get to school.

Reluctantly he left, his car moving off slowly until it reached the
first traffic lights before he sped off. I looked at my watch. Damn!
Time was ticking.

I felt defeated. I was losing hope. Why was this even allowed
in Singapore? When the middle-class who cannot afford to have
cars are desperate for a ride and cabs decide to do a vanishing act
right when we most need them? How else would we get to our
destination? Fly? Teleport? There should be a law against this.
Selective passengering—if such a word even exists.

The last cab with a green signage caught my eye. I flapped my
arms like a drowning heron looking for rescue. It was a pale blue
taxi. It stopped where I was, and the driver rolled down his window.
I wasn't going to let him go so I stepped forward and reached for

the handle on the door, ready to open it and dive into the backseat regardless of where he wanted to go.

The driver moved his car by a few inches. He was in control.

Where you want to go? The driver barked.

To school! I responded just as loud, trying to assert authority. I didn't want to give away the information of my destination until I had gotten into the car and he couldn't get rid of me then.

I peered into the car. It was the driver who had driven Peter and I before. He recognized me and flashed me a conspiratorial grin. This must be karma, I thought, and died inside.

Aha! Uni student want to teach Uncle lesson today har? The driver cackled.

Uncle, please, I need to go to NTU. Have classes now, I implored.

You lucky Uncle in good mood. Just finished laksa, the driver said with a hint of a burp. I didn't need to smell it to know a whiff of his after-meal would permeate the air-conditioned taxi within minutes. I held my breath. Losers can't be choosers, I told myself. Okay lah, get in! The taxi driver yelled.

I thanked the driver three times when I got in and twice when I reached the university. Despite the bad traffic, the slower speed of driving due to the slippery road and poor visibility from the ongoing drizzle, I made it to my class five minutes past the start of the lesson. Throughout the journey, I was too embarrassed to talk to the driver. The radio was playing Nat King Cole, The Beatles, Patsy Cline, Cliff Richard, The Carpenters. The music of my grandparents. Old-fashioned nostalgia. Had I been too presumptuous about him? To assume he was ingratiating when it could have been a generational difference?

I decided, when the cab swung into the lobby of my university building, I would be a better person. I would eat my own words.

Sorry for last time, Uncle. I was talking nonsense. Don't mind me, I said with remorse.

Girl, you know, Singapore now, Uncle cannot recognize. Everything looks different, roads and buildings keep changing. Singapore machiam like changing clothes, always something brand new or colourful. I also cannot recognize what it looks like before.

You so young, don't judge what you don't understand. Driving taxi is a service. I make customers happy. They make me happy. You haven't started making money yet so you don't know how hard to make a living.

I know. I know.

Last time, you know how much your friend tipped me?

He tipped you? I said, pleasantly surprised. Peter knew it wasn't necessary to tip in Singapore.

He gave me fifty. No need to give back change. Good man. Boyfriend like this can keep.

He did that? I raised my voice.

He said to buy presents for my grandchildren. You didn't hear?

No, I didn't. I wasn't paying attention to their conversation then. I had been staring out the window and counting the cars go by. I had been following the passengers standing in the crowded bus going at the same speed as us whose eyes were staring at me with scorn, despising me for being in a car while they were squashed like sardines. Most days it would have been me in their place, holding a bar support myself, shoved elbow to elbow, waiting to be disgorged out of the tubular bus while my eyes were plastered to the small screen of my smartphone—my personal Pulau Innerworld—to shut out the rest of the world.

I didn't know he did that. So nice of him, I said.

Yeah, can keep for boyfriend. Not bad. Quite handsome. You lucky girl!

Exiting the taxi, I ran all the way to the seminar room. I wasn't the only person late. The lecturer had started talking about Henri Lefebvre and how space was something that could be produced to create political meaning and agency. Space. I was trapped in a room in a university on an island where space was condensed to the monotony of motions. Space was used for utilitarian purposes. Space in my world was the opposite of the space of infinity, of outer space, of black holes, whorls and multiple galaxies. I knew only my cage and its metallic bars. I needed a projection. Something beyond the present. Beyond the lack of climactic seasons, the machinery of theorems and tests, beyond the train rides that turned me into one robot out of a hundred robots in a capsule shuttling from one platform to another. I shut her voice out. My mind became still, peaceful. An image floated out of this serenity. *Eisblume*. I smiled, took out my smartphone and started texting.

Hey Peter, how's the vacation so far? Are you missing Singapore? Singapore misses you.

I paused as long as my courage could endure. I heard my professor's voice in the distance. I tuned her out again and returned to my phone, typing the rest of the message. *Pity we didn't have more time to hang out. Write back when you can.*

I heard the rain pelting on the roof. The cold room started becoming unbearable. Goosebumps pimpled my arms. Be bold, be honest, I told myself.

I signed off the message, *I miss you*, then pressed send.

I froze. Did I just externalize my thoughts? Could I delete it?

No. I couldn't. Had I just put myself out there? Crystallized an idea that had been floating around formless in the air? I blushed and giggled softly. Outside, the wind whistled aloud. Foool . . . Foooool, I thought I heard it say.

I took Peter's picture of the *Eisblume* and made it my screensaver. Something blossomed inside me. I listened to the professor and smiled at everything she said. The rain droned on to an acoustic murmur; a symphony amplifying the sounds of nature, drowning the mechanical words of theory, intellect, scepticism, empiricism. Ways to prove what exists with the whys and how-tos. The lecturer repeated: If you don't have enough points to substantiate your thesis statement, your argument isn't going to be very solid.

In my private reverie, I rewound scenes of the past, the private moments I had shared with Peter. I relished the jokes he made— even the awful ones that were meant to be humorous but turned out flat like roadkill. The more I reminisced, the more I turned Peter into something endearing. Maybe, just maybe, I had been focusing on the wrong side of him. I needed to examine him on the flipside. Notch up more points to make Peter a convincing argument.

What for? For the funny way he makes me feel. For the wistful way his face crops up in flashback and I don't know why or how it happened.

The rain seemed to have stopped. Someone opened the door to use the bathroom and the sounds of laughter from the corridor spilled into our room. A giggle came from the back of the class. Sounded like a girl, flirting with the hunkiest guy from the class who played rugby, water polo and tennis. The jock who couldn't be ignored. He who had no fear or qualms about the limitation of spaces. All spaces big and small were conquerable to him. If the world were the Bermuda Triangle, he was enthroned in the middle of it. From the way he looked smugly at me, I was to him, most definitely a square, like many others in his peripheral vision. Some spaces, even within the same plot, would never overlap, never connect. Sometimes it took imagination to leap out of the ordinary, to muse over shapes and spaces you couldn't quite grasp yet—these were unknown territories, unfittable puzzles, seasonal eccentricities.

The lecturer finally cracked a joke, a dry, lame witty joke about I don't know what and three people laughed. My phone beeped with a new message. It was Peter. There were only two words. It read:

Me too.

I stared at it too long, remaining stationary, thoughts congealing. The words dissolved while the screensaver with the *Eisblume* appeared from out of the dark of pixelated corners: odd-shaped, frosty, uniquely petalled by the spikes of beaded ice crystals, a budding bloom of nature's artisanal science I would never know why or how it happened that way.

Chapter 7

The Elephantine Apple

Grandma would love a family of elephants, Wilhelm said, pointing to a teak statue the size of his palm. The curved wood was polished till it shone when light fell on its spine. Next to it was a pig with wings, its snout pointing upwards, smelling the sky for rain.

Come in and take a look, the shop assistant's lilted North Chinese Mandarin welcomed us. I smiled perfunctorily and waited for Wilhelm to step in before I did. He was the tourist. I was just following.

I curved my spine, cocked my head this way and that, trying to peek at the price. $120 for the elephant. $100 for the flying pig. Four legs good; but two wings better.

It's a steal, I winked at Wilhelm. You should get it. Skip two dinners, miss the Night Safari. Window shopping on Orchard Road is free.

Steal? Wilhelm raised his voice. I don't want to steal anything!

I don't know if he was mocking me, or if he didn't know the expression. But I had communicated long enough with him to guess that his Swiss German English, as I called it, had its limitations. Some sentences sprung whole from him perfected. Some were mimicked from television, movies or popular culture jargon. Much of it was translated semantics. Sentences structured with different word order. Gendered articles. Nominative, dative, accusative, genitive endings. *Am Freitag kannst du ihm das Buch geben*: In Friday can you him the Book give. Properly translated in English: You can give him the book on Friday.

No, I said, it's an expression. Not to steal but it's a steal. Meaning, something's so cheap it's like stealing it. I meant it ironically.

I have a bigger one, double its size, from Krabi, Wilhelm looked at me smugly. Half of the price.

So if you buy this, your grandmother will have two. Mommy and Baby Elephant. Sweet.

Best things come in threes. I'll need to buy a third, Wilhelm groaned. But my luggage allowance will be over the limit. Coffee from Vietnam. Peppercorns from Cambodia. Tea from Myanmar. Two kilos each. And now elephants.

My eyes searched the display shelf. How about this, a bronze thimble? Old little ladies like to sew, don't they? I offered.

The price tag read $50, which made me raise my eyebrows.

She's eighty-six. I don't know if she can see the hole through a needle.

Oh.

Besides, she doesn't want anything too foreign, Wilhelm said, then corrected himself. What I mean is . . .

We were standing in a kitschy shop in Chinatown, and I was more local than the shop assistant, a foreign import like the souvenirs she sold.

I know, I interjected, my father the proud Chinese who considers the sandwich an unthinkable substitute for his rice meal thinks all food should be eaten cooked—sashimi and salads too.

Wilhelm smiled wryly then shrugged, Last thing I want to do is carry this thousands of miles across the ocean, give it to her, and she'll keep it in the storage for years and years. I'll remember it but it will be exotic junk to her.

I understood what he was trying to insinuate. His grandmother, in her eighties, and my dad, who had just turned eighty, were from a generation whose childhoods were touched by the last, major epochal war—World War Two: one in Europe; another in Asia. She, who knew the slogans to a fascist regime even through a crackling radio; and he, through the food rationing and rampant fear of being Chinese in Japanese-occupied Singapore. Their burdens were different from ours. History tainted by the colonization of weapons and blood. For our generation, our problems were capitalist materialism and not travelling enough. Fear of being killed and fear of not upgrading to the latest technological gadgets were two vastly different concerns.

Besides, Wilhelm continued, got to spend the remaining Singapore dollars on something special.

Like what? Drink more, get wasted? I said flippantly.

Wilhelm had been in Singapore for slightly over a week and was, according to him, out in the clubs most nights. I refused to join him until today, when we had decided to finally meet over a late lunch. His Southeast Asian escapades were coming to a close, and he had left Singapore as the cherry on top; the last pit stop to savour while he devoured the rest of the Far East first.

Maybe get someone a present.

Not for Grandma?

Do you sew? Wilhelm leaned into me.

His T-shirt grazed my arm. I knew his eyes were locked on mine but I couldn't lift my head up. I looked at the grey silver thimble. There were in fact two elephants on it—one carved into the body of the metal like fresco, another perched on top of it. Twinned creatures with the same fate of serving the thumb of the owner who liked to sew, a seamstress or tailor who could turn a piece of useless fabric into a fully functional garment to keep a person warm, make that person fashionable. Thimble plus needle and thread plus fabric equals dress or suit or pants or shirt. The purpose was clear. Unlike the overlapping oft-tangled threads of human relations.

We were standing really close now, almost touching but not quite. Our flesh never made contact, one giant swaying to and fro in a dancing parody with a dumpy tree. Families do. Lovers do. Friends do. Even strangers rub skins by accident. I reckoned it was considered strange in his culture to be so standoffish, as if one of us was diseased by a dermatological anomaly. I tried hard to play the role of the Asian prude, if he actually believed it as much as I definitely didn't.

But we just wouldn't allow ourselves to touch. Our skins were an inch apart, polarized by static.

I lifted my head and gazed at him. His eyes fell on the thimble immediately. Then he glanced at me through the corner of his eyes, nervously.

No, I don't, I answered him.

I had a question of my own, but it wouldn't come out of my mouth. Once, I had tried it with another man, asked the obvious, pushed for an answer, and the unstable threads of our nonexistent relationship unspooled, ribbons curling out of control. We never spoke again. It was beautiful when the mystery was in the box, covered with secrets; the moment it was opened, I peered into a gust of furious locusts. We still saw each other, but at a distance, each two-second stare a monologue, an accusation.

Now, with Wilhelm, I found myself at the exact moment, tension so thick I could feel the air within the four walls of the store stiffen to a ganache. Maybe I was thinking of chocolate because I was hungry. Or maybe because he had just given me a box of Swiss pralines.

Whatever it was, we would not see or touch or talk about the elephant in the room, the ginormous invisible we-both-know-it-but-let's-ignore-it fact that we somehow, subconsciously acknowledged that any reference to it through words would make it concrete, make this thing between us dirty.

We were both engaged to someone else. We shouldn't even be here at all. *Aber wir wollten.*

* * *

The night he left, I didn't manage to say goodbye to him. I wouldn't call him. He didn't call me either. What was there to add? Or subtract?

We were modern-day pen pals. We communicated. Then something grew out of language. But electronics was a poor substitute for the corporeal. What appeared like friendship from the closeness of technology was nothing more than cells multiplying into billions of whorls and zones and black holes that echoed and absorbed memories and fantasies both real and unreal.

Many times, I was lost. Sometimes he was lost too. Communication cut up by a buffering broadband connection, unspeakable thoughts, cultural chasms. Who really knew? Who kept count? Everyone was on the blue wire trying to find someone who spoke the same language, who could translate lostness. Everyone was looking for a world beyond their own, plucking out of the air, a feather of an unusual colour, something to marvel at, because it was fresh, different.

I had breathed in his presence while he was here. Then he was gone, on two wings and a tail, jet setting off. Like the flying pig. Air pork. Bak kwa. I should have insisted on him smuggling a sealed packet in his luggage. No way he would be able to find it in Bern. Each time someone I know fairly well is on a flight somewhere, I'd like to visualize what they are doing at that very moment. Imagine I'm being teleported to them, or them to me. Airspace: liminal zone, borderless continent, countryless, passportless; for the winged fugitives of dreamers. Have they fallen asleep? Neck at right angles to their shoulders, head lolling around? Are their legs feeling cramped and restless? Are they in the toilet? Hoarding toothbrushes? Are they refilling on free alcohol? Watching the third movie in a row with bleary eyes and jet lagged brains, each storyline bleeding into the other, narratives crisscrossing?

I couldn't really say he was a friend. I couldn't say he wasn't either. He was more to me than someone in the same city. People you can visit in half an hour but won't. That is the trouble with the internet. False relationships turn real. Real relationships evaporate; concrete fades to abstract.

I'd met him at a conference. We were in different fields. He was an unemployed twenty-something trilingual architect who really dug Rihanna and hated wine. I was a confused thirty-year-old historian with interests in Sanskrit and Soviet paraphernalia; and a Star Wars fanatic who occasionally crocheted to relax. He came with friends. I came with colleagues. A banter over tea break turned into an hour-long discussion of meaningless jokes over funny memes and viral videos.

Towards the end, metaphors of the sexual seeped in, and we continued our bawdry language. We analysed 'Wrecking Ball', 'Blurred Lines' and 'Pour It Up', reminding both of us of naked flesh and breasts and gyrating groins. Our chosen celebrities were our proxies, rubbing one song against the other salaciously while our tongues engaged in intercourse, using language as a striptease. Two strangers holding cold cups of black coffee, drinking words oozing out of each other's mouths. This is how seduction happens. Even if it is never admitted, never spoken of again; this is how two strangers know they have cast the web to ensnare each other in a moment of need—and someone heard and listened, and held out an open hand. Fingers intertwined between the gaps of the web, behind the shadows of conscience, of decorum.

Then sex happens. Between the flesh or as atoms hovering in the air. The elephant in the room we wouldn't talk about, growing larger the more it was ignored.

* * *

What is it we are doing? That was the question I'd wanted to ask him.

Wilhelm didn't buy the elephant thimble at Chinatown. We were famished, and the detour at the souvenir shop had delayed our lunch. I had planned to take him to a quaint, cosy place I had found on hungrygowhere.com, but frankly, Chinatown's signage is a mess of garish colours and contrived exotica; one shop looked the same as another.

Are we lost? Wilhelm had asked when we tried to make our way out of the souvenir shop. The drizzle had turned into a downpour. The view in sight now a blur, I couldn't see the sign for my street, let alone the next; or navigate.

I stood next to Wilhelm. We were like two figurines hard and cool as china, fragile with a single drop, paralysed, immovable. The rain, a hypnosis; he and I, each in our reverie. In mine, I imagined this.

There is the exit.

There is signage.

If you take this route, you end up on one path, meandering through rocky terrain, maybe a river or two, fight a bear, kill it, skin it, wear it as a trophy coat to tide the winter through.

If you take another, you end up in the steppes of nowhere land, swathes of grassland forever growing and disappearing, no habitat in sight.

Then there's the urban jungle, concrete heights of grey stretching to the clouds, cars flying into highways, humanoid automatons on conveyor belt, mouths mumbling binary code.

I'm always lost, I wanted to say to him but swallowed the words. The Google Map on my iPhone was the size of a chicken nugget squirming around the weak 3G signal.

I think we're close, he said, pointing to the map on his Galaxy. I leaned in to look and held my breath. I didn't want to smell him, didn't want the tactile part of his bodily senses to infuse me, confuse me further. It was enough for me to see and hear him. Touch was out of the question. Taste was illicit, another dimension. If you smelled something and you liked it, it might be the start of a craving, like food.

We walked down Temple Street briskly, getting partially drenched, my vision blurred by raindrops. I couldn't see the sign. I couldn't see the road. I didn't know which way to go.

Wilhelm was about to bump into me when I saw it and yelled, There!

The sign hung from the second floor of a shop house, right above the screaming neon lights of a karaoke bar on the lower floor. Lucky Paradise Restaurant.

Guess we're lucky after all, Wilhelm joked, to find paradise.

Hell, I muttered, I wish paradise weren't so full of contradictions.

He heard me. Why? What do you mean?

We were still walking in the rain that had petered down. A flash storm to slap me wet in the face. Soon the clouds will part, the sky sunny, and all will be forgiven.

Eve and the apple? Snake? Paradise is a place for dark souls to corrupt the good. The playing field is not even. Never was, and Eve got the short end of the stick for doing what's natural. Eat when she's hungry. Giving in to her craving.

And who do you sympathize with?

Eve, of course! Her instinct got her into trouble. Why should it? Should she have skinned the snake? Grilled it and eaten it instead?

Ah yes! Anything grilled is good, Wilhelm smiled with relish, I agree.

We have to cross the road, I said, pointing in the direction of the sign.

The cars kept coming one after another. I took my time, waited for them to pass. A minute became five. There were no traffic lights. It was a short street. Wilhelm walked ahead of me then took my hand, pulling me to the road. A moped flew past, swishing my skirt, making me jump.

What is it you are doing? I sputtered, eyes on our entangled hands while words spilled out like beads tumbling out of a broken rosary.

Following the sign, he said, pulling my arm as we dodged the front of a car, wormed around the back of a taxi, and avoided a motorbike that had appeared out of nowhere. Then he added, And being the snake.

We had crossed the road. The gaudy purple and green lights of the bar on the ground floor screamed into my eyes. My mind was screaming too. But nothing came out of my lips.

I stared at him. He looked serious then laughed.

Just joking! he said. Come on. Ladies first.

I knew he had answered the question I had wanted to ask him all along. I walked up the shadowed, dingy stairs while he followed behind, and as the smell of something grilled wafted down, all I could think of was whether he was checking me out from behind. My skin, wet from the rain, opened its pores to the heat of the enclosed space as my bare legs kept moving, and I no longer knew whether what awaited us in Lucky Paradise was an apple to be devoured or the elephant we could pretend was still invisible.

Chapter 8

Honey Flour Chocolates

Honey, flour and chocolates. The three gifts he gave to her. Honey to nourish your soul, he said. To lubricate me, you mean, she thought.

Flour, ready mix, just pour in 200 ml of water, stir and bake. German farmer's bread, or *bauernbrot*, you can't get it from Singapore, he said. Flour made her think of 'flower' and immediately joy rose from her heart, much like yeast.

Since everyone loves chocolate, I got you one from Germany. *Moser Roth*, I grew up eating this. Uses the best cocoa, tastes super, and is good for your circulation, he said. She stared into his eyes, felt the rush of his sweet gesture, thinking, I can get addicted to this attention you give me.

That was how Rainer was brought up—to be nice to nice girls. In a tiny nook of a medium-sized suburb in big-city Hamburg, Rainer was sandwiched in a family of two sisters and a matronly mother who baked, roasted and spooned organic purees into their golden lips. Rainer had learnt how best to soothe the quicksilver moods of feminine emotions by being a gift bearer. Even a used toy car gift-wrapped and tied with a ribbon was enough to make his younger sister squeal at age six. Frivolity, Rainer understood, was anchored to strong emotional needs that could win over a girl's loyalty.

The word 'nice' did not mean much to Josie. She had been shoved and pulled quite a bit; and been called god-awful names on too many occasions. She wasn't used to men who behaved like that, giving her things that were useful, fortifying, unless she counted Brand's Essence of Chicken. That she received once, in the midst of her final-year bachelor's degree examination by a boy who wouldn't become her boyfriend because his niceness irked her. It took her a long time to understand boys like that turn out to be good boyfriends, and even better husbands.

Thank you, she said almost too softly.

You're welcome, he replied, somewhat disappointed, wondering, were the gifts too . . . sundry?

She was confused as to why he was confused. Couldn't he detect from her tone? She was immensely touched. How could she amplify her gratitude?

Rapshonig. What does this mean? she asked, picking up the jar of murky, buttery honey, making sure she raised her voice slightly to sound girlish and delighted.

I don't know, let me check. Rainer looked it up on his phone, searching for a translation.

Josie knew by instinct what it was. But the word was too brusque to say out loud and it would taint the mood, puncture the setting with violence that didn't belong. She was familiar with that world and didn't want its intrusion.

Rapeseed honey. They're very common during summer in Germany, he said, then showed her a picture of a bright yellow field on his smartphone.

So beautiful, she responded. Rape. Seed. She twirled the words in her mouth like sand gnashed in a sandwich. What tragic words, what brutal metaphors for such cheerful flowers. Birth of Violence. How dreadful language can be.

* * *

Two summers ago was the first time Josie had seen real-life rapeseed, and what a sight it was! Fields of continuous, picturesque strips of yellow blooms on green, grassy hillocks flashed past her window through town after town on the Eurail train on her five-week backpacking trip. She didn't want to miss her stop, so she kept her eyes wide open and her ears alert for the announcement of her station while her mind went into shutdown. She wasn't alone, but even with a travelling companion she didn't want to miss her stop in an unknown city where the locals spoke a language foreign to her.

The scenery was hypnotic, the cabin stifling and the sun outside burning while millions of yellow flowers danced on her eyelids. Compounded by the monotonous burr of the train, an hour later, her eyes surrendered and she shut them finally. If only for a while, she told herself, if only for a little rest.

Even while Josie dozed off, her mind had captured the gaiety of the mood of the idyllic sunburst summer while she dreamt, though the quality of her dream suffered, for she couldn't drift into deep sleep, oscillating between wakefulness and dreaming, as her head drooped and raised repeatedly like a nodding sycophant.

In the dream, she was on a train, almost like this one, though it was speeding much faster, ten, maybe twenty times faster—so fast, things were flying off the tables and children had to be held down to their seats by their parents lest they flew off too. Josie felt her pelvis squeeze. She had an urge to urinate, so she got out of her seat to find the toilet. With her hair flying backwards, the skin on her face wobbling with the force of the forward movement, she tried to claw her way, seat by seat, down the aisle, towards the sign that blinked the word, 'damen'. It was red, occupied, so she stood hanging on the metal bar of a train door for dear life, looking outside the window, the panoramic view of yellow meadows swimming past her.

The train entered a tunnel. Josie looked at her reflection in the window opposite her. The woman in the reflection looked back. Josie checked her hair. Was it in place? She flattened her fringe then volumized the sides of her shoulder-length bob. She leaned forward, checked her eye bags. Were they decent or should she apply some coverage? Josie kept an eye on the toilet sign, still red, turned back and saw the woman in the reflection starting to cry. Within seconds, she was wailing like a banshee with a bone-chilling howl between sobs. But Josie wasn't crying; the woman in the reflection was.

The speeding train started to wobble, jerking the passengers back and forth. Josie was flung to the other side of the train door. The train exited the tunnel. The fields of gold were back. The train doors threw themselves wide open while the train was still moving. Josie found herself hurtling towards an open door, spat out of the train into the open. She screamed, flailing arms and limbs as she was ejected out forcefully, landing abruptly on the cushioned flowerbeds of the rapeseed harvest.

Then she woke up in fright. Where am I? Josie thought, her mind scattered and out of sync with her body.

Are you alright? the man sitting next to her asked. He was drinking from a thermos flask. It belonged to her—that she recognized. Her naptime nightmare had briefly made her forget he was her husband. Her present was coming back to her now.

Mmm, she mumbled, and relaxed. Just a dream, I'm alright now.

Want a drink? he offered. Oops, I've almost finished it.

Where are we now? she asked, turning to him. The dark curls of his hair, chocolate eyes; she found comfort in their familiarity.

Almost there. Maybe half an hour more, he said, putting his headphones on. He was tuning her out. That was familiar to her too.

She wanted to ask him if she had been crying in her sleep, but it was too late now. He wouldn't be able to hear her. She could tug at him and force him to pay her attention but he was already bobbing his head to the beat of whatever was in his head, eyes shut, tuning into himself.

Better use the toilet now before the crowd gets to it, Josie thought, and got out of her seat. The train was moving at its usual speed; she was not defying the forces of motion like in her dream, so she moved purposefully, quickly, getting into the toilet cubicle and shutting the door. Once shut, the toilet light came on, a startling white. Josie looked at her reflection. It was her alright; her eyes were a mess, her mascara having run, giving her black smudges on her eye bags. It was as if she had had a big cry. Josie sighed, took out a tissue, wetted it then wiped away the evidence of her outpouring. She returned to her seat, giving her husband an accusatory look.

When the train reached Berlin, Josie and her husband got their bags from the overhead compartment and alighted from the train. They each had a map and a copy of *Lonely Planet Western Europe*, and as her husband started to refer to the map of the metro, Josie decided she was too agitated to wait for a better time to nag.

Why didn't you tell me I was crying earlier? My mascara was messed up. I looked like a panda, Josie snapped.

You were? He turned to her and inadvertently let out an ill-timed yawn. I didn't hear you crying at all.

What do you mean you didn't hear? She was getting upset.

I had my headphones on, he replied. It was loud.

Well, couldn't you see my mascara had run? She retorted, vexed.

He peered at her face. No trace of evidence in sight.

You look fine to me, he pointed out.

I cleaned it up! Earlier, when you asked me if I was okay, didn't you see my eyes were a mess? Josie fumed, her anger and voice rising concurrently.

Her husband looked at her indifferently. It's always something, isn't it, he thought, always blaming me for everything.

No, I didn't, he replied coolly then walked away from her, yanking his luggage along violently.

* * *

The day she flew across the living room, she knew she had it coming. How the conversation had started, what had triggered the argument, even how it ended on a sour note—none of it mattered. Though who threw whom across the wide stretch of a ten-foot rectangular room was obvious. It was he, her husband, the man she married who weighed double her size. He held her by two arms and flung her with great force, sending her sailing across the parquet floor to the other side of the room where she landed with a dramatic flop on the floor. Josie remembered she had once thrown a doll that way as a child. She was now that doll.

It always began with an accusation. One of them was in a surly mood. It was either her PMS or his comedown from something he had smoked.

Can't you pay for the groceries this time? He demanded from the sofa where he was sitting.

I did, I've already bought it, I'm cooking dinner with it. You pay your share, we agreed. Josie reasoned with her husband as she stood facing him. The living room seemed to have shrunk, all of a sudden. She could hear him breathing.

I don't have the money, he replied dismissively.

Then how come there's extra beer and wine in the house? And you're obviously smoking something. Where's the money to buy *all that*?

It's not *your* business what *I do* with *my money*, he sneered.

Yes it is. We split the rent, we split the bills. Then I do all the cleaning and the cooking. I don't even earn that much. You can't spend on what you enjoy and pretend that bills are my problem! Josie shouted.

You buy what you like. I don't even eat the stuff you buy, he said, defiant.

Oh yes, you do. Almost every single day.

Yes, and they suck, he said with a smirk.

Josie was dumbstruck.

I cook better than you, he added. Admit it. You burnt the chicken last time.

Only on the tips of the wings! Only that!

Twice you tried making something with flour; they were a disaster. The muffins were flat and hard. Like rocks. What's the other thing you made? Bread! You really aim high.

You told me to add more baking soda, she seethed.

Don't blame me for your mistake. And how did it turn out? It collapsed in the middle, remember? Good job, Iron Chef.

You try baking bread, know-it-all. It's not easy as it looks. At least I try different things. You just make the same things over and over again.

I rest my case. I do cook better than you. And what I cook I'm pretty damn good at. Plus, I've never burnt anything. And that . . . is . . . a . . . fact, he reiterated smugly.

So if I cook every day and you cook once a month that makes you a better cook? You win me? She felt herself getting hysterical.

He raised his voice: I cook more than that! You know that!

Well, why don't you go to the store and buy the fucking groceries, carry the six fucking bags of groceries from the store to the bus stop, take the bus, and walk half a fucking kilometre back home with five fucking kilos in each hand. Why don't you do that? You're a man, you're big and strong. Why the fuck don't you do that? Josie yelled, her mouth running faster than her thoughts.

That was when it happened. She found herself being held by her arms, his fingers coiled around her flesh, both of them trembling with rage, and in one shove, one unblinking, unthinking moment, Josie's husband pushed her across the room; and as she was thrown backwards, still in shock, the only thought in Josie's mind was *Did I deserve this?*

The aftermath was probably just as shocking to her. He did not come running to her when she fell. He did not pick her up with contrite or beg shamefaced with the words her pride wanted to hear, *I'm sorry I wasn't thinking I don't know what came over me are you alright please forgive me I'll never do this ever don't leave me I'll do anything you want I need you I love you I can't live without you.*

No, Josie's husband just walked off, still in his tantrum, skulking off as a raging bull would, being denied its red flag. Even when she sat on the cold floor weeping in fits, he did not go to her. She understood he was punishing her for her behaviour. He was denying her kindness; even if what he had done was on impulse, he should have followed up by trying to recover the situation based on reflex or pity.

Only when her crying had subsided, when Josie had stopped crying for ten minutes did he appear, a forlorn figure who said nothing to her about what had happened but moved among the furniture as usual, an animal sniffing for table scraps, his movements familiar, audible; his presence telling her he could stand her now so he was back in the instant, he wasn't going away, he still wanted to be with her.

At a moment like that, Josie regretted not following her impulse to bolt. She stayed, went to the kitchen, put the kettle on and stared out the window while the water came to a boil. It was not the first or the last time she would have to lick her wounds on her own.

* * *

Usually for teatime, Josie enjoyed a pot of red tea and something sweet. One of her favourite snacks was muah chee—a Chinese version of the Japanese *mochi mochi*—made with glutinous rice flour and dusted with peanut powder, if she could lay her hands on some. Sometimes it was chocolate, milk chocolate preferably, or even better, pralines.

Rainer had given her dark chocolate, *Bitterschokolade*, an 80-gram slab of rectangular bittersweetness he had wrapped in two paper towels inside a blue-orange Aldi plastic bag, snuck it between two pairs of jeans in his luggage, smuggling it in all the way from Germany on his last work trip back home, together with the packet of flour and a sticky, leaked jar of honey.

You can't get these here in Singapore, he had told her then, in all earnestness.

I grew up eating these chocolates, and this is our typical local honey. You know, the same flowers they use to produce canola oil or diesel. It's our flower power, Rainer chuckled, beaming with pride.

You use flowers to make diesel? No kidding, Josie queried, genuinely surprised.

Ja. Don't underestimate what these little flowers can do to generate horsepower for new generation automobiles. Earth friendly too. Good old German engineering. You know diesel comes from the name of Rudolf Diesel, a German scientist who invented the first plant-oil engine for cars?

No, Josie didn't know that, and no, she didn't have the heart to tell him either that she could get most of the European produce here—even the gifts she was cupping in her hands—in high-end artisanal boutique shops or bakeries sprinkled liberally all over the red dot island she called home. Worse, she didn't have the heart to tell him she disliked, no, loathed, dark chocolate. It defeated the purpose of eating chocolate, which—according to her—had to taste sweet and creamy with a lingering taste of cocoa. Dark chocolate was intense, it masked the nuance on her tongue. Her life, she felt, was bitter enough. No need to rub it in.

She kept the bar of dark chocolate from Hamburg for as long as she could, stashed inside the depths of a drawer cabinet where the sun wouldn't shine, and her mind would forget about it. The next time she saw it, it was on the coffee table in front of the television set; half of it anyway, the other half on the lips of her husband, melting into the cavernous dark of his mouth.

What are you doing? her raised voice startled both of them.

Eating. What does it look like I'm doing? he garbled, eyes on the TV.

Chocolate? At midnight? Are you insane?

No!!! he yelled at the TV. His home team had missed a goal. He was watching premier league soccer.

Do you even know that's not yours? Josie chided.

Her husband ignored her, eyes following the little legs running from left to right on the flickering screen.

Hey! I said, whose chocolate is that? Swine, Josie grumbled, walking to him and grabbing the chocolate on the table, waving the wrapper in his face.

Hmph? Josie's husband broke from his trance. Move! he slapped her thighs lightly. She had blocked the entire TV screen, standing in front of his view.

It's MY chocolate. Who said you could eat it? Josie said.

I'll buy you one tomorrow. Now can you move!

Josie moved. She was upset beyond belief. It was a gift and sure, she hadn't planned on consuming it, but it was still hers. Hers! She owned this bittersweetness, all of it, all tiny squares of charcoal brown that she had no intention of savouring.

Yes!! Yes!! G-O-O-O-O-A-A-A-A-A-L-L-L-L-L-L-L-L!!!!

Josie's husband leapt to his feet, punching air fists, then fell heavily on the sofa, triumphant with the scoring. He laughed and hooted, texted into his phone something congratulatory to someone and ate more chocolate.

Josie had sunk into the sofa on his other side, holding the half packet of chocolate he hadn't consumed. She looked at it. It didn't look as dark as she thought it would. She peered closer and saw what it was. White spots had colonized the entire chocolate bar. They were minute and aplenty. Ugh, Josie thought, feeling disgusted. She turned the wrapper around. Sure enough, it had expired nine months ago. Had to be the damp in the kitchen, she thought, that and the humid tropical climate.

Hey! Josie tried to catch the attention of her husband, who was now engrossed in a game on his phone. His face was in fight-mode, battling imaginary enemies, winning unreal medals, tallying up meaningless scores.

Screw you, Josie thought, and rose from the sofa. She threw the rest of the chocolate into the bin, went to the washroom and started to remove her makeup. A cotton wad soaked with her milk cleanser, she dabbed at her eyes; her vision getting poorer as the cream left a thin film on her irises when there were vigorous loud knocks on her door.

You finished?

It was her husband, hurrying her as usual.

Not yet, she mumbled a little louder for his benefit.

I need to go. Come on, her husband said, insistently.

Wait! she said and started to remove the last traces of the red stain on her lips. She splashed some water on her face to remove the grease, patting her face dry with a towel then quickly applied a cucumber kaolin clay mask on her face, avoiding her eyes and lips.

Her husband opened the door. It wasn't locked.

Got to go. Now. Come on! Can you move? he pleaded, half-barking at her.

Josie could see he was serious. She knew what it was but didn't tell him. Not yet. Let him suffer a bit, she mused to herself.

Alright. What's the hurry, funny bunny?

Stomach ache, he muttered, pushed her out, banged the door shut, and Josie thought she heard an explosion coming from inside.

She hurried away, chuckling to herself, nose wriggling. Swine, she said under her breath, knowing it was an extremely bittersweet moment she would be able to savour for months after that. *Orr be quek*, she muttered in Hokkien, sniggering.

Five, ten, fifteen minutes later, Josie's husband still hadn't emerged. The mask on her face had almost hardened. Her face could hardly move. She knocked on the door.

How long are you going to take? she said loudly, avoiding too much lip movement lest the mask cracked.

A while, go away, he answered weakly.

Hmph, she grunted, audible enough to let him hear her displeasure.

With nothing to do but wait, Josie parked herself in front of the TV. An old rerun episode of *Everybody Hates Raymond* was on. Deborah and Raymond squabbling like a duck and chicken about inane domestic duties used to make her laugh, but now, not so much. It was quite painful to watch comedy mimicking real life drama; it was funny when it happened to other people, the antics of fools and the foolish. Not funny if she had experienced it herself. Marriage took a lot of work, unpaid, ungratifying work, like chucking the logs of an entire forest just to keep the spark of a flame that had ignited a long time ago from extinguishing.

A Volkswagen ad came on. Anything vaguely German always reminded Josie of Rainer. It had been a year since she last saw him when he had quit the company and returned to Germany. They hadn't communicated at all for some reason. She, out of a strange sense of moral decency; he was now a father, and they were both married while their so-called friendship was in a grey area. No need to complicate matters, Josie had reasoned.

News about Rainer had emerged during lunchtime gossip. Her colleagues told her, months after Rainer had left, he had gotten engaged to a Bavarian *fraulein*, married, and was the father of an infant boy soon after. There were whispers of a shotgun marriage. It wasn't Josie's place to judge him. He had gone on to become a family man, a *familienvater*.

Josie was proud of him still for taking the plunge. There was nothing between them. Friendship, definitely. Romance, likely not.

Or was there?

Was there a behavioural code for nice boys like Rainer? Did they give presents regardless of romantic potential? Josie didn't know. They had several work lunches, being colleagues after all, in restaurants full of other co-workers. Then there were two dinner dates that were meant to be with two other colleagues who had fallen sick, one to food poisoning, another to flu, so dinner ended up with just the two of them, the appearance of which looked like a date between a married woman and a single bachelor. Great repartee they had, Josie admitted, but there was always something amiss. Something Josie couldn't articulate except blame on a lack of chemistry.

Maybe there was a moment between them, something sweet, like honey; something that rose from the mixture of their odd-fitting personalities like yeast that grew without control; or something bittersweet, with a potentiality that had expired.

Whatever it is or was, Josie was above all, grateful. Rainer had gone on to live his life with someone who fully deserved all his niceties, who wouldn't call him 'swine' and for whom he would nourish her soul and stomach, Josie thought poignantly, and he would be a wonderful father, giving his son night feeds while his tired wife slept or changing diapers when she took her time with her dinner. Rainer would be the kind of father, Josie imagined, who would take paternity leave so he could stay home with his baby while his wife went off to the mall to pamper herself with a manicure, a new hairdo or shop for new shoes and dresses, maybe a pair of jeans that would finally fit after childbirth.

Josie thought of all the things Rainer's wife would have that she didn't or couldn't have. The kind of life that was meant for her but since then she had to settle for less. Perhaps that was the kind of life nice couples ended up having, instead of the shouty mess she found herself stuck with day in, day out, smelling the shit from behind the door of the en suite bathroom in her bedroom.

Thirty minutes later, Josie's husband still hadn't emerged from the bathroom. She whipped out her smartphone and checked her emails. A couple of ads from her credit card company, a travel booking website and a Facebook notification were quickly deleted as Josie scanned what else was new in her life.

There it was. An email, fresh and unexpected, from the person she had been thinking about. It was Rainer. She clicked on the bold subject line with a sense of thrill.

Hey beautiful! How's everything? Been thinking about you lately. Want to video chat sometime? Bored every day, working nonstop. The weather here sucks. Cold and grey and nowhere fun to play. Miss the sunshine in Singapore. Miss the nice ladies like you. ;) Rainer

Josie stared at the email long enough to let the meaning of it sink in. No nuance. No game. No pretence. An open invitation it seems, Josie thought, for mischief. Too easy, too crude. What happened to the sweet, civil gentleman she remembered him as? Couldn't he at least pretend to be one so she could also play along?

She couldn't resist. She was amused, flattered and predictably baited. She typed a reply.

No video chat function. Hate to Skype. What's up, golden boy? Still charming the beer ladies? Haven't heard from you since forever. Let's stick to email, for now. Nice of you to reconnect.

Josie sent the email then deposited her phone on the coffee table. Swine, she muttered, all of them swine. Yet, in spite of herself, she couldn't contain the smile curling on her lips.

I'm finished! Josie's husband yelled. He had obviously finished his bowel business. A minute later, he strolled into the living room; a sweaty, beleaguered hulk. He stared at her caked mask and snickered. Josie knew he was headed for the sofa so she sprung up from her seat, avoiding him, shuffling quickly to the bathroom where she could finally continue with her ablution.

The stench was overpowering the minute she got in. Ugh, Josie grumbled as she held her breath then gave up, returning to the living room with utmost reluctance as she sat down on the side of the sofa as far as possible from her husband.

Do you like my present? he asked cheekily, eyes twinkling at his wife. Smells like roses, doesn't it?

No, smells just like you, Josie replied with a sigh, resting her head on a closed fist, her elbow planted on the arm of the sofa.

You like it, admit it, he teased, pulling her close.

When you live with shit, you get used to shit, she deadpanned, pulling away and with great resolve, went back to the bathroom, holding her breath as much as possible. Josie was tired; she wanted to go to bed.

She turned on the shower and stepped in. This should wash off the smell in the room and the mask off her face, she thought, and began to rub away the dissolving chalky clay away from her cheeks, nose, forehead and chin. She then soaped herself liberally from the neck down to her chest, stomach, pelvis and limbs, down to her soiled soles, forming soft white clouds of rose-scented bubbles that drifted her mind off to somewhere far, far away, somewhere filled with fields of gold, sweet decadence and better days ahead where the pliant, magical hands of a confectioner will concoct a ravishing and delectable fantasy that has no place in her humdrum and embattled existence.

Chapter 9

The Scents of Sweat

Two women, noticeably expatriates, one platinum blonde and the other a glossy brunette, bump into each other while shopping for shoes at Aldo in Westgate Mall. One is pushing a stroller, a space-taking vehicle that could mow down naked toes in sandals, the push-the-baby-while-I-jog MPV-equivalent, the Quinny Zapp Xtra. The other woman dangles a mustard leather Gucci handbag on her arm, her right elbow sashaying at the same time as her left leg.

Small talk is about to ensue, that's obvious. I watch them from my seat at Coffee Club, safe behind my glasses as I sip on an iced tea, calculating their moves.

Elena!

Cathy.

They hug, skins touching, their lips barely grazing the surface of each other's cheeks. A baby's leg sticks out, followed by a fist grabbing bunches of air pockets. Cathy waves her baby's hand away.

What are you doing here? Cathy asks, eyes brightening.

Even from where I'm sitting, I can see Elena stiffening.

Nothing. Just walking, shopping. You? Elena says, casting an eye on the baby.

I'm bored to tears, just me and the bub, you know, day in, day out. Geoffrey works all the time. I like to get out and about.

The baby whimpers, kicks two legs in succession.

I know, Elena answers flatly.

She doesn't know. She's not a mother; I make a guess, intrigued by these two. I turn my head so my ears pick up more pieces of the conversation.

Are you going to stay here longer? Do you want to grab a coffee? Cathy asks, pointing her chin towards the café in my direction. She sees me looking at her. I avert my eyes quickly to the nearest artificial fern.

I don't know . . . I'm . . . in a hurry.

Oh! Work is it?

Work? No, no, not work.

The baby has started crying, leaning forward enough for me to see that it's a well-fed, pudgy girl, attired in pink. She's grabbing onto Cathy's dress, yanking it sideways.

How about later on? I'll be around. I don't mind waiting, Cathy persists. I haven't spoken to another adult for weeks. I'm about to go mad, she laughs lamely.

Elena takes one step backwards. Cathy follows her rhythm, steps forward towards her. The baby is holding onto a dangling Lamaze turtle toy and chewing on it, salivating and grinning at the same time.

Perhaps . . . , Elena starts tentatively.

In an hour? Two hours?

This weekend? Elena offers kindly then checks her phone. Oh wait! I'm not free this weekend.

When did you start working? I thought you had problems getting a work visa?

It's not work.

Oh. That's right. You said that already, Cathy replies sheepishly, laugh lines breaking into a fine web from the creases of her eyes. Sleep deprived mommy, you know, I can't retain information.

I'm sure you must be tired, Elena deadpans. As if she needed to express some kind of sympathy, she continues, You have someone to help you? A nanny? Helper?

We have a cleaner. She comes round three times a week. Our apartment is too small to have a live-in helper. Penthouse suites are great if you are single, you know, not for families like ours. When the baby cries, everyone wakes up. Even the neighbour's shih tzu.

A girl with an overpowering scent of peach perfume squeezes past my table. She's in a tiny skirt, white, that swishes while she walks. There's a lot of skin, so much so I look up at her and stare hard. She gives me the kind of smile that puts a lump in my throat.

S'cuse me, the white-skirted girl says kittenishly as she glides in an imperceptible dance, blending into the sea of incoming shopping traffic. It takes me a moment to gather myself. Then my eyes return to the two Caucasian women.

Take my number, Cathy is insisting to Elena, who reluctantly presses some buttons on her phone.

I think I have it somewhere.

Are you sure? I don't have yours.

Hmm. No, I don't have it. It's K-A-T-H-Y, right?

With a C, not K.

My eyes search through the crowd for the girl in the white skirt. There are many girls—some in skirts, some in shorts. But that same girl is no longer around. A spontaneous smile by a young girl like that, not older than twenty, to a guy like me, in my late-thirties, can fill my mind the entire day. The unconscious teaser, like a drop of honey, lingers like sweet lychee lust that smells of after-rain grass and the mulch of mud.

Shall I call you or do you want to call me later? Cathy asks loudly. Her voice interrupts my reverie. I return my attention to them.

Best if I call you. In case I'm occupied.

The baby has pulled the toy off the stroller and throws it on the ground. She gurgles and grimaces, then finally whimpers.

Bye baby, Elena holds onto the baby's right fist and shakes it gently. She smiles genuinely, as if preferring the baby to the mother.

As she leaves, her Gucci bag swings to the movement of her body. A slender, tall and classy lady, in her thirties maybe, the sensuality of her moves is nothing compared to the bendable limbs of the lithe teen I had earlier in my imagination.

Cathy pushes the stroller brusquely off, picking up the toy as she chides the baby softly. I see them vanish from sight as the mother digs around the bags hanging on the stroller, brandishing a lunchbox from which she whips out cookies that she hands to her hungry child who ravishes her treat.

I lean back in my seat, boredom setting in. The straw in my drink is bent. I unbend it, bend it again then lift the glass to let the cold condensation drip on the table, away from the coaster; I have an uncontrollable urge to make a mess. The brown of the table turns darker at the spot where the moisture seeps into the wood.

Hi, a voice says.

I peer up, expecting to see a waiter. It is Elena. I jerk backwards, confused.

Huh? It is the only sound I can muster.

You were watching us, Elena says coldly.

W-w-was I? I stutter. I detect an indiscernible accent from her. Heavy, low-throated and mono-tonal. Russian?

May I? she points to the empty seat next to mine then sits down before I can answer. At such close range, I can see the roots of her hair are brown. The entire length of her very long and very straight hair is shimmery yellow straw.

I don't know why the next line that comes out of my mouth is this, but I thought, perhaps she's an assassin; I'm in deep shit.

Are you going to kill me? I ask, voice trembling.

I've seen the movies, the Harrison Ford thrillers where he runs from start to finish, all because he's at the wrong place at the wrong time. That's me right now. My heart sinks, just thinking of the debauched life I have always dreamed of but never dared to live.

Elena bursts out laughing. She turns to me, exuding all her femininity then intones huskily, No . . . unless you want me to.

The waiter comes by my table and picks up the plate splattered with crumbs. Earlier, I had gorged myself on a big slice of chocolate cake. The evidence of my rapacious frenzy is cleanly swept away.

I watch Elena put a casual arm around the chair where my canvas satchel bag is. Getting more confused by the minute, I try different questions.

Are you soliciting? Are you offended I was looking at you? If so, I'm sorry. What *are* you?

What's your name? Elena says, her eyes lazily scanning my features.

Me? I blurt, racking my brain. Shall I give an honest or a fake response?

Yes, name. What is it?

Mick, I half-lie—it's actually Michael, but I can't think of a better alternative under duress.

Alright, Mick, Elena says. I'll call you.

She picks up my phone from the table, dials her number, which makes her phone ring, so now we both have each other's numbers.

Okay, job done.

She stands up to leave. At such close range, I detect perfume, a lingering scent of something musky with rose. A woman's scent. Instead of feeling aroused, I am afraid of her. I've seen one too many hardboiled crime movies where the beautiful damsel in distress turned femme fatale ends up killing the hapless male protagonist. Moreover, Elena is so blonde she fits the bill.

And Mick? Elena winks at me, only slightly. Don't be strangers now, alright? Ciao.

I watch the curve of her spine sway to her hips, as the glint of her Gucci logo warns me with a metallic gleam, and all I can manage is a weak wave from a lowering arm.

* * *

Go. Go. I tell myself for twenty minutes after Elena has left. But I can't move, obeying a stunning woman who has given me no cause to fear her except my fear itself, irrational as it is, based only on instinct; fed too much on popular culture tropes of femme fatales such as the likes of her. The ones who lure a man into the bedroom all pumped up with virility, then eat his head, or chop his manhood off, or impregnate (always possible in sci-fi stories) him to make an interspecies hybrid to colonize earth.

At that very moment, who would pass by outside the café but the young girl in the white skirt. She stands in full view where I can see her, oblivious to my presence, unlike Elena earlier who had watched me hawk-eyed. The white-skirted girl taps her phone with a self-satisfied grin plastered on her face that makes me want to lick it suddenly. Another immodest idea comes to me when along trots a young strapping youth glowing with an athletic tan, his torso and biceps muscly in his tight Aeropostale tee. He scoops her up with the kind of urgent embrace that tells me I stand no chance whatsoever. Their arms hook around each other, they lean in, kissing nose to nose in their sickeningly sweet adolescent romance. And just like that, the couple whisk themselves off to conquer the world. I sigh deeply—there's my youth gone down the drain.

The phone beeps. I look: ELENA. Fuck.

Hello Michael.

It's Mick.

No. It's Michael. I saw your name on your bag, she chuckles faintly.

I swivel my head quickly. My bag does bear my name embroidered on it—Mother's gift to me five years ago on my birthday. Damn you, Mother.

What do you want? I ask rudely.

You look like a man who wants to make some spare cash, she says in a way that makes me suspect she must be laughing inwardly.

She is right. I am freelancing as a graphic designer. I do need to make some spare cash. Not selling my organs though!

It's none of your business, I reply, brave behind the camouflage of the phone.

Listen. It's simple. You know the woman I was talking to just now?

Who?

Don't pretend. You saw her. The one with the baby. Cathy.

Is that her name?

Yes. Cathy. Now, listen. In half an hour, Cathy is coming to the café where you are right now. She will take an empty table. You will go to her, be nice to her, talk to her.

I start laughing.

Listen to me now, Michael. Go talk to her. Or better still, listen to her talk. She likes people to listen to her. She can talk a lot. Especially about herself.

Excuse me. I don't know you and I don't know her. Why on earth would I do that?

I'll give you $100. Easy gig.

I stop my chortling. I ponder her offer seriously. Just talk to a woman with a baby and get paid?

What's the catch?

No catch.

Now, I mentally calculate, if I talk to the woman for two hours for $100 that works out to, what, $50 per hour?

How long for?

It's up to you and her. If she likes to talk with you, you can go on forever. If it's for an hour, then so be it.

I thought, That's not bad, $100 for an hour? I try to sound indifferent as I answer, Hmm . . . let me think about it.

There's nothing to think about. She's on her way. Remember to be nice to her. Treat her like a lady.

Then when I finish, how do I get my money?

You already have it, Michael. It's inside your bag.

My bag is open. I peer inside. There is a note with a one and two zeros that doesn't belong to me.

Don't get me into trouble, Elena. I don't break the law.

I can hear her easing up on the phone. A nasally laugh breathes out of my phone speakers.

You don't get yourself into trouble. I'm paying you to talk to a beautiful woman. You should thank me.

Right. A beautiful woman with a baby. There's nothing there for me, I disagree with a snort.

We'll see.

Out of the corner of my eye, I can see the mammoth stroller headed towards me—or the café, that is. The sleek brunette bob of Cathy's hair hugs her gamine face. She looks younger than I thought, in her late twenties at most, her face bare of makeup, with startling light grey eyes. The sun exposure on her fair skin makes her cheeks burnished with a dark pink while she has minute laugh lines around her eyes; nevertheless, an evidently attractive lady.

Oh, she's here, I whisper into the phone.

Good. Now, before I forget, Michael. She's there to meet me actually. I'm going to text her later I can't make the appointment.

She may be disappointed. Then you go and talk to her, befriend her. Don't scare her off. Be a gentleman. You look like one. I trust you'll do your best?

I look like a gentleman? First time anyone has said that of me, I thought, amused.

Alright now, work your Keanu Reeves charm on her. Ciao.

And then she hangs up. My phone in my hand, bribe in my bag, iced tea finished, bladder about to burst, a woman with a baby to seduce—now what step shall I take first?

* * *

The baby takes the first step. From three tables away, she hurls a bottle cap her mother has given her as a temporary toy; a flying blue plastic object lands right at my elbow. She gurgles with glee. I am impressed with her aim. Her mother is aghast, and when she looks in my direction with great apologetic eyes, I know the timing is now.

I'm terribly sorry! Cathy calls out from her table. She admonishes her infant with mock gravity, arms gesturing, whispering to her child, explaining civil conduct to a baby who is clearly triumphant over her hand-eye coordinated motor skills. An athlete can perform sports whenever she wants.

It's perfectly fine. Babies, I shrug it off with a wry smile.

I bend down, pick up the bottle cap.

Do you want it back? I ask Cathy.

No, no. Don't trouble yourself, she shakes her head and a hand.

Maybe the baby wants it back, I say, pointing at her child whose plump fingers are opening and closing in anticipation of the object I bear in my hand.

Louise! No! Cathy says sternly to her baby, one finger raised as warning. The baby ignores her, whimpers to me, fingers clutching and unclutching faster.

I stand up, move towards their table.

May I? I ask Cathy, the cap in my fingers dangled in front of the child who has started to mouth: Me! Me!

Cathy sighs. She takes the cap from me, cleans it on a paper napkin and hands it to Louise.

Thank you, she says.

I think fast. I need to stay and talk to her as instructed. Can't leave her table empty handed. What excuse shall I use to stay where I am?

Louise takes another aim and hurls the cap at my empty table. It bounces off the tabletop and lands on the floor. The baby bubbles over with joy. Cathy and I look at each other. We laugh. I walk over to my seat, pick up the cap and return it to her, placing the cap in front of her.

Louise! What did I say? Cathy scolds.

Louise gazes at her then at me. I bend down to her level and say with mock sternness, Naughty. She pulls off my spectacles.

Cathy is horrified. She opens her baby's tight-fisted clutch and tries to pry my spectacles away with much effort. She returns them to me. We both see that one side of the frame is slightly dented. Her look is priceless.

I cannot believe what she has done! I cannot . . . I am so, so sorry! Cathy is no longer pretending to be mad at her child.

The infant looks terribly scared. Her mother has the kind of crossed face reserved for special days when baby has gone overboard. Today is that day. Louise starts to cry.

It's fine! I try to reassure Cathy. In my mind, I know it's easy enough to unbend the metal frame. It will never get back to its original shape, but it can be adjusted for continued use. It will feel awkward, but what's done is done.

I unbend the metal to show Cathy that the damage can be reversed, then put my spectacles on—hide the defect, be the nonchalant hero.

There. See? I said, turning my head side to side.

Cathy is sheepish, embarrassed.

Can I at least buy you a drink as apology?

Bingo! I grin widely then reply, Sure.

What would you like? Mister . . . ?

Michael. And you? I pretend to ask.

Cathy. And this is Louise, the midget monster.

We shake hands. I shake Louise's hand too. It feels grimy with crumbs.

Coffee or tea?

I'll have Perrier. Give the baby another bottle cap to practice her aim. Consider it my sponsorship for her career in discus throwing.

Cathy bursts out laughing, a girlish *hur-hur* that seems to reverberate at the back of her throat.

I'll be back with your water. Keep Michael company, will you, Louise? And oh, your things are still there. Are they safe? She points to my belongings where my table is.

Yes, you're right. I should have them with me. Shall I join you then?

With pleasure. I could use some company.

Me too, I say, our eyes meeting under the odd lighting of the café that is too dim for reading and too bright for something clandestine.

A couple of seconds pass. Cathy frowns, her brows gather closer to each other. Behind my spectacles, I hide my emotions, show nothing. She doesn't know I'm on a mission, and I don't know anything about her yet. But I will.

Already I'm confused before I have even begun. Women do that to me. With or without a baby.

* * *

I'm at the café again with Cathy. Louise is being taken care of by a part-time nanny, the same woman who cleans her apartment and moonlights on the side as a barista and bus driver. This is our third time here; our first time alone, just the two of us. We both know what we are up to, though we don't articulate the words.

Did you finish reading it? I tease Cathy. We sit apart like most friends do, while our legs are closer than they should be; sometimes they touch ever so slightly.

I couldn't find the time. I'm halfway through, she smiles lopsidedly.

It's one of my favourites.

I've seen the film though. Does that count?

They're similar but very different. The language of Kundera is hard to transpose on the screen.

Lena Olin was very beautiful, I remember. Daniel Day Lewis was, oh my, in his prime.

The hat.

Yes, the hat.

We both smile, each remembering the prop in a scene of a film we had seen at separate occasions in our lives.

It's better to read the book first then see the film. Now you know how it ends, I speak softly, touching her shoe with my shoe. She doesn't move her foot. The contact makes us both comfortable and uneasy at the same time.

I can't figure out what the title means, Cathy says, almost breathily.

The Unbearable Lightness of Being . . . a philosophy. Lightness versus the heaviness of life, of burdens, of love, of existence.

What's light? What's heavy?

To travel light. To live light. Not to have worldly possessions, of long-term relationships. Heavy is the opposite, to want materialism, to own another person, to have the institutions of marriage, of bonds, family. The characters go through the book trying out both lightness and heaviness. Eventually, even the theory of living light is unbearable; it leads nowhere. It is an idea of an ideal that doesn't live up to its promise.

A heavy life . . . that's good?

Well, I don't think the author offers a solution. The title does suggest a preference for lightness since he puts it there. But he doesn't let the reader off easy, so maybe that's why he reminds us it is unbearable. Humans do crave rootedness at the end of the day. No matter how much we want to float away, to crave freedom. To have unlimited amounts of it, is like being glutted on all-you-can-eat buffet.

Does this mean we shouldn't crave the alternative?

Don't think that's Kundera's message, I respond.

I don't mean for Kundera.

I pause. Cathy is expressionless. I feel movement under the table. It is her ankle brushing past my feet.

Kundera . . . I start but can't finish saying whatever it is that I have no idea what the words are to begin with. My thoughts somersault.

Cathy's ankle retreats. Her shoe is back next to my shoe. The woman is perplexing me.

Cathy . . . I begin, then abruptly stop.

Cathy sighs, a profoundly deep sigh emanating from within her entire body. She sounds like she is expelling the heaviness from her heart. I wait for her to speak—or to make the next move.

But she doesn't. The minutes pass as I watch her sip her cappuccino. My iced tea is sweating from the glass, the erect straw bent out of shape, sideways. I feel emasculated just looking at it.

I tell myself I'm not doing anything wrong. I'm a friend. We have been commiserating—she has been talking while I've been listening. Our rendezvous is this: two strangers who have met fortuitously—I was stoned by her kid—and we found comfort in each other's company. Just conversations. Nothing more. Nor less.

I place my hand on hers. She reacts, about to retract when she decides to be stationary. Her eyes dart from left to right for the presence of someone she knows. I don't let go.

What's wrong? I urge.

You know.

I don't. I honestly don't. I'm your friend, I say, gambling my luck on higher stakes. Tell me.

As my friend, she says, coming to the table, playing my game. You should know about my marriage woes. Geoffrey doesn't come home. Well, he does, if midnight when the house is dead asleep, is considered coming to a home.

It might be work, I suggest, standing on the side of her husband to goad her into saying more.

It might be an affair, she says with a hint of anger and sadness.

How long has this gone on?

For almost a year.

Every day?

Most days. Sometimes he's back early. Like at nine. He's fine with the baby. He's fine with me too.

And?

He doesn't want to . . . you know . . . we don't . . .

Oh.

I shift my foot so it's parallel to hers. Our skins touch. A tremor of heat travels from foot to foot. Without warning, she plants her legs against mine so our shins are kissing skins. I jolt involuntarily. I can see she is pleased.

What do you want to do about it? I ask, implying about her marriage.

I don't know, Cathy answers coquettishly, referring to our current situation.

This is heavy, Doc, I make a joke. She knows I'm talking about Marty from the film *Back to the Future*. I have seen the film twenty times. I've made her promise to see the film when she can find the time. I've been playing the middle-aged mentor; her cultural barometer of the classics.

Or it could be light. Depending on how you see it, she replies.

I almost choke on the spittle welling inside my mouth. The phone beeps with an incoming message. I check to see who it's from. It's Elena. I make sure Cathy doesn't see it, tuck the phone away in my satchel.

I haven't seen the film yet. *Back to the Future.* Do you want to join me? Cathy says, her innocent tone too contrived to be genuine.

Where? I ask, guileless.

My house.

Oh. Okay. Sure.

Are you fine for time, Michael?

I'm fine for time for a request from my crush. Especially if it involves something heavy and a little lightness of nothing. In any case, baby Louise will be around. I'll behave myself, and so will Cathy. Two friends and a baby and a TV. Platonic enough, even without the husband in sight. The cleaner aka nanny may even be around.

Lead the way, I joke.

If you say so. Perhaps later you will know your way around better than I do.

My jaw drops. I have no witty comeback. As Cathy stands to get out of our cramped seating arrangement, she brushes her body against mine. I smell her. No perfume but the natural scent of a woman's healthy perspiration mixed with adrenaline.

The baby's at a birthday party for the rest of the afternoon, by the way. Hope you don't mind.

Cathy eyeballs me with her wide whites and her piercing irises that make mine dilated. I can't walk, rooted dumbly while I watch her skirt sweep past my thigh. Her pinkie hooks onto my pinkie before sliding off, releasing it. I didn't even know that tiniest and unimportant part of my body could be erogenous. I shiver a little.

I'm beginning to think that Kundera is a true philosopher for the lightness of one is choking the dark heart out of my weightiness.

Come.

Cathy's loaded one-syllable command shoots through my ear and inside my spine and down my groin while the phone inside my bag quivers again and again. To save my soul, I reach for the phone to read Elena's new text message, giving Cathy a wait-signal as she dithers about outside the café: *What you waiting for? She wants you to take her like a man! Grow some balls and do it!*

I look around to check where Elena is; she's across the café in a retail shop selling dresses, stalking us. I frown at her, angry. She ducks away from view, disappears among the colourful fabrics.

Truth is, I want to leave with Cathy. An urge is an urge. But having seen Elena spy on us has a strange, unintended sobering effect. My superego takes over. Do I want to be the asshole breaking up Cathy's marriage? Do I want to be the bad man ruining Louise's childhood? Am I capable of cuckolding another man, even if it's someone whose path I'll never cross? In the midst of all this, my id creeps back. What does it matter? It's just nature taking its course. A healthy man and a beautiful woman giving in to their normal, bodily functions. The body cannot be starved when it is hungry, when it hungers. Precisely, I am a free man. I am human. I am light. I am light. I am . . .

Cathy! Wait.

She turns expectantly. She sees the look of apprehension on my face. I am paralysed by the turmoil acting out inside my head. Immediately, despair spreads all over her face. I can feel her ache even from a distance.

I understand, she says, turns and walks away.

Wait! I call out.

She struts back to me, face in my face. I am breathing her again. A woman's sweat and her hot breath. Her smell, oh god, her smell. I try not to get influenced.

I'm ready for this, Michael. I think you are too. I'm not afraid. I don't care anymore. Don't you get it? I'm too young to wither. Too young! Too . . . energetic!

I gulp. My mouth so dry as though I ran a mile and back in five minutes. Dehydrated by lust so insistent all my pinkies are going *c'mon c'mon!* Instead, staring at the lovely mirage of a woman whom I can only describe as a seraph—a dewy-eyed angel made flesh by my fantasies—I can only feebly utter a white lie that doesn't make sense even as I hear it coming out of my mouth.

I have an urgent meeting, I plead with Cathy. My boss just texted me. If I miss this one, I'll lose my job. I've been missing the last few.

I know I'm so close to perfection, to smelling the insides of this person. But something just won't allow me to move in the direction she—or I—wants. I know I will regret this the moment she leaves. I know. I know. Fucking idiot.

Fine, Cathy sighs and about-turns. I don't believe you, but fine. Call me when you are ready. Doesn't mean I'll be waiting.

She huffs off in a fit of flurry, humiliated. I stare after her receding back, wondering what divine gift I had just declined then smell my fingers from the scent she left behind when I had her hand in mine moments ago.

* * *

Why didn't you go with her? Elena demands to know when we meet. You don't like women?

Maybe I'm a good person, I retort.

Elena chortles. I am a good person too! That's why I bring you two together. I see only sparks but no fire. How disappointing.

I want to tell her she's an evil witch, conspiring the downfall of more than one innocent life. But I hold my tongue.

Cathy is wrong, you know, about Geoffrey, Elena says.

Wrong about what?

He is not having an affair.

How do you know? He tells you? I ask, sarcastically.

Because he is with me.

I choke on the ice that is crushed in my mouth. I sputter.

He's with you and he's not having an affair? Do you think I am stupid or are you stupid?

Elena sighs deeply. What's with women sighing all the time? So much drama, so little action.

I am in love with Geoffrey, Elena says, as if her words paint the picture any clearer. Geoffrey doesn't love me. He comes to me, to talk, sometimes, just for company. Whenever he wants, I am there for him. But we don't have sex.

Like I believe you.

We sleep together, lie in bed, until he feels relaxed. No sex, no hanky panky. Just . . . company.

As a man, I find that hard to stomach. I taunt her. Why? Why would he spend all that time with you when he can't benefit from you-know-what?

He loves his wife, Michael. He thinks he doesn't.

Is Elena for real? A fool with a fool. I'm the bigger fool for getting in the middle of this foolish folly. My brain is exploding. Kundera, you moron!

Fine, he loves his wife. Why would he want to be with you? Ignore his hot young wife?

Because Michael, Geoffrey, wonderful man that he is, is impotent. For no reason, after Louise was born, he finds himself completely impotent. And so, he's depressed. I've known him and Cathy since we came to Singapore. The baby was born two years after. He has a crisis. I will gladly let him use me. But he wouldn't . . . I would . . . but he wouldn't . . .

The nuts and bolts are creaking into place. I'm beginning to see the picture now; the machinery, the springs that operate the piston. A lot of innuendo comes to my mind, I can't help it—I've declined the flesh of a very succulent peach that has opened itself to me. All I have to do is follow the lead, take a bite, and luxuriate in its exploding juices. What possessed me to reject the golden opportunity?

You're screwing with me, Elena. Why the hell did you get me involved in the first place?

I can't help if I'm in love with a man who doesn't love me back. I want to punish him, make his wife fall for another man, leave him. I want Geoffrey all to myself. He will never leave her, you know? And Cathy? She's lonely, desperate. Anyone can see that. You were simply at the right place at the right time.

Elena realizes what she has said when she sees my darkened face. She tries to compensate.

I wasn't sure if you were her type. It surprised me actually.

What am I to you? An experiment? I snapped.

Oh, Michael, I told you, I am not a bad person. We cannot help what the heart wants. Or when, or where. Or why. Love is a mystery. I wish it wasn't so . . . complicated.

With a married man? You should have stopped yourself, I chide her, trying to recover my hurt.

You fell for a married woman too. Was that ever your intention?

No. I never said I'm in love with her.

Hmm . . . , Elena paused for effect. If you don't love her, why didn't you want to sleep with her? It's because you love her that is why you cannot do it. You care about her, you don't want to hurt her. Or . . . you don't want yourself to be hurt. Because you know you will never have her.

I stare at Elena, stupefied. I did feel stupid. She continues.

I can bet with my life, Michael, that you will never stop thinking of what you cannot have with her. You want her but you don't want her. Your desire for her is based on a paradox. Admit it.

Deep down, I admit it. Kundera is a master of the imperviousness of human desire. His words, his metaphors explain myself to me even when I think I know it all. Fact is, I know nothing until I have tasted both the light and the heavy scent of what human relations steeped in strange misdeeds are capable of doing. Some of them smell light as a peach. Some are heavy with musk, redolent of roses. Some are halfway tensions tugging between the two, like limbs entangled, like sighs expiring inside the breaths of each other, floating and sinking simultaneously, like organs suspended and inserted, a compressor machinery at work, pounding up and down, grinding again and again like groundwork, setting the foundation for a home that may not last the years of mortgage set in stone.

Cathy never calls back. I believe she expects me to make the move. I can't call her back either. Conscience weighs me down like a stone around my neck. To forget about her, I find a new mall to hang out at, seek out a different café to people-watch. I grow my hair out, ditch my spectacles, put on contact lenses, change my dull workpants for edgier clothes. Find a girlfriend who wears a perfume like ocean breeze, with a hint of lilies and a note of basil that reminds me of Italian cooking.

I forget about Cathy. But I can never forget that day, so close was I to taking over the burdens of a person I hardly knew. True, Elena was right, I cannot stop ruminating over what could have been. Mind over matter, I remind myself day after day. One day, when I'm married, now that I'm forty, I'll truly know how to balance the burden I've only read and heard about from between the stale vanilla scented sheets of a musty book.

Chapter 10

Fresh Blood

All I saw was blood when she first appeared before me. Her cheongsam, in a screaming scarlet, collared at the throat and falling all the way to her ankles with a slit rising to the high of her thighs, exposed her lithe, bare legs. When she said hello, my mouth opened, and only soundless dry air came forth. She caught me staring so I shifted my eyes from her thighs to her hips to her bosom to her bare shoulders and then to the doe eyes of this alluring gazelle. She towered above me in her four-inch stiletto heels, her womanly curves tucked inside a dress that was too tight for her but just right for me.

Good evening, Sir! Welcome! She greeted me warmly. Her words sailed melodiously up and down my spine. How can I help you today?

I had made no future plans except to wander aimlessly into a few casino hotels to gawk at their opulence. I vaguely remembered seeing gold varnished statues, Swarovski crystal chandeliers, water fountains with jet streams dancing acrobatically to some tunes by Debussy or Strauss or Queen. Orgasmic anthems climaxing to pyrotechnic displays of fireworks and a big musical flourish.

I don't know. What can you do here? I asked.

Do you want to play a game or two at the casino? she smiled, showing lots of teeth, inching closer. She smelled sweet, with a lingering jasmine perfume. I recognized the floral note. My wife wore the same.

What else have you got?

We have plenty of retail shops for you to relax and buy something for your family. We have many restaurants if you feel like dining. Are you a guest here in this hotel, Sir?

No, I'm not.

That is perfectly fine. What do you feel like doing?

What I felt like doing was too illicit to be broadcast to her so I settled for the prosaic. I'll maybe gamble a little, I've never done it in a casino before, I said, watching her reaction.

As expected, she opened up warmly, as if she had closed a sales pitch. I was to be that newbie gambler likely to lose a tonne of money before dinnertime.

Then let me show you to a table, Sir, she cooed, touching my arm gently before releasing her touch. It had the effect of controlling me, this easy lamb to slaughter. I followed her meekly. That slight body contact lingered in my mind. I watched her sashay in the tight red dress, watching her tiny waist and ample hips. She seemed the fertile type. I wondered if she had kids. She turned abruptly to me, How do I address you, Sir?

Larry, I blurted out quickly. My name was, in fact, Harry. I didn't know why I lied.

My name is Sally, she responded, almost too smoothly, her smile now a thin snake on her lips. She pointed to her name tag, as if to affirm what she had said, See, Sally.

Now, I know a liar when I see one. I had given a fake name and so did she. Hers was verified by a name tag. Mine was unverifiable. She prodded.

What will you be playing, Sir? Any preference?

Sally brought me to change my money to chips. We then walked to the gaming tables. I surveyed the thick crowd of tense heads, most of them Asian with some Caucasians who either looked like serious players or had come along for a joy ride that was beginning to turn joyless. I was big on playing poker online, but the stakes at the tables were high. The minimum bet was HK$1,000. The blackjack tables seemed less tense, more convivial, obviously tourists among veteran card players. I knew my blackjack. It was either an easy win or an easy fold. Less high stakes than poker. I sat down at a table with three people, two of them middle-aged ladies with dyed bronze hair and a man in a jacket that hung limply on his shoulders. He seemed more apprehensive than the women, who stared at me as I sat down. Nobody smiled, except Sally, who stood near me and put her hand on my shoulder, keeping me under her spell. She spoke.

Is there anything else you need?

I looked up at her with a lump in my throat.

Would you like a drink, Sir? Beer? Juice?

Beer. Heineken.

Coming, Sir.

Sally made eye contact with the others at the table, greeting everyone. They ignored her. She leaned into my ear and whispered.

Don't worry. I'll rescue you if you're losing. I'll tell you when to stop. These are regulars. They don't lose. Have fun.

She took her hand off my shoulder and strutted off to the bar where she placed my order with a waiter, leaving me with a sweet floral scent of her skin and hair, and all I could think of as I placed my first bet with a rush of adrenaline was that this was definitely one game I was about to lose.

* * *

By the time I lost HK$20,000, I knew I was sinking so fast no appearance by Sally would save me. She was nowhere to be found. The players at the table had started to relax, chat among themselves in a thick Putonghua accent I instantly recognized them as mainlanders from China. Even the women were smiling at me from time to time—with the arrogance of being winners and the sympathy of being female. I wanted to get up, stop my losing streak, walk away. But a part of me kept thinking I could recoup my losses. Just one more round. The next one will be different. Again, another shameless defeat.

My phone vibrated with a fresh text. It was my wife. *Don't go to the casinos and gamble, OK? I'm warning you. We need to save for our Xmas trip to Zurich. Did you eat any Portuguese egg tarts yet? Don't forget to get souvenirs for the kids and relatives.*

The text message had the effect of sobering me up. I was drugged by the effect of being surrounded by these people who were playing with money as if they were trading with fake money at a board game. I felt impulsive, emboldened by each ponderous second and minute as I agonized over whether to fold my cards or to go on. I had won only one round. That one round was enough to spur me on, make me feel invincible. Sally turned up just as I was about to start a fresh round of loss.

Sir, would you like a break? she asked. Perhaps you want to eat something?

I turned to her with desperation. She had appeared at the right time. My angel, Sally.

Okay, I said feebly and stood up to follow her.

She took me out of the gambling area, passed several retail shops towards a café. I didn't know Sally at all, but I was already annoyed with her. I said rather curtly, What took you so long?

An imperceptible laugh escaped from her lips. You from Singapore, Sir?

How do you know? I turned to her, surprised.

I can tell from your accent.

You Filipino?

Yes, Sir. I worked before in Singapore, Sir.

Marina Bay Sands?

It was Singapore's one out of two legal casinos. I assumed she had been working in the same industry.

No, Sir, she murmured, and all traces of the amiable disappeared. She said something to the service staff at the café before speaking to me. Here, you can have your dinner. Enjoy.

And then she walked off. I sensed that I had slighted her. I ran after her.

Wait!

Yes? Sally gave me a disinterested glance.

Thank you for helping me earlier, I said, with sincerity, Would you like . . . to have a drink with me?

This was a gorgeous woman who looked like she had been bought one too many drinks in her lifetime. Her eyes were clouded over by a kind of sadness that betrayed the vulnerability in her. She was no longer red cheongsam lady but fake Sally with real problems.

Sure, she mumbled.

We sat at a table in the corner. Men kept turning to look at her. She didn't blink once. Male adulation was a response that the head-turning dress on her body was designed to elicit. I should count myself lucky for having her choose to sit with me.

I looked out for a ring on Sally's finger. There was none. I, on the hand, wore mine, which she noticed right away.

Do you want to eat something? I asked her.

I'm fine, she shook her head, A pineapple juice will do.

I ordered her a juice and a sirloin steak for myself with a glass of red wine. The steak took fifteen minutes to arrive. In that time, I watched her sip her juice, leaving red lipstick stains on the rim of the glass. My food hadn't arrived, I had lost money, and I was hungry. Watching her made me hungrier than usual. I had to break the ice.

How long have you been working here?

Two years.

And before that? You were in . . . the Philippines?

I wanted to say 'Singapore' since she had mentioned it earlier. But I didn't want to state the obvious. I didn't want to embarrass her in case it reminded her of a past she might not be proud of.

Singapore, she replied. Five years.

Wow. Long time.

She stared at me, her long mascaraed eyelashes defiant. She seemed to channel anger at me.

Yes, I was a maid, she spat out the words. It was out in the open.

I see.

What could I say to change the atmosphere back to what it was before? I had made her repeat her history that had no meaning in the present.

Well, you're in Macau now, I said and shrugged, hoping she would notice it.

Yes, and I serve gamblers, she laughed sardonically.

Serving is maybe not the right word, I corrected her, You host your clients. You're like . . . a casino concierge.

She burst out laughing. You Singapore men are so straight.

What do you mean 'straight'?

You do this one way, only one way. You think that way, only that way. So simple.

Excuse me?

I happened to hold a master's degree in Predictive Analytics and a management job in one of the Big Four accounting firms and was promoted four times in the last seven years. I hardly saw myself as 'simple'.

Nothing, Larry. Your dinner is here.

I ate in silence. Sally watched me the entire time.

I'm a mother, you know, she mumbled, staring listlessly into space.

I kept quiet, and continued eating. Experience had taught me to not interrupt a woman when she was about to open up.

My son is sixteen. I want him to go to college.

If her son was sixteen, then how old was she? I peeked at her from the corner of my eyes as I chewed the meat. Thirty-three? Thirty-five? She looked at least ten years younger than whatever age she was now.

He got a girl pregnant. She was fifteen.

You're a grandmother? I blurted, swallowing the meat quickly.

She died giving birth last week, she said, eyes turning red and moist.

Oh. I'm sorry.

So now I have to work harder. Pay for college. And the funeral.

That's kind of you.

She's my best friend's daughter.

I'm so sorry.

This is what happens when you have no self-control.

My dinner was almost finished. I poked at the Vichy carrots and peas with my fork and wondered who she meant by the pronoun 'you' in her statement. 'You' meaning people in general? 'You' meaning men? 'You' meaning herself in a different perspective, seeing herself as someone else?

If I'm taking your time from work, please let me know, I said, looking up from my meal and told her in a gentle tone. She had intimated her history to me, a stranger, without any persuasion on my part, while I'm not entirely sure what for.

You are my work, she replied.

What?

She gave me a piercing look that said more than what was needed to be uttered.

You mean you're not just a hostess? I croaked. The red wine was making my throat dryer than usual.

I'm flexible.

My phone vibrated with a fresh text. My wife. Again. *Can you believe the maid just burnt your work shirt? The one I bought for your birthday! On the breast plate where the logo is! I'm going to make her pay from her next salary. Also she broke the crystal champagne glass today. I'm absolutely furious!!!*

Flexible, you say? I asked and raised my eyebrows at Sally.

She nodded. I gestured to the waiter, paid for the meal and led the way out of the casino; Sally followed me meekly and wordlessly.

* * *

She was very flexible as she said she would be. In that hour, I had temporarily forgotten the losses I had incurred at the casino. Two weeks' wages I would have to justify to my wife. Fuck it. Sally was worth every dollar of a reckless gamble.

My hotel is not as fancy as yours, I said, apologizing for the three-star hotel I had booked. I checked out her creamy body. Underneath the scarlet dress, she was pale and smooth, with a pliable belly—a tell-tale sign she had given birth before. Macau is only a day trip, I'm actually on a work trip to Hong Kong, I explained.

Larry, it's fine, she said, yawning.

My name is Harry, not Larry, I admitted.

Her eyes sparkled. My name is not Sally either.

What is it?

Guess.

Guess?

It could be any name under the sun. I racked my brain hard. What's a common Filipina name? I made some wild guesses.

Maria? Angela? Lola? Teresa?

Madonna, she intoned.

I bit my lips to stop myself from laughing.

Yes, I get that very often. Not the best name to use in a casino. Mother of God watching your every move in a place of sin.

I had thoroughly enjoyed and tasted the nakedness of her body as a married man. That was a sin. Throwing money down the drain for a couple of cards at a wrong turn didn't seem so sinful in comparison.

Sally/Madonna seemed to know what I was thinking. She stood up from the bed and started to dress herself up. I watched her as I lounged on the bed, one arm supporting my tilted head. Her alabaster skin, smooth as a Venusian statue, was more magnificent than the gilded lion statues I had seen in the casino lobby. More elegant. More classical than all the faux antique replicas and designer décor I had witnessed that day, stumbling upon one five-star hotel to the next, lost in the money trail of one posh gambling den after another.

I have to go, she said softly. She turned her back to me, her zipper undone, Can you zip me up?

The zipper went all the way down to her derrière. I wanted to touch her there but I knew the moment was over. Before, she was eager, passionate and hungry, tasting me like the sirloin steak she had smelled earlier but hadn't eaten. Perhaps she really was famished. I wouldn't know for sure. She would be too polite to admit.

I affixed the zipper to the teeth. The two clasped together and bit as one, one jagged tooth overlapping the other while I pulled the zipper up with one hand in a smooth fluid motion, feeling the tension rising upwards between the metal and the fabric as I pulled down her red dress with the other hand, listening to the sound of the familiar and satisfying *z-z-z-i-i-i-p-p-p* as the zipper reached the top where her nape was. She bent her neck demurely to the side during that time, parted her hair to the front where it cascaded to her breast plate, and now she flipped her tresses back. I held her by the arms and turned her to me to take a closer look at her face—her lips were pillowy and no longer rouged, her eyelashes having clumped and a few fallen on the sheets, her nose upturned and perky, her eye bags evident of sleep deprivation or stress or long hours at work, yet I still found her mesmerizing. I leaned in to kiss her. She pushed me away.

I have to go, she repeated her words, You have to pay me.

I held back a sigh, got out of bed without a shred of clothing to find my wallet. I crouched bare assed on the floor searching for my wallet, hiding my nakedness that I was suddenly self-conscious of. The rolls of my belly fat tripled and quadrupled the more I bent and dug for the goddamn wallet inside my pants' pocket. My companion turned her head away. She was already dressed; she was slowly putting on her mask. Madonna was easing back into the performance of Sally. Back to the world of Macau and what it had to offer her that Singapore couldn't.

I gave her what we had agreed on before we started stripping off our clothes, before we removed our layers of masks and became the animals we were, throbbing with the fresh blood under the skin of our bodies.

I watched Sally adjust her curves to the tightness of her scarlet cheongsam which immediately transformed her. On her lips, she repainted a new coat of rouge stained in the colour of dried blood. Turning to face me, she purred.

See you around, Harry Larry.

And then she was out the door. I felt a bit of pain smarting on my neck and touched the spot. It burned. I rubbed my fingers over the sore area and looked at my hand. There was blood. I went to the mirror, examined the wound. She had left me a souvenir I would have trouble explaining to my wife and kids.

Chapter 11

From the Ocean Deep

Wenyi's third week at her new job meant she had settled down to a routine sufficiently enough to regain her usual appetite. Lunchtime at Dhoby Ghaut was a manic affair. By twelve, the office workers in the area had crawled out of their air-conditioned holes to populate any eatery within a five-minute walking distance. It was half-past twelve, ill timed; most of her favourite haunts would be snaking with queues by now. Such a shame. The meeting had gone on far longer, and before Wenyi could jot down the last bullet point for that day's minutes—the damned cells on the Excel sheet were shifty little buggers!—the team was dismissed, and everyone had skittered off to their separate ways. That was how she found herself alone with no one to dine with. As usual.

It was fine, Wenyi consoled herself, as she was the noob in the team, having joined them a month ago—although, at thirty-five, she was more experienced than her millennial co-workers. She also knew she was socially too awkward to fit in an existing clique, and not zealous enough for anyone to volunteer to buddy up with her. She had gotten used to her solo lunches—the first week of mayhem had whizzed past in a daze; the second week allowed her some breathing space; and she was now knee deep into the fourth day of week three. Plaza Singapura, being nearby, had become her regular lunch spot by default for she rather enjoyed the seven minutes of brisk walk in the blazing noon sun—a total of fourteen minutes of exercise both ways. This was the part of the workday she actually looked forward to. It invigorated her to be among strangers milling about aimlessly in the shopping centre, with its glitzy showcase of products she would never think of buying and its many dining options she could never decide on. Everything about the mall was shiny, thrilling, beckoning to her, so very different from the serious and sluggish office atmosphere she couldn't wait to escape.

The morning marmalade jam sandwich Wenyi had consumed at seven o'clock had digested hours ago. All she had left with in her tummy was a hearty acid waiting to disintegrate anything she would next swallow. She sauntered past one restaurant after another, perusing their lunch menus quickly. Ground floor, Nam Nam, $9.90 for a beef pho and bottled water—the restaurant had run out of lotus tea and the other complimentary beverage option was Vietnamese coffee, but she wasn't a coffee drinker. So, no. Second floor, Bangkok Jam, $12.90 for a green curry with rice set coupled with iced lemon tea. A combo she liked, but it always gave her a dreadful post-lunch food coma, making it impossible for her to focus on work. Nope. On the same floor, Nana's Green Tea, $16 for a cold bowl of salmon don with a matcha drink. A wise pick for most days, but today, the idea of cold rice and raw fish didn't tempt her. She was in that kind of premenstrual crampy mood that called for something warm to soothe her stomach and appease her disgruntled soul.

* * *

Please, come take a look!

A woman called out to Wenyi. She had a big fat scrunchie yanking back her medium-length hair and was practically shoving a menu into Wenyi's hands. Wenyi was so famished she was gliding along the mall's marbled floor tiles like an aimless wraith. Her indecision was prolonging her hunger pangs. It had been fifteen minutes since she had stepped into the mall, and she hadn't settled on a place to lunch. Her knees were giving way; she felt light-headed. She felt stupid for having passed three perfectly reasonable options that she would have no qualms about choosing on any other given day. But today was different. Today was twelve hours after she had come to the conclusion that he had ghosted her. Her Facebook crush, the guy she had religiously texted on Messenger for three whole weeks: two hours daily; one hour in the daytime and one hour at night; the rare kind of a man who had made her feel wanted. *That guy.* The one whose account she couldn't locate on her Facebook any longer. He had blocked her or disconnected from the app. She had spent the whole of yesterday waiting for that green dot to appear beside his picture on her Facebook Messenger. What would today be like? She was afraid to know.

Wenyi glanced through the menu quickly. Her glazed eyes registered nothing. She looked up and saw the restaurant sign. Haidilao, meaning 'deep sea fishing'. This was a popular hotpot restaurant; hot soup, hot rice, hot food. A favourite haunt of families and friends to gather and dine in large groups. Saliva pooled inside her mouth. She looked to the woman with hope in her eyes.

Can one person dine here? Wenyi asked.

The woman could not hide her disappointment. Perhaps she was expecting Wenyi to book a table for a lunch party.

Yes, of course, the woman managed a smile, We have a special menu for single diners. You can choose the type of soup base you want and the different platter options.

Wenyi was hesitant. Dining in a hotpot restaurant alone? Even to her, it seemed a little odd. Perhaps she would settle for a steaming hot bowl of beef pho at Nam Nam after all. It was a cheap lunch, and the broth always offered her comfort.

She was about to turn her heel and walk away when the woman sprang to life and bustled Wenyi with a sudden fervour. 'Come, come in and take a look!' There was a flurry of excitability around the woman that roused Wenyi from her low energy stupor. As the woman led the way, Wenyi followed after, dutifully, gratefully.

The restaurant interior was lush, modern and dark, with touches of chinoiserie. Ceiling lights were dimmed to set a kind of romantic mood Wenyi envisioned would suit a dating couple. She would have gladly booked a place like this for her and Steven; though Steven lived in Michigan, not Singapore. Only two tables were taken by small groups of diners. Wenyi was ushered to the back of the restaurant, a quiet corner that was more than ideal. She sat down, put her handbag down on the empty chair beside her and propped her elbows on the table. The woman whisked off and, in her place, a waiter appeared, presumably to take her order.

Nihao, I am Xiao Kang. I will be serving you today, the waiter said, his mid-range voice soothing and melodious, Shall I offer you some recommendations for what you may want to eat?

He presented her with the menu, opening to the page for lunchtime options. Wenyi peered at her waiter. Young man in his twenties, his hair swept back and up to display his broad and unlined forehead. His cheeks were moderately high, his nose sharp as his chiselled chin, his thin lips shiny and succulent. An average build though visibly athletic, with taut, sinewy muscles hidden discreetly behind a white long-sleeved shirt, folded at the cuffs that is neither too tight nor loose. As he flexed his fingers to hold on to the stylus on the smartphone he is using to jot down her order, Wenyi detected a strong wrist, visible veins pulsing through his olive skin. She nodded her head to respond to his question.

Is anyone joining you today, Miss? he asked breezily.

Wenyi shook her head. I'm alone, she replied, to which he nodded. A trained smile manifested on his lips.

At this point, he gave her a cursory glance. Their eyes met for two seconds too long. The waiter peeled his eyes away before she could do so. What was that? Wenyi thought, flabbergasted. Did he just channel me a vibe?

We have four types of soup you can choose from, Miss, he said, We have mala, tomato, herbal chicken and mushroom. Do you have any preference for what you would like today?

Wenyi stared at the options on the menu blankly. She knew about the types, but she hadn't been to Haidilao before, even though it was a famous chain with hundreds of outlets across several countries. For one reason or another, she just never found the time nor opportunity to do so. She gestured towards him; he leaned in to listen.

Is your mala here very spicy? I have to work later.

Ah!

He gave a quick nod as if he understood her situation: *Customer has work after lunch, a lighter option would be preferable.*

You work in an office around here, Miss? Your dress is so nice.

This old thing? Please. Wenyi lamely dismisses him. Yes, I work around here. Not far from Plaza Sing.

I can tell you are the kind who went to college. Am I right? You have that look.

Wenyi peered at him quizzically. What look?

Smart girl look, he tried to hide a smile, like you read many books.

He was right. She was a bookworm. Always has been, always will be. Books were the faithful companions that took priority over platonic and romantic relationships in Wenyi's life. Books allowed her to travel to other places beyond the shores of Singapore; they let her inside the perspectives of characters unlike her. He spoke, interrupting her thoughts.

May I suggest the herbal soup? Many customers like this option. It is good for the stomach. And it has just the right amount of taste, not spicy, not bland, not too overwhelming for our customer's palate.

Sounds good.

Alright, one herbal soup. About your platter, Miss, do you prefer meat or seafood?

What do you suggest?

He gazed at her directly now. She had invited him to do so, and he did. The moment registered in her brain as somewhat illicit. She felt her shoulders and neck burn; this radiating heat that rose from inside of her, escaping her skin cells like steam leaking out of the gaps of potholes. His eyes were kind, black marbles with a hint of a glint, blessed with the type of sooty long eyelashes women would kill for.

You seem a little under the weather to me, he diagnosed her accurately, Perhaps our beef shabu shabu? Some red meat would give you some energy?

Wenyi blushed, though she was certain he couldn't see it under the darkened lights. She was so pleased with how acute his observation was that it made her smile. He noticed.

Yes, I am feeling quite tired today. Didn't sleep well, Wenyi confided, as if he was a friend. A waiter and stranger, Xiao Kang had somehow managed to make her feel comfortable around him within minutes. Sure, I'll take the beef then.

Alright, Miss. Would you like to order our condiments? It comes with dessert. And how about a drink?

Wenyi calculated that her meal, after GST, would come up to thirty dollars. It was shrewd how the restaurant had lured her in with a basic lunchtime deal of $15.90 that turned out to be only the price of the platter. The soup base cost $7. The condiments would cost an additional $4. A drink would be an extra few dollars. No need. In her bag was her bottled water. She declined both the condiments and the drink.

After repeating Wenyi's order to her, the waiter left her table. By now, she was beyond hungry and would devour anything. Just bring me my food now, she thought, slightly annoyed, hoping that this wasn't one of those places that would make their customers wait twenty minutes for their food.

A minute later, the waiter reappeared. He produced a red cloth napkin and an apron. He leaned in to speak, his voice gentle like a lute.

This is to cover your bag so it won't get dirtied. May I?

Wenyi nodded dumbly as she watched him tuck a cloth napkin around and over her three-year-old Esprit faux leather bag that cost her no more than $60. This was a gesture that was rather extravagant for something that wasn't. Next, he opened up the apron and offered it to her.

And this is to prevent spills on your dress. Shall I help you?

He gave her such a genuine smile she felt embarrassed. Wenyi did not know how to respond without rejecting him; the waiter took his cue from her and gently nudged her into raising her arms as he placed the apron around her without touching her the slightest bit. His discretion was as professional as it was skilful. At close range, she took the chance to smell him. He had on no cologne, no perfume, no olfactory trace of cheap hair products. It was the most refreshing, natural scent ever. A pheromone of a clean human body with undetectable bodily effusions.

She thanked him as he finished. She was hooked, she thought, and gulped with a tinge of shame.

Here is a wet wipe, and disposable gloves if you need them, the waiter continued, If you would like to tie your hair—I notice you have long hair—I have here a hair band for you. In case, you know, of the smell.

This is unreal, Wenyi thought. What other parts about her body was he going to notice? As Xiao Kang stretched his hand out to offer her a black hair band, adrenaline rushed inside of her. This pulsing, healthy, tanned boy-man with the firm butt she had noticed when he left her table earlier and returned bearing these gifts was impossibly swoon worthy. Could she *tabao* him back home?

It's okay, I don't need to tie my hair, Wenyi said, asserting herself. I just need my food.

Only five minutes had passed since she had entered the restaurant. Although the restaurant had sent her a distraction, food was on Wenyi's mind. Nothing was more primitively urgent than hunger.

I'll go check, the waiter said then left her for a short while. He reappeared with a cup and a sachet. Miss, your food will be here very soon. Here, I have brought you some tea, while you wait. His voice turned uncertain. Is ginger tea alright for you?

I didn't order tea, Wenyi declined. She didn't want to pay more than necessary.

Oh, I know, the waiter reassured her, before leaning in to whisper. This is on the house. Please don't tell the manager.

Oh . . .

Ginger is good for the stomach. Boost you up. Unless you don't like ginger . . .

Usually, Wenyi didn't. But ginger would be ideal for the strange cramps she was feeling which, anyway, were subsiding. In place was a fuzzy feeling that was stimulating and confusing. It felt like hunger and something more. She was rather confused. She needed food. Then she would know what her stomach problem was. Then she could think straight.

She thanked him for the tea. He opened the sachet and poured out the granules into the hot water in the cup, stirred it with a spoon and presented it to her. This level of service was unprecedented in any of the restaurants Wenyi had ever been to. Or ever will.

He left her and reappeared again, this time with a three-tier trolley bearing her lunch. He first popped the hot pot with the herbal soup into the allocated slot on her table, set up the platter of vegetables with its assortment of mushrooms and cabbage, the plate of beef shabu shabu and a warm bowl of rice. He explained that she could dip some of the vegetables into the soup first and the beef as and when she wanted to consume it. Wenyi grabbed her chopsticks, but before she could start dunking the ingredients into the pot, he interrupted, Would you like me to cook your lunch for you?

She glanced at him bemused. He could, actually, but she wanted the space to devour her lunch. Eye candy could not satisfy this hungry cow. *Move along, handsome*, Wenyi thought, and waved him off.

The beef, lightly swished in the hot soup, melted in her mouth. The mushroom soaked in the herbal flavour and tasted divine. The cabbage wilted softly yet retained its crunchy stem and paired so delightfully with the fluffy jasmine rice, each grain well separated by skilful steaming. Bit by bit, the lunch that went down Wenyi's throat and commingled in her stomach sent forth a delicious sense of comfort and pleasure. Midway, she sat back in her chair. The waiter took this chance and shuffled back towards her.

Her table was for four diners. One chair was being used for her handbag. Two other chairs opposite her were empty. He gestured to the empty one facing her.

Miss, would you like a teddy bear on this chair? We offer this service to our customers if they feel like they need a companion.

Wenyi couldn't help but laugh. The waiter waited for her reply.

Teddy bear? Why do I need a toy to sit at my table?

He grinned with utmost politeness. Some of our female customers like that. If you don't want that, it's alright. We want our customers to feel comfortable at Haidilao.

There's a lot more he could do to make her feel comfortable, though a teddy bear wasn't it. She decided to find out more about him.

* * *

There was nothing left. Her bowl, the hotpot, the platter. Wenyi
had eaten everything up with gusto. The waiter had left to give her
privacy, so she could enjoy her meal. He now returned. Seeing the
destruction left on the table, he smiled. A very much sated Wenyi
smiled back.

How was the food? he asked, presumably to gather
customer feedback.

Delicious. Exactly what I needed.

How would you rate our service today, Miss?

Excellent! Best service I've ever had.

Oh, that's so kind of you, so glad to hear that. Be sure to give us
five stars on our feedback survey later, the waiter said and beamed.

I'll do that.

Shall I clear the plates?

She nodded, sitting back so he could begin his work. As Wenyi
watched him remove the plates and bowl, she decided this was the
right time to snoop.

Can I ask, where are you from? You don't sound like you're
from China.

It was apparent to her that he wasn't Singaporean either. There
was a trace of an accent she couldn't detect, unlike the woman with
the scrunchie, whose thick Putonghua accent gave her nationality
away instantly.

I'm from Malaysia.

Oh . . .

But of course. The laidback, gentle demeanour. The olive skin.
The face that looked like he could pass for a local. Wenyi prodded.

Which part of Malaysia? If you don't mind me asking.

From Bentong, Pahang, Miss. It's a small town. Not sure if you
will know it, he said shyly, picking up Wenyi's used chopsticks and
spoon and placing them on the trolley.

No, I don't know. Is it near Kuala Lumpur?

Yes, it is. You been to KL?

She shook her head. Her idea of a small talk was stringing along
ideas that made sense until questioned. She was more ignorant than
he had expected.

Our town is known for growing and exporting ginger. Have you heard about Bentong ginger? It's very famous.

Again, she shook her head and smiled wryly.

My family grows Bentong ginger. We are farmers. We always have a lot of ginger at home. When my mom and sisters have . . . you know . . . problems with their stomach, they will take some of the Bentong ginger, crush them with a pestle and mix them in hot water and drink from it. It helps them. Also for all kinds of problems.

Wenyi realized this man was attuned to her bodily discomfort from years of watching his female relatives. His home produced the treatment that he witnessed as being effective for women. A farmer's son, now a waiter in a hotpot restaurant, transplanted from a small agricultural town in Malaysia to a modern metropolis. Something about his narrative was rather thrilling. Like *Tess of the d'Urbervilles*. The tropical version. Wenyi continued her questions.

You left farming in your hometown to come to Singapore?

Yes.

Why?

He sighed, staring at his hands wistfully.

Farming is hard work. I wasn't good in my studies and I can't find another job. A friend recommended that I try to find work in Singapore. So I did. So here I am.

You like to be a waiter?

He looked at her with such directness she was taken aback. Yes, of course, he replied, forcing a smile, Haidilao is the best employer. We are treated like family here.

Pushing the trolley now laid out with her dirty dishes and utensils, he turned towards Wenyi, Hope you enjoyed your experience today. Come back again! And then he left.

The next and final time Xiao Kang appeared that day was to present Wenyi with her bill, which she had to pay at the cashier counter at the door. Wenyi decided that her meal was worth a $4 tip. It was generous, considering her meal was under $30. She made sure to fill in the short survey form at the counter to praise the socks off Xiao Kang so that the management would recognize his worth and pass her tip to him. He had earned every penny of it.

As the cashier finished up Wenyi's electronic transaction and survey and passed her the receipt, Wenyi tried to catch a last glimpse of her waiter. She saw that he was already assigned to another table, where he had begun his exceptionally caring and diligent service.

Before she could wait for him to turn his head so she could say her goodbye, the scrunchie usher had orchestrated a fuss around Wenyi, bustling her quickly out of the restaurant with a loud and resounding 'See you next time!' then disappeared back into the restaurant's dark and moody interior.

* * *

Two days later, Wenyi revisited the restaurant. Then four days later. A week later; and then a fortnight. Each time, Xiao Kang was serving another table. Sometimes, she would try to catch his eye, offer a smile to test if he remembered her. The response was always the same. Either he would return a trained smile like the professional wait staff that he was, or he would ignore her, being too busy with whatever he was doing at that moment. The treatment she had received that first time she saw him was beyond special to her—for she felt there was a connection between them—was sadly not to be repeated.

One evening, she had to work an hour late. The damn Excel sheet had given her trouble again. Everyone had left and it was just her, so she finished what she could and, checking her bus timetable, slammed down her laptop to call it a day and made a dash for the bus stop. The next bus would arrive in seventeen minutes, but if she caught this one arriving in four minutes, she would be home before eight.

As fortuitous matters go, who would appear at the same bus stop was none other than her favourite waiter! She recognized his chiselled jaw and those sooty eyelashes from far—and that veiny sinewy wrist she had sometimes imagined grabbing her by her own thin wrists and slamming her against a wall, where he would roughly plant his wet shiny lips all over hers, ravishing her like she had devoured her beef shabu shabu with an appetite to parallel hers.

Xiao Kang was not in his waiter's uniform. Garbed in a distressed denim jeans and a white tee-shirt that was a size too tight, his gelled hair now tousled and floppy, hair strands teasing one eye, he looked like a runway model straight out of a magazine. Wenyi took a sharp intake of breath. How could he look more gorgeous than he already was? In this context, where she was not a paying customer and he did not have to service her, she felt suddenly inferior. Income, status quo and educational qualifications boiled down to nought in the face of youth and beauty.

He hadn't noticed her despite her standing seven feet behind him. Xiao Kang wasn't alone. He was chatting and laughing with a young man like him, tall, boyish, in black jeans and a pink shirt with sleeves rolled up. His face was even more handsome than Xiao Kang's though with a softer profile, smoother complexion and more plummy lips, as if he had makeup on. Wenyi was so fixated on the duo and trying to eavesdrop on what they were saying she realized her bus had closed its doors to the last passenger and sped off.

The next bus that came along, the two men got on it. Wenyi, impulsively, decided to follow them. When they climbed the stairs on the double decker bus, she did the same; they settled on a seat midway of the bus while she chose to sit right behind them, even though there were hardly any passengers around. They were already engrossed in conversation and did not notice this strange woman behind them, picking up every word she could overhear.

Parts of the conversation revolved around a dinner party. Another part was about a shoe sale happening that weekend. The oddest experience of Wenyi eavesdropping was how Singaporean Xiao Kang sounded. Any traces of the Malaysian accent she had heard in the restaurant was replaced by the unclipped, lazy enunciation she herself was guilty of, coupled with the use of local lingo that clearly marked Xiao Kang as a local. *bo liao. wah lao eh! sibeh sian!* He was using these phrases as dexterously as someone who had served his national service. Maybe he was just a gifted linguist?

His friend in the pink shirt, on the other hand, spoke with the Malaysian accent which she could detect. His voice was mellifluous and soft, the tonality of his speech eerily similar to Xiao Kang's in the restaurant. Wenyi clung to the side of her chair, her face turned to the window in a futile attempt to hide her identity. She need not bother, for the two men were blithely unaware of her presence and could not care less about her. They were seated shoulder to shoulder, both of their broad backs occupying the entire back of the chair.

You should stop working, the pink shirted man said.

It's fine, it's not that hard work, Xiao Kang replied. The money comes in useful. The extras, especially.

They really buy it, don't they? These women? These customers? The companion turned to face him, pouting. Throwing money at you like a gigolo.

Xiao Kang could be heard sighing. I don't do anything with them. They want to give, they give. Should I not accept their money? Their tips? It's for us, anyway.

You're not the only male waiter there. Why are you so popular? What do you do to these women?

Laughter emanates from Xiao Kang's mouth. It sounded steely, cruel.

It's easy. I play the role they want. The poor farm boy who misses his home, who has nothing while they have everything.

You mean, you play at being me?

Xiao Kang turned to face his friend with a grin, leaning into him where his lips almost touched his companion's cheek. A hot, breathy silence ensued.

I'm so good at being you I can become you. I know you from *deep, deep* inside out.

Wenyi sat back abruptly. She could see both men's shoulders move as one hand grabs another's hand, or at least she thinks it's a hand. The bus was in the opposite direction of her flat, speeding towards the west of Singapore. She lived in the north in Yishun. She pressed the bell. BUS STOPPING appeared on the red LCD panel at the front of the bus. Wenyi shuffled her body out of her seat. The men's shoulders stopped moving. They caught the back of her as she moved down the aisle to the top of the stairs where she was about to begin her descent to the lower deck of the bus.

Wenyi couldn't resist. She focused her eyes on Xiao Kang. He stared back. There was a glimmer of familiarity in his eyes. His eyes perked up as if he had made a sudden mental connection of who this woman on the bus was. She was so disappointed in him, in her idealization of this man, that she wanted to cry or scold him in front of other passengers. The imposter. The heartbreaker. The scoundrel. In essence, he had done nothing wrong. He had not cheated her of anything except hope. He parted his lips as if he wanted to say something, changed his mind and clamped his mouth shut. Wenyi smiled. His secret was out. She looked at his friend, who returned her gaze with clueless indifference, noticed Xiao Kang staring at her, and a look of contempt overcame him. *One of his lover's stupid women.* He must be thinking.

Wenyi cocked her head up by way of saying goodbye. Xiao Kang turned his head away. His lover grabbed Xiao Kang's chin, forced his cheek towards him where he planted a wet, loud smooch right on the lips. Wenyi climbed down, one foot at a time until she reached the bottom. The bus screeched to a halt. The back door hissed wide open. Wenyi, along with the other alighting passengers, was spat out of the long, heavy vehicle where she landed feet first on the pavement. Her face felt hot. She could not lift her chin up to look back at the bus receding from her line of sight. It was late and she was hungry. Her parents would have finished their *tabao* dinner and nothing would be left for her. She would have to find the correct route to get back home, eat, shower, sleep and restart a new day tomorrow.

Chapter 12

Underneath the Ruins

She couldn't see the whole picture, either the heads were cropped out, or the feet disappeared out of the frame. The lens on the camera phone could only fit the group in as much as parts of their bodies and parts of the ruins. Aisha put down the phone and thought for a moment. She would have to go down the steps much more, so everyone in the group could fit into the photo, in order for the Ruins of St. Paul to appear behind them, even if it was only a cropped version of its imposing presence, for there was no way she could capture sharply the faces of the people and the architecture of Macau's famous landmark in a single frame. She tried her best, and while halfway down the steps of the ruins, she took a series of shots.

Daw jeh leng lui! chorused the tour group of young adults as she returned the iPhone to the lady who had approached her for assistance, first speaking to her in rapid-fire Cantonese, then realizing Aisha's Asian-looking face was not Chinese but from another culture, switched to English instead. Aisha smiled obligingly. She didn't know what they had said to her earlier, presuming some form of thanks in their language. They were tourists, obviously, and she herself was one too. This time, that is.

Someone waved at her enthusiastically near the spot where the group had been. It was an attractive young girl, a teenager on the cusp of adulthood. She had jet black hair that shot out of her head like wires out of control, tempered only by the fact it was waist-length, so the weight of her long untameable curls pulled them down and put them in place. She looked Chinese or Asian, mixed with some racial ambiguity that was hard to pin-point, for she had light brown eyes like Aisha's, though these days coloured lenses were the rage, and they could be that.

The teenager spoke in English, Can you take a picture for us? Her arm was clasped around an older man. He looked Chinese, with an unsmiling face that seemed visibly embarrassed about asking a stranger to take his photo.

Aisha returned to the spot where she was earlier and framed the picture. The man looked old enough to be the girl's father. When she was done, she gave a thumbs up, signalling she had finished and that they were to retrieve the smartphone from her. As the usual effusive thanks was given to Aisha and the trio departed separately, Aisha observed the couple from a distance. The young girl stood on her toes and kissed the man on the lips. He hesitated, partly due to the lack of privacy, partly aware of their age difference in view of the public. But he couldn't resist the pure enthusiasm of a woman still full of childish fervour and returned the gesture. Their kiss lingered longer than it should, while tourists, residents and lovers flitted around them like butterflies up and down the aged stone steps, looking for a sweet-smelling sanctuary to land their tired feet.

* * *

The Kazakh walked through Senado Square, reminiscing over how she used to do this many, many years ago in the company of a man not unlike the one she had just met. Meng. That was what Aisha called him, truncated from Nam Meng. Like the man earlier, he was in his thirties, and she was about the same age as the teenage girl. Seventeen and straight out of Almaty, she had won a string of awards as a gymnast in acro-sports. She had been enticed to come to Macau for the money. There was to be a new resident circus-entertainment show, and Aisha had been handpicked to join them. It wasn't the right time, for she could go on to win awards in her field, but travel and money, and her father's worsening spinal problems and increasing medical expenses meant she should try to switch careers, even for a while. So she signed a two-year contract with the show, though Meng's appearance during her stay in Macau complicated an otherwise practical situation that she had been unprepared for.

Aisha recognized the Starbucks sign and popped into the café. She was about to sit down when she saw, from the corner of her eyes, someone waving at her. It was the same girl from earlier. Aisha smiled. The girl gestured towards her. Aisha frowned, tentative about her intentions. What does she want from me? she mused.

Do you want to join us? the girl said, beaming.

Aisha felt perplexed. This was an unusual request. She didn't want to intrude.

The male companion nodded to Aisha. He was giving consent to the invite.

Join us, he echoed the words.

Aisha sat down as instructed. She was confused yet curious and flattered that they had chosen her again.

What do you want to drink? Let me get it for you, the man said, standing up.

Cappuccino, please, Aisha replied. No sugar.

As the man left, the young girl rattled off a series of questions.

You're so pretty! Where are you from? You're not Chinese, are you? Are you here on holiday? Have you been to Macau before? Are you hungry? We can get you some food too. We can take you to a restaurant if you like. Do you want to try Macanese food? Portuguese food? Have you tried them before?

No, not Chinese. I'm Kazakh, Aisha said slowly, trying to remember the sequence of questions she had been bombarded with. No, she added, I'm not yet hungry. Ate a lot during breakfast. And yes, I've been to Macau before. I lived here for two years.

Aisha paused. That part of her history was something she was not yet willing to reveal. She hardly knew this person. Or this couple. They were tourists in the long and complicated life of Aisha. No simple snapshot of her Macau experience could justify how she had felt then, or what she had been. She fell silent all of a sudden, caught in a forgotten memory that was slowly emerging from the dark ruins of her mind.

What is your name? Aisha asked, turning the tables of the inquiry.

Chloe. She picked up her iced caffe Americano and took a swipe at it with her lips. What about you?

Aisha. She saw the perplexed look on Chloe's face. I'm Muslim.

Oh.

It was a singular word dense with meaning, in which Aisha detected surprise, trepidation and cultivated indifference. It was the appropriate response, usually garnered from people who had met her for the first time. Aisha's face and religion seemed at odds to people who didn't know anything about her region culturally or historically.

I'm not religious, Aisha explained, trying to ease her companion's discomfort. Not very, anyway.

Ah.

Chloe's cappuccino-bearing male companion appeared. He sat down as he passed Aisha her coffee. He put his arm around the arm rest of Chloe's seat, marking his territory. Aisha sipped at her coffee.

Aisha here is from Kazakh, said Chloe, turning to him.

Aisha waited for the part where she would say 'and Muslim' but it never came. She interjected.

I'm not from Kazakh. I am Kazakh. My country is Kazakhstan.

Nice country, the man said.

Oh, Aisha was taken aback. You've been there before?

No, I want to. Your economy is booming. Lots of business opportunities, oil, gas, construction. Lots of new hotels coming up.

Aisha was pleasantly pleased. The man knew his current affairs. His female companion was young, impressionable, inexperienced. He was a man of the world. Cosmopolitan and cultured. Definitely educated. In that instant, he reminded her of someone from a long time ago. Sitting across from her in a café just like this. She smiled at him.

You should visit then. It's a beautiful country. Plenty to see.

If the women are as beautiful as you, maybe I will, he said with a barely containable laugh.

Chloe didn't look amused but didn't look particularly jealous either. Her eyes were hungry for more information. She continued questioning.

Are you travelling alone?

Yes, Aisha replied.

How cool! But why?

How was Aisha supposed to answer a question as that? She was single without a companion, hence, she travelled alone.

I like it. Besides, she added, trying not to paint herself as odd, I've lived here before. I know this place well enough.

What do you do? Chloe pressed on.

I'm an acrobat.

What? the two of them blurted at the same time.

I used to work for Cirque du Soleil. I was a gold medallist. I can walk on my hands. Do you want me to show you?

Chloe nodded her head vigorously. The man was sceptical. Aisha looked around her. It was after lunchtime and the crowd had petered out. She stood up, removed her shoes, pushed a few tables and chairs away to clear the space while the waitresses and diners looked on in puzzlement and flipped her body to do a perfectly straight handstand. Chloe grinned proudly. Aisha lifted one palm and placed it forward and then the next until she had covered the distance of the cleared space with her hand walking as she had promised. The crowd applauded and cheered. Someone whistled. Aisha wasn't done yet. She bent her body slowly like a clam closing its shell and went as low as she could go without touching the floor, then opened her legs wide and straight like chopsticks going in different directions, swivelled her buttocks and swung her legs back on the opposite side and balanced her body and legs using the strength of one hand. Her biceps strained without effort. She focused on the present moment, blood rushing to her brain, veins visible on her forehead, pulsing and pink. The crowd relished the free show. She decided to show off a hand-balancing trick, placing both palms firmly on the floor, curving her body like a prawn slowing being cooked then bringing her feet towards her face where she waved her toes to the delight of the audience.

When she was finally done, she resumed to a handstand position and flipped herself back to her feet. Her heart was pounding.

Adrenaline was coursing through her body. She looked at Chloe's male companion. He had the same expression as the man who had courted her in Macau long ago. She recognized desire no matter if she was thirty-seven or seventeen. Her throat was dry after the demonstration.

Chloe's companion passed Aisha bottled water. You look like you need a drink, he urged gently.

Aisha swallowed the clear liquid in gulps. Thank you, I appreciate this.

Wow, you really are an acrobat! Chloe blurted out loud. I've never met an acrobat before. You are amazing!

I've been doing gymnastics since I was four, Aisha said as she sat down.

Her companions and the wait staff had reshuffled the furniture back in place. Everything was back to normal.

Tell me more. I'm only a student. I can't do what you do. I can only jog and swim. I am nothing like you. Isn't she incredible? Chloe gushed to her companion. He nodded vigorously and leaned forward to kiss Chloe's neck.

Aisha turned her head away from the sudden intimacy between the couple. Perhaps what she had done had created arousal in the two of them. She heard giggling and smooching. She had to talk, to drown the sounds.

When I was seventeen, I came to Macau for work. I had just won a gold medal from a competition in Poland. Then Cirque du Soleil talent-spotted me. They wanted me to perform in a new show opening at one of the casino hotels. I thought, why not? I've never been to Asia, but I've always been mistaken for one. I'll fit in. Right?

Aisha's companions had stopped cuddling to listen to her. They were huddled in an embrace, rapt and attentive to her words. Aisha went on.

For the first six months, I had so much trouble fitting in. It was terrible. I was young, like you now, desperate to fit in, to be liked. The acrobats were fine. It was the world outside the show that I felt loneliest in. Pretty soon, the older acrobats would couple up. I was the only one left that didn't have a companion.

Then what happened? Chloe's male companion interrupted.

Then I started walking around the city alone, exploring places, looking for something I didn't know what it could be. For a few months, I was fine with that. I ate alone, walked alone, shopped alone, enjoyed my own company. I was seventeen. I was growing up, learning to enjoy my own company. Looking back, I think I was quite brave.

Yes. I could never eat by myself. I would be too anxious, Chloe chipped in.

You get used to it. You start to observe other people, wonder what other people's lives are like, stop worrying about your own, you know? It can be liberating.

I agree, the male companion said and nodded sagely.

One day, I was in a café such as this, minding my own business, having a coffee like now, but alone. And then I met this guy, Aisha said, trailing off, tripping down memory lane. A part of her that had been suppressed was surfacing without effort. She was conscious of the two strangers in front of her. But they were strangers, weren't they? They wouldn't know anyone she knew, would they? Would she dare tell them her past?

Aisha continued, signalling to Chloe's companion.

He was like you. Chinese, in his thirties, good-looking and very smart. He came to talk to me. He was the son of someone very rich, very powerful. I couldn't resist him. So knowledgeable, so widely travelled. Went to Harvard. Spoke French and Portuguese and English. Cantonese and Mandarin. Always with nice shoes and suits. I guess for a seventeen-year-old, it was a crush between us that we mistook for love. If you thought my acrobatic skills are good now, you should have seen me at seventeen.

A waiter came and took the empty cups away. Chloe had removed herself from her companion's arms and leaned forward, eating up everything Aisha had to say. Both of them kept quiet, waiting for the punchline, if there was any. Aisha felt a sense of her former self unburdening. A taut feeling in her heart was loosening as she told her story for the first time, having kept it to herself for years. At her age, she didn't mind if anyone knew. That was in the past. It made her what she was now. She needed to navigate through a forgotten history in order to find new ways towards her future. Out with the old; in with the new. She wanted to speak, and words rolled off her tongue with ease.

Anyway, we hooked up. This guy and me. We lasted six months. Or five or seven, depending on when we started dating and when we stopped. It was the best time of my life. I think it was the same for him. He was so alive, so happy with me. We were like best friends who couldn't keep our hands off each other. There was so much passion and connection between us. I can still remember him when I close my eyes.

What happened to him? You two broke up? Chloe prodded, impatient to get to the end.

In a way, I guess. He left. He stopped contacting me. I never heard from him.

But why?

Chloe furrowed her brows. She was too young to be dumped so heartlessly, but she knew it was a process that was unavoidable in life. Like acne or wrinkles.

Aisha looked at Chloe and her male companion. His eyes were sympathetic, waiting for her to finish her story. Life's like that, his expression seemed to say. The two thirty-somethings had crossed enough hurdles in their separate life journeys to know it didn't matter who had rejected whom in a relationship. Heartbreak was a solitary and painful outcome that was always difficult no matter who had initiated it. There was no healing that could be done in companionship, no matter how much support one had. The body was a singular entity belonging to a single human being. Suffering of the heart and mind was to be endured. Time was the only true antidote. The only difference was how long one needed to heal completely. For Aisha, she never did. She simply pushed the pain deeper into herself until she couldn't remember it anymore. The problem was, she had never truly forgotten. The memory bubbled forth like a latent volcano that had decided to awaken the minute she walked the streets of Macau where the events had occurred.

Because . . . Aisha hesitated, calculating the risks of revealing something so private. She decided to let it go, let it out in the open. She wanted to move on, grow up from the teenaged self she had hidden behind the closet. In a bare whisper, she said, he made me pregnant.

Chloe gasped. Her companion cleared his throat and sighed in a way that made itself known he had half-expected it.

Then what happened? Chloe pressed on.

I was petite. I kept on working while my belly grew. Then in my final trimester, I got off the show on an ankle injury. I wasn't sure if the company would allow it. I think he must have helped me, talked to somebody at the top. I never knew. And then I gave birth. At the ripe old age of nineteen. I never told anyone. Not even to my parents.

Was it a boy or a girl? Where is the baby now?

A girl. She was the most beautiful thing I had ever seen. I don't know where she is now, Aisha sighed and let out the bad air she had trapped inside her for all those years. Her body was expelling a ghost inside her; she was being released from the secret that had been eating her up, that had haunted her in her quiet moments of despair.

How come?

I gave her up for adoption. I had to. My parents would have killed me. My lover didn't want me, or her.

Did you give her a name?

Yes, but I don't know if she still has that name, Aisha said, longingly. Aliyah. My daughter. Wherever she is in the world.

What happened to the man? Is he still in Macau?

I have no idea. I don't want to know, to be honest.

You're not curious at all?

Yes. But I was burnt badly the first time. It took me a long time to forget him then. I don't want to repeat the same mistake.

What's his name? Chloe's companion asked.

Aisha looked at him without blinking. She wondered, in this small city, whether everyone knew everyone. Even if it did, it didn't matter. She couldn't be shamed. But he could.

Nam Meng. I called him Meng.

Chloe let out a strangled cry like a frightened crow. She dropped the drink she had been holding onto the carpeted floor. The black beverage seeped into the maroon velvety carpet and turned it to a dirty brown-purple. Her face was aghast and white. She stared at Aisha with a tortured look.

What? Aisha asked, picking up the plastic cup that had fallen. What's the matter?

Chloe's companion sat up suddenly, putting his arms around his teenaged lover with the support she needed. He faced Aisha grimly.

That is her biological father. Chloe is adopted. She found out who her biological father was from her adopted parents.

Aisha dug her fingers into the arm rest of her sofa and tried to breathe. Chloe glared at the mother who had given her up. Tears welled up for both of them. Chloe tried to control herself, but her sobs came out faster than she could speak. Aisha looked at the daughter she never knew. She felt herself drowning and surfacing at the same time, breathless, heart in her throat, water gushing out from everywhere around her.

Chapter 13

The Fix

The luscious cherry tomato exploded in Dahlia's closed mouth as her back teeth bit down hard on it. She shuddered. The sweet tang of the citrus fruit overcame her, as did the aroma of basil, mozzarella cheese, olive oil and tart balsamic vinegar; each of these minute ingredients triggered her taste buds in a complex and captivating combo. Paul tucked into his own serving of the Caprese salad his wife had made for lunch. A wave of pure pleasure washed over him, as it did for Dahlia.

Hmm . . . so good, Paul managed to slip the words out without spurting out the juices swirling between his sealed lips. It felt like there was a party going on inside his mouth.

Dahlia could not help her smug reply. Told you. Grown in our garden some more. Totally organic.

They were in their garden, seated around a cast aluminium round table with matching chairs. The backs of the chairs were not cushioned, and Dahlia could feel the metallic ornate pattern biting into her bare flesh. Sure, the patio furniture set she had picked two years ago was exquisite when situated in her lush, tropical garden, but it was a dud when it came to comfort, especially since she liked to wear as little clothing as possible in her own home. It was a hot day, and she had on her backless batik dress, which was cooling for the weather but not a cool choice for this goddamned chair.

You look beautiful, Paul said, in between bursting tomatoes and cheese between his lips and taking sips of his Californian Chardonnay.

Dahlia nodded by way of accepting his compliment. She knew she looked gorgeous. Why shouldn't she? She had spent a tonne of money and hours at the salon primping, pruning, tanning and waxing to emerge a bronzed goddess. But she didn't usually look this way. In fact, she did it just for him. For this weekend. He turned to her, puzzled.

What's the occasion? We're at home. Are we expecting guests?

I just want to look special. For you.

Aw . . .

Paul pulled his lips into a cute pout then placed his hand over his wife's, giving it a good squeeze.

Maybe later . . . , Dahlia started, but before she could complete her sentence, her husband interrupted her.

. . . I've a great idea. Shall we rent a yacht? You look perfect for the occasion.

She fought back her frown, instead, turning the lines on her face to a smile. She shrugged. Dahlia had in mind a sweaty and sexy tumble upstairs in their bed. Not a boat ride as he had suggested.

Paul continued, I'll call Penelope and Rahul. They will be more than happy to join us.

The names of his college friends made her cringe. He didn't see it, having turned his head towards the incoming figure of Gloria, their domestic helper. She took away their salad plates first then brought out the main course. Roast lamb with potatoes. Dahlia had spent the last three hours cooking it. She was trying hard to seduce her husband through his stomach. Paul's face turned delighted.

Ooh . . . I could smell the rosemary when I woke up this morning. Nice job, honey.

Sir, Gloria said as she placed his plate for him. Ma'am, she addressed her mistress as she served Dahlia her lamb then disappeared into the kitchen through the patio door.

Paul started to text someone on his phone. Within three back-and-forth messages, he was finished.

All set, he said to his wife. They are coming. Today will be a glorious Sunday, you'll see.

It pained Dahlia to know that she had to see those two, especially Rahul. Her heart quickened and sank. It had nothing to do with him, though. It was the mere mention of his name, this very name, that grated on her nerves. Dahlia picked up her cutlery and started to slice the soft, brown meat she had been roasting since morning. She stabbed at a morsel with a fork and placed it on her extended tongue, withdrawing it into her wet mouth where she got her canines to work on this tender, sweet flesh, grinding it over and over before a satisfying swallow. The dish was a success. Dahlia sighed inwardly. She was cognizant of how much effort it would take, for as long as she lived, to keep the secret from her loving and doting husband. She turned her head sideways. The burial ground for Coco was in sight, next to the shrubs and in front of the skinny trees she can never remember the name of. Paul followed his wife's gaze.

Poor dog, he lamented, I feel bad for not being around when he died. Thanks, honey, for sending him off.

Dahlia mustered a weak smile. He didn't suffer, she assured him, he went off with love, I made sure of that.

* * *

Paul and Dahlia hadn't had sex for nine months. That was the first and primary problem. In nine months, a couple could have procreated and delivered a baby. Well, not for this couple, who had decided not to have babies anyway. Paul was not sexually interested in his wife. That was the secondary problem. Dry spell or not, the two had infrequent, dispassionate, mechanical intercourse during the times they did. This was bewildering to Dahlia who, despite her outward repressed appearance, was a horndog when it came down to dirty business. Both of them were attractive, in good shape and had the kind of relationship others envied. Take Penelope and Rahul. Those two bickered like bitches in heat, declared their loathing for each other, but continued to stay married for ten years. Three babies later, Penelope still had lust for Rahul, as she intimated to Dahlia, describing their lovemaking as acrobatic and out of this world. So, despite their differences, the couple stayed married but not, as Penelope put it, out of love but habit.

Dahlia never knew whether to feel sorry or envious of her. Paul *loved* her; he always showed it and told her often. Ever since junior college, they had known each other as friends first then confidantes, and became intimately acquainted when they both turned twenty-five. This meant kissing, strictly. By then, Dahlia had gone through four boyfriends, two serious and long-term and two just for the fun of it. Once she and Paul started to develop feelings for each other, they had coitus one time before getting engaged then marrying soon after. That one time was a litmus test for her. She needed to know if he had the whole package. For not only was Paul good-looking, but he had also made his fortune from being a self-made entrepreneur. He was, on paper, in all senses, a fantastic catch.

Granted that one time coitus was brief—it lasted only ten minutes—Dahlia felt there was chemistry between them. There had to be some, for she had longed for this man in the interim years when they kept up their friendship while staying chaste—she attributed it to him being a lapsed Baptist, some lingering guilt or shame that kept him at bay from her.

It happened in a room that was completely dark. She was unable to see his face or expression as he came. He didn't call her name either. He always called her honey or baby, childish words that used to endear him to her but soon lost their thrall. A dream man, he was, to Dahlia, but there was always something off about their relationship. She couldn't put her finger to it. Still, he adored her, and brought her the most lavish gifts whenever he returned from his overseas work trips. The most kind, generous and loving husband a woman could ever ask for. Yet, he couldn't satisfy her in the bedroom.

That was the bugbear that kept on bugging her.

* * *

Dahlia didn't need to marry into wealth. Her family was not poor, no, not at all. The Low family ran a funeral directing service since the time of her granddad, passed it on to her father, and now, she was in charge. Her two sisters had no interest in dealing with corpses or other people's grief. One married a Frenchman and moved to Bordeaux; the other stayed a spinster and worked as an auditor. Dahlia had the right personality for the job, her father had noticed right off the bat. She could empathize while staying unstirred when she came up close with the families of the dead in the funeral parlour. She said the right things, and often, said nothing at all; knowing how to toe the line between getting emotionally attached and detached at the same time. Most of all, her father saw that she had no qualms seeing a dead body. Even as a child, her fascination was clinical and curious. Average in academics, she had no ambition for the high-flying jobs her university mates were aspiring for. What's more, the girl could talk like a boss. She was shrewd with money and was unafraid of older or taller men who towered over her. The confidence and business acumen that Mr Low gained from watching his own father at work was imparted to his own daughter. By starting Dahlia early with informal apprenticeship, he had been grooming his youngest child with an entrepreneurial education since he had first spotted her talent.

No, Dahlia didn't need the millions that came with her union with Paul. Besides, they were too busy with work to enjoy their fortune. Now, at thirty-five, she had been running the family business for a decade. She had a solid team she could trust to take over whenever she was busy. From working seven days a week in the first year to now four days a week, Dahlia enjoyed the freedom of being a small enterprise businesswoman receiving a regular paycheck. She could have gourmet lunches and lavish dinners with her friends and husband whenever she wanted. She could shop at any high-end store without blinking an eye. Premium vacations, jewellery buying, filling roomfuls of designer shoes and handbags—all these had become routine to Dahlia. No kids, no fuss, a cushy, perfect life. Then Paul got Coco, an Alsatian puppy that grew too fast and too big, but with a temper tame like a turtle. Dahlia hated the dog. She was the victim of a dog bite when she was nine and never forgave all dogs for their ability to hurt her.

So naturally, Coco became collateral damage.

* * *

One of Paul's best mates was from work. As an employee, Chester was a wizard with numbers, helping Paul keep his taxation accounts kosher. He crunched some figures and taught Paul to trim the team while raising bonuses and kept up the profits, pleasing the stakeholders immensely. Within four years, Chester had become Paul's right-hand man and made VP. It was not unexpected that Paul's business trips, particularly the ones that lasted a month or more, included this sidekick. Each time her husband returned from these trips, Dahlia swore he glowed, perhaps from the tan of a beach he had visited or the glee of discovering more moneymaking tricks. She never asked. She was happy to bask in the aura of her handsome husband.

Yet, in their presence, Dahlia often felt left out. A third wheel, she once told her husband. He laughed out so loud spittle came flying out of his mouth. Paul assured her he would include her in everything he did, even his business meetings, if that was something she wanted. He said it in a way that was so guileless that she didn't think he was trying to condescend her. Frankly, she was fine with her husband being close to his colleague. She just wanted the one thing he seemed to be most unconcerned about. But each time she touched him sensuously, he simply smiled and removed her hands. In front of Chester, that was awkward for her, but she did it anyway; stroking the hardened biceps on Paul's arm or attempting to neck him while ruffling his hair. She knew her PDA was a tad excessive, but Chester was a family friend by now, not just someone from the office. He wouldn't find her actions indecent, she told herself. After all, a wife had her needs, and she had every right to display her desire.

But it was when they were alone, at home or in a hotel, with no prying eyes, that her husband's lack of interest in her stung her most. On a particularly warm day in July, when Gloria was having her weekly day off and there was no one in the house, Paul again gently nudged Dahlia's hand away as they were on the sofa watching a movie with a love scene that grew increasingly erotic.

What's wrong? Dahlia blurted. She finally had enough. Could he not see that she wanted intimacy?

We finish the movie first. I want to know how it ends.

Paul then stood up and brought two tubs of Ben & Jerry's ice cream—a matcha flavour for her and a Belgian chocolate for himself.

They tucked in as they finished the movie, which had as lame a finish as the plot. It was a waste of two hours. Dahlia checked the clock. In an hour's time, Gloria would be home, and there goes her chance at the kind of shrieking sex she had been dreaming of.

So, Dahlia nudged her husband. How about now?

Sure. Meet you in the bedroom. Need to use the toilet first.

Dahlia was thrilled. She went upstairs and put on lacy undergarments and lay on the bed, waiting. The minutes ticked by. There was no sound in the house but the dog's whimpering, perhaps crying for food. Fifteen minutes later, she got fed up. She went to find her husband, still locked inside the guest bathroom downstairs.

Paul, she said, rapping on the door. What's going on? Are you coming or not?

Paul let out a visible groan. Diarrhoea, he mumbled, I think it's the ice cream.

Dahlia wanted to kick him. He was the one who wanted the ice cream. And now, look what's happened.

She wondered what she could do now. There was nothing sexy about a man with the runs. It would be futile to push for her agenda. Then she heard the keys jangle, the lock turn, the door open. Gloria had returned. Dahlia wanted to tell her to make mint tea for Paul to soothe his stomach then realized to her horror she was wearing only her bra and panties. Quickly, she climbed back up the stairs before her maid could notice her and shut the door to her bedroom. Coco's whimpering stopped. Gloria had fed the dog. As Dahlia heard the flush of the toilet coming from downstairs and the sound of a door opening, she put back on her clothes, disappointed yet again.

* * *

Trouble started with the first recessed ceiling lightbulb burning itself out while Gloria was dusting the shelves. The sudden sizzling and sound of a pop shocked the poor woman. Then, one of the door handles for one of the rooms came loose. A myriad host of household problems started occurring one by one. Two of the rusted hinges in the kitchen cabinet corroded further, misaligning the cabinet doors when closed. A framed poster in the living room fell off along with the nail. The shower head in Dahlia's en suite bathroom cracked. Not to mention one too many drain holes that had drainage issues.

That week of discovering these faults occurred at a particularly bad time for Dahlia. It was December and Gloria had already planned her annual two-week home leave to Batangas for Christmas. Business at the funeral parlour was brisker than usual, and Paul was overseas, returning only in late January. His excuse? Opening a branch office in Ho Chi Minh City to expand into the Vietnam market. He had promised Dahlia he would make it up to her for Chinese New Year. What choice did she have? A big house coming apart that needs fixing while her maid and husband are away. Perfect timing.

Gloria was quick to offer a solution. Her Bangladeshi boyfriend knew someone in the same dormitory who was a nifty handyman. He could fix anything in no time. She felt awful, knowing some of these issues had been around for weeks, and had made no attempt to tell her employer. Besides, this guy would be cheap and quick, Gloria promised, and she would write Dahlia a list of things that require fixing.

Dahlia knew she had to pay this guy with money under the table. It's not as if she didn't have the money to pay a professional, but really, she was much too busy to manage the situation. In two days, Gloria would be gone, and the funeral of her latest client was complicated by the grieving family being too large and too finicky. So Dahlia closed one eye to engaging the services of Gloria's contact, a man who turned up at 10 a.m. sharp that Sunday.

He introduced himself as Rahul. Dahlia stopped herself from smiling, for what coincidence it was that he was named the same as Paul's close buddy. She made sure not to display any sign of friendliness, putting on a stiff, blank face. She was hiring him for his services, no need to be chummy. Dahlia stepped aside to let the man through her main door. Rahul was used to such treatment from people in Singapore. There were rich people who showed kindness and were generally cordial. Then there were those like this lady whose face he couldn't tell was indifferent, hostile or bored. He had

been asked to turn up with his toolbox if he wanted to earn some
extra cash, so that's what he did. He was a problem solver with his
hands. And he was masterful with it. How an employer looked at
him was not his concern.

There was another reason why Dahlia didn't want to smile. For
as Rahul came through her door, she felt the wind get knocked out
of her. Here was someone who looked vaguely like Tiger Shroff,
a celebrated Bollywood actor whose stud factor was through the
roof. Leaner and shorter, Rahul had a subdued expression that made
him seem coy, contained. She tried not to compare him with Tiger,
knowing they were worlds apart; in fact, she and Rahul were not of
the same league either. But once the teasing thought had germinated
in Dahlia's mind, she couldn't shake it off. She was only too pleased
that she was alone in the house with him, free to luxuriate in the
beauty of a copycat.

Follow me.

Dahlia told Rahul as she led him from the hallway to the dining
room. She had a long list of things that needed fixing, almost sixteen
items. He stood erect and awkward, gazing at her with a certain awe,
waiting for this rich young lady's instruction.

Gloria told me you are good with your hands, Dahlia said. You
can fix anything?

Before noon, Dahlia had to return to the funeral parlour to
oversee that complicated wake. She could leave the task to her team
if she chose to, though there was no reason to delegate. She was
available that Sunday; and the grieving family kept texting her with
queries. It was imperative that Rahul fix all the items by this weekend.

I try, replied Rahul softly.

His voice was low and sonorous. It sounded like a cross between
an animal growl and the burr of a motorbike. It was sexy as hell.
Dahlia pictured Tiger half-naked from the waist up, displaying his
greased, shredded torso as he leaned against the beast of a shiny
Ducati, bedroom eyes calling for her to come over.

Is one hour enough? Dahlia asked, rattling off the item list.
Lights in the living room and corridor, kitchen and toilet downstairs.
Clear drain pipes in all washbasins and the drain holes. Secure door

handle in master bedroom. Repair shower head in master bedroom en suite bathroom. Fix cabinet hinges in kitchen—quite a few. Replace nails for the painting in the living room. And repair several unwieldy drawers.

Rahul shook his head. Maybe two hours?

You can come back again?

He shrugged his shoulders. When?

Dahlia checked her work schedule on her phone. Tomorrow?

Rahul scratched his neck and made a slight frown. He was not available, Dahlia could tell.

I'll pay you $100 for today, and $100 for tomorrow. How about that? Dahlia proposed to him.

She could him see him thinking. His eyes narrowed. $200 for today, $200 for tomorrow, he negotiated.

Dahlia liked where this was going. He was playing a game; she was up for it.

$120 for each day, she said firmly.

$180.

$150. Final offer.

Two days $300? Rahul's low voice went an octave higher.

Dahlia was amused. She nodded her head. The power of money could buy over anyone's time, Dahlia knew from being a boss. Had he insisted on his original fee of $200, she would have easily given it to him. It was petty cash to her.

Okay, Rahul said firmly. Tomorrow I come after work. Night time okay?

The mere mention of night and the accompanying imagery of cloaked darkness with this man alone was quite a scintillating idea. She nodded affirmatively, and set out to walk Rahul through the house, pointing out the places he needed to be to fix the problems in her wide and spacious bungalow. Rahul whipped out his power tools and promptly got down to work while Dahlia stood observing him. This was a perfectly normal scenario to the handyman; for clients often wanted to make sure he wasn't cutting corners.

For the entire hour, Rahul bent over this and that while his newest client watched him like a hawk. Pretty soon, his T-shirt was drenched in sweat. He started to relax and began to sing softly to himself. When the first half-hour had passed, he took a break. Dahlia offered him a Coke which he accepted, guzzling down the fizzy canned soda hungrily, chin raised to the roof, eyes closed to savour such simple enjoyment. The act of stretching his torso meant Dahlia saw how well-built he was. Without malice, Rahul directed one eye at Dahlia, returning the gaze on the woman who had been staring at him since he entered her house. Her face turned hot. Dahlia broke off eye contact. She was now thirsty herself and, fumbling with the fridge, grabbed a bottle of Perrier and poured herself a glass. The bubbles of the mineral water leapt up and about, bounding in and over the glass. Dahlia drank all of it down, letting loose fireworks of sparkling molecules inside her mouth. When Rahul gave her a shy smile, thanking her for the drink before resuming his work, it was all Dahlia could do to yank herself back from throwing herself at him.

* * *

It was bound to happen. Rahul left half the work undone for the next day, so he could earn the other $150 the lady had promised. Dahlia didn't ask how he had managed to get out of the dormitory on a workday. She knew foreign workers had restricted movement, or rules they had to abide by. The fact that he was there in her house was all it mattered. He arrived at 9 p.m., expecting to leave at ten. He would earn his quick buck and still have time to catch the MRT back to his living quarters.

Rahul crouched then sat down on the kitchen floor, getting ready to repair a kitchen cabinet door below the countertop. His bum was on the floor while his legs, bent at the knees, were spread wide open as he held a cherry-dyed plywood door with his hard knuckled hands, attempting to remove and replace a rusted silver hinge. Dahlia leaned against a wall, checking him out. In her hands were a bowl of strawberries that she munched on absentmindedly. It was like watching a movie, live—Tiger Shroff, in her kitchen, fixing her up. This time, she permitted herself to smile at her delicious reverie.

Five minutes in, Rahul received a call. As the conversation went on in Rahul's foreign tongue, his voice started to change. It sounded like distress to Dahlia, despite her not understanding a word. When he hung up, he was very much altered, a different person altogether. He stared into space in a state of disbelief. Concerned, Dahlia tried to rouse him.

Rahul!

This was the dreaded face she had been accustomed to in her line of work. The pure and gut-wrenching shock of someone who hadn't yet accepted a terrible piece of news. She squatted down so she was eye-level with him.

Rahul! She snapped her fingers in front of his face. Hey!

He turned blankly to her. He couldn't seem to register who this person was or what on earth he was doing in a stranger's place. In a split second, his face cracked, sudden awareness. He broke down, sobbing. Then, realizing he was shaming himself in front of a woman, he covered his weeping face with both his hands to try to contain his outpouring.

Dahlia knew what had happened even if he didn't say anything. She put down her fruit bowl on the floor and patted him between the shoulder blades. She could feel the taut muscles beneath her fingertips. When that didn't have an effect, she made firm circular motions with her palm, massaging his back to try and calm the man down. This seemed to work. Rahul's sobbing came to a halt. He looked up at her with tear-soaked eyes, childlike, lost. She saw that they were bloodshot. She also noted his eyelashes were luscious, black and long.

Do you want to talk about it?

Dahlia stopped touching his back, removed her hand. It seemed like the right time to stop, lest he thought she was coming on to him.

My son . . . Rahul's voice trembled, he died. My mother call to tell me.

Oh.

That was worse news than she had anticipated. She had assumed the bad news would be related to a parent or relative, not child. She murmured gently.

I'm sorry for you and your wife.

Rahul shook his head. My wife already dead.

Oh.

She couldn't think of anything else to say. Still, that was not exactly bad news to Dahlia. The man's tragedy was her gain. She was not really thinking about his pain anymore. Usually, she was well versed in keeping in the moment with her grieving clients. The empathy she would express. The serenity she would ensure they had. In the wicked corner of her mind, she was reminded of a scene from a movie. Tiger, tears flowing down from his cheeks, holding on to the hand of his desired one as chemistry flowed back and forth between the two.

From baby, my son always sick, Rahul blubbered, I work hard, send him money, for hospital, for medicine. He only two years old. Why this happen? Why? Why doctors don't fix him? Why God take him, not take me?

Dahlia harnessed her most kindly funeral director's voice, a specific timbre of a sound she would typically use to soothe the grieving.

Your son is now in a better place. No longer suffering, no longer in pain. He knows you love him. Always remember that. Always. You have given him so much love, more love than you can ever know. He feels your love. You must know this. Believe that he is taking your love with him to a better place. Your son is on a journey. You will see him when your time comes. Know that he will always be with you, in your heart, your mind, your soul, in the sun that shines on you, the wind that kisses you, in the air all around.

It was the same spiel Dahlia would say to her clients. Different variations, similar themes. Content shuffled and reshuffled to fit the audience depending on their religious and cultural affiliations. Her speech had a powerful effect on Rahul. His big black eyes grew wide, awed by this strange lady in a huge and fancy house who was now taking pity on him and showing genuine kindness.

Impulse drove him to grab Dahlia's hand with his rugged hands. Their faces were inches apart. There was a glimmer of reckoning on his face that informed him how attractive this lady was. Dahlia felt slightly unnerved. She tensed up. A married woman's fantasy was not reality—that she could tell apart. Rahul's facial expression dissolved from grief to relief to an unexpected, desirous lust. Dahlia blinked. She could feel him channelling vibes towards her. She felt stirred, warm in places she couldn't deny. When he lunged forward and wrapped his lips around hers, she knew this would be a solid one hour that neither of them would speak about later.

* * *

It didn't take one hour. Twenty minutes later, they uncoupled, silently putting back their clothes. Rahul had exerted himself so much his shirt was a wet rag. He asked if he could shower and have a change of shirt before leaving. There was still work to do around the house, but neither spoke about it, and it seemed inconsequential at that very moment.

Dahlia took him to the en suite bathroom in her bedroom. She wanted to give him something nondescript that her husband had not worn in years. As Rahul showered, filling the room with the familiar musky scent of shower gel and shampoo her husband often used, Dahlia selected a pair of Calvin Klein briefs, a black Tom Ford tee and a pair of Hugo Boss jeans, all of which Paul had multiples and would not miss if she gave them away.

As Rahul stepped out of the shower, she was dismayed that he hadn't closed the sliding cubicle door for the shower. The bathroom floor was now flooded.

Here, take this, she said to him, turning her head away at his nudity as she passed him the set of clothes. Under the bright LED bathroom light, Dahlia could see that Rahul was not as aesthetically sculpted as her husband. Paul had a personal trainer who helped him gain designer abs and muscles in the right places; and a nutritionist's carefully crafted diet to ensure he reached his goal. Rahul's build was working class rough; bull solid, hulk-like, like a tough T-bone steak that had been overcooked. Paul was photogenic, a hunky model; Rahul was a swarthy, sweaty Santa Claus who had climbed down her chimney to gift her a one-night encounter. No doubt Rahul's passionate vigour earlier was appreciated, but Dahlia could not do it again with this man. She had lapsed in discretion and wanted to end the night quickly.

When Rahul was dressed, Dahlia softened. In her husband's clothes, Rahul was a good copy. Like Paul. Like Tiger Shroff. A man of unfixed identity she could project her perverted fantasies on. He fixed her house. She fixed his persona. Or at least, that was what she thought.

Dahlia's bathroom was large. Rahul's phone rang again. In his eagerness to answer, he tried to make a quick run for it. The marble tiled floor was completely wet and slippery. Rahul lost his footing and slipped. The heavy sack of his body fell backwards with a loud thud. Dahlia gasped. She rushed towards him. A trickle of blood oozed out from his head towards the drain hole. Rahul was unconscious. Dahlia shouted his name again and again in panic. There was no response. The tables had turned. Instead of him fixing her, she would have to fix her fixer. But how?

* * *

Her instinct was to call an ambulance. It was the ethical thing to do. But something changed her mind quickly. For someone who was so young, Rahul's rather dramatic fall had made him stop breathing. Dahlia was beyond disbelief. This man was not more than thirty, thirty-five. He had lines on his forehead, scattered white hair on his sideburns. His dead son was two, but he could have married and fathered late. Over the next half-hour, she sat down beside him, getting her bum wet and soaked through. Rahul was really not breathing at all. She knew a dead body when she saw one, how the warmth on the skin slowly faded to cool.

Regaining control of her senses, Dahlia snapped to attention. She dug around the trousers he had come to her house with. They were scattered to one side of the bathroom, lying limply. She found his wallet and opened it, sifting through his cards for an ID. She found his work permit card with his photo, name of employer, occupation, work permit number, date of issue and expiry and some other details, but no birthdate. There was money and calling cards and an ATM debit card. Dahlia knew this was the most crucial evidence about Rahul. It was the first thing she had to hide or destroy.

During the time that Dahlia had her rendezvous, she had let Coco into the garden. The dog had a kennel and often slept there on balmy nights. This evening, Dahlia had made sure the Alsatian had a large meal, which she had given him before Rahul's arrival. The gentle beast didn't bark once even with Rahul, a stranger, around. It was not a territorial animal, and not very smart. Because of that, Dahlia had completely forgotten about Coco, a feminine name that Paul had insisted on for his stupid stud.

She left Rahul to check on Coco. The light from the kitchen flooded into the pitch-black garden as she swung open the door to the patio. Coco looked up sleepily, whining by way of hello. Dahlia let go of the door. She strode to the patio table with chairs and took a seat. She sat in the darkness, the back of her head lit by the faded orange glow from the kitchen. Dahlia started to think. Coco had grown too big for the kennel, its oversized limbs and head jutting halfway out. The dumb dog must weigh at least 60 kg. When stretched out paw to paw, it would be over 1.5 m. It could fit into a coffin. For a human.

Her ideas generated fast. She could see the sequence of actions unfold in her head, step by step. Dahlia stood up. She went back to the kitchen. She took Coco's favourite canned lamb and poured the contents out into his food bowl then mixed the lethal rodent poison that had kept the rats out the entire year. This she gave to her husband's dog, where the smell of wet slop awakened it. Coco devoured the food, licked the bowl. Dahlia sat down on the patio chair and waited. She watched the animal retch and writhe in pain, crying for mercy. When the deed was done, Dahlia walked over to check. No sign of breathing, no sign of life. She then walked over to the garden shed, took out a spade and started digging an area of soil she had decided on. Close to the shrubs and the ugly trees, Dahlia dug and dug for hours until the hole was perfect.

* * *

It was fortunate that, due to the grieving family's shilly-shallying, there was an empty casket assigned to her client sitting in Dahlia's hearse parked in her house. They had vetoed against the design and choice of wood; and had asked for a replacement. This pinewood casket was to be returned, which was why Dahlia had it with her that day.

Dahlia moved fast. She dragged Rahul's body from her bedroom, down the stairs, past the living room, kitchen and out the patio door. He was heavy, but Dahlia was wiry herself. Taking kickboxing and Muay Thai lessons for the past year to pummel away her sexual frustration had come in handy. She deposited Rahul inside the hole she had dug. It was a metre deep, a metre long and half-metre wide. She folded his body neatly to fit the space, dropped his wallet and toolbox in with him then covered the hole with soil till there was a neat hump. She dragged Coco's carcass and placed it inside the casket inside her hearse. Over the next hour, she removed all traces of dog vomit from the garden and Rahul's presence in the house, scrubbing and cleaning till no trace of misdemeanour could be found. By then, it was almost three in the dead of night. She filled up a death certificate for Coco using her company letterhead, gave the dog a fictional pet name, signed it with instructions then drove the casket to the crematorium. First thing in the morning, the family pet would be incinerated. Dahlia returned to her house, depleted and promptly fell asleep on the living room sofa.

The minute she woke up the next morning, she planted the seeds of some herbs, fruits and vegetables over the fresh covered soil where Rahul's body lay. The seeds were gifts from Penelope, but Dahlia hadn't found a use for them before; now, it was more than useful. Next, Dahlia ordered a burial sign for Coco from a supplier who didn't know her. When delivered, she secured the sign on the mound where Paul could see. It would take months for the vegetation to grow to size, in which time, she would be solely in charge of caring for the edible garden. Paul wouldn't go near the plot, Dahlia knew; and Gloria would be more than happy to not bother if instructed.

And so, the organic garden flourished. The basil, rosemary, coriander, curry leaves, peppermint and many other scented herbs and plants sprouted in weeks. When Paul came home, the tomato plant was still barren but soon, tiny red plump cherry tomatoes started to pop up everywhere. It kept on giving, week after week, even as Dahlia fed her husband the vegetables she sowed and harvested with great care. While fond of Coco, Paul was not particularly attached to the dog. It was something nice to have around, but not an object he dedicated much time and affection to. He wanted to replace it with another; but Dahlia, not wanting an animal that would forage the earth, resolutely said no. Instead, she went and got a sable Bombay cat that sat around all day staring at her with yellow evil eyes. Dahlia was fine with that. At least the feline was smart. This one would keep Dahlia in check. She needed that kind of critical judgement to keep her on the straight and narrow.

Chapter 14

Old Man Young

She thinks I'm deaf or dead, but I see and hear everything. One eye is blind, for sure, but I can't argue with God. A sacrifice for everything He's given to me so far in life—I have lived to the fullest. To give half of my sight, I'll let him have it. Have been counting down to the abyss since my numbers started climbing up. Eighty. That's two decades away from a century. That's four generations away from this young girl taking care of me.

Been there, done that, my little friend. I see her doing things she thinks no one knows what she's up to. I'm a living corpse to her. So, I shut up. See no point in even telling my son about it. He comes so much less often now, with the baby on the way. Number three. Good genes, my son. Comes from his mother. My smoking and drinking years are all way behind me now. You can see their wreckage on my skin, in my voice. I croak when I speak. I'm dry as the bark of a century-old Casuarina tree. Used to be brown, tanned, now I'm grey, mottled, like an animal growing spots—a bit white here, a bit black there. Once, the girl pinched my arm, a patch of flesh the size of a fifty-cent black disc, rubbing the loose skin between her fingers just to see if it would come off. As if she's trying to rub the stain off laundry. My good glaucoma-free eye looked at her. She barely gave me a glance, merely mumbled. With one finger, she prodded the spot, pushed my thin skin till she touched bone, kneaded and circled the spot. It was going nowhere. I'm not even sure when I first got it, or how it grew larger.

Sometime after I smoked my last Camel, on that very day, when my voice was coarse as a used sputtering motor, the spot simply appeared and stayed, taking over the space of the other age spots and scars. The tiny colonizer wasn't malignant, I was told, a year after it had grown to this size, when Ben took me to the hospital after his eldest son turned six. Now that his other son is six, he's too busy to come round which, I suppose, is a casualty of being a young parent. I wouldn't know. I was nothing like my son. Ben knew how to change his sons' diapers—I saw with my own eyes. Ben fed food, teaspoon by teaspoon, into the mouths of his children when they were so small they couldn't chew yet. I saw that, and squirmed. I've never so much as stuffed a crumb into my children's mouths. A woman's job, my own Pa always said.

Ben's mother did everything. I mean everything. All that and the cooking and cleaning and taking the shit I threw at her. The words I said to her about how she wasn't a good enough mother. How she was a wife who didn't know how to sweet talk her husband. How she always cooked a little too salty, or not salty enough, cooked too little food, or too much. I was never happy enough. She took it all in. We quarrelled, of course. Gek was no wallflower. A librarian, she was the quiet type, book smart, and dumb enough to have met me when she was twenty-two and fell for my glib tongue.

Back then, my voice was a weapon. An instrument I played to my advantage. I charmed so many ladies—rich ones, beautiful ones, easy ones. Not sure why I picked her. She wasn't even in the same dialect group as me. Maybe it was the conqueror's instinct. Heard Teochew girls were pretty, delicate flowers for the picking. Gek was so quiet, with black eyes like two round spots that grew large as fifty-cent coins the instant she saw me; I knew this girl would be happy in my palm, lapping up everything I fed her.

For years, Gek's eyes would pop up each time I called her name. Oi! Gek! Where's my slippers? Gek! Is dinner ready? But decade after decade, her rounded eyes became less round, less widened, less bright, less sharp. They became clouded over, milk in her eyes. Ten years ago, when I called her name, Oi! Gek! Eat rice! Gek! Watch out for the bicycle! I didn't know if she heard me or saw me or cared who I really was. She knew I was the same man in the same house. But she was long gone, like her eyes were long gone. A crazy mix of blue and white and brown all floating around unsure which way to flow. She used to mumble aiyah, aiyah, diam lah just to shut my voice out. Towards the end, before she completely shut me out, and her eyes didn't recognize me anymore, I remembered her muttering aiyah, aiyah over and over again, like someone who had lost a lottery again, the lament of one accursed with bad luck.

* * *

I don't tell Ben, but she calls me Oi! when it's just her and me. It reminds me of the way I purposely refused to use Gek's name. So, in a way, it doesn't feel as bad as it sounds, to be called by your maid like a nameless stranger, Oi!

In front of Ben, to whom the maid deferentially refers to as Sir, she remembers to address me as Mr Young. She updates Ben about my health and daily habits, or whichever part of my mundane life he bothers to know, which I suspect is very little, since Juliet is always in a hurry to leave, and Ben has to scold one of the boys who are always fighting or breaking something.

Sir, yes, Mr Young exercise. Every morning six o'clock. We go garden, playground, yes Sir, he walk himself. I hold him, Sir, he no fall down. Mr Young eat food okay, sometimes more, sometimes less. Tingkat man come every day. Pass motion also every day. Blood pressure still okay, Sir. Mr Young like young man, Sir, very strong.

Which is just bull, if you ask me. I can see, though fuzzily. I eat enough, soft food like tofu, porridge, or sometimes overcooked rice, fish yes, steamed not fried, carrots and potatoes very well, sometimes chicken if its shredded thin and small enough. The kind of food Ben gave to his sons when they were four, or two. I don't know at which age kids stop eating soft food. She calls an old man eating like a young child strong? I suppose I have enough strength to keel over. Got to watch my steps. Walk slow, take it easy. Haven't decided how much I should trust this girl. She's only been here nine months. My moles know me more than she does.

No Sir, I no use phone daytime, only nighttime when he sleep, Sir. Yes, I take good care of Mr Young. He like my father.

At that, the maid reaches out and pats my arm gently with her hand. She smiles widely, mumbles something to me. Her acting is not appreciated. Ben doesn't care. I don't care. Ben looks me in the eye and says, Pa, how are you? Doing okay or not?

When Ben was fourteen, I asked him the same thing, How are you? Doing okay or not?

He had a large gash on his leg from where he had fallen from the bicycle, going full speed to school, took a short cut where he hadn't been before, swerved at the sight of a running stray cat, and collapsed in a heap right at the spot of some broken concrete jutting out of the floor. The gash was gauzed and taped over by the school nurse, but he was wincing even when he got home. I was chain-smoking at the time, back from work, whisky in one hand, seated in my armchair. I blew a cloud of grey smoke in his eyes—the boy had had an accident, phoned me in my office but I directed him to his mother whose librarian job was, in my mind, more flexible to take time off. As an engineer, I was always needed. A cog in a machine couldn't be plugged out at will just like that, for a teenager's non-fatal mishap.

Painful lah! What do you think? My fourteen-year-old had shouted at me from the sofa where he was sitting. His words pierced through the nicotine smoke. I saw him finally when the clouds parted. Gek was frying in the kitchen, as usual. From the living room, I could hear the sound of something sizzling and the pots and pans clanging away, the smell of garlic mixed with the smell of cigarettes. I leaned forward and peered at his dressing: white oblong with a red sun; a Japanese flag. The smell of Dettol. My finger reached out instinctively to touch it. It stopped an inch before it decided it wasn't such a good idea.

What do you want? Give me more pain? Ma! I'm hungry! Ready or not? Ben tried to stand up quickly but his injury slowed him down. He cried out in pain. I reached out to touch his arm but he pushed me away and forced himself to move quicker, wincing with each step, hobbling on one foot bit by bit till he got to the kitchen table where Gek had brought out the first dish. Chinese spinach with garlic and ginger. Ben made a face.

It's good for you, makes you stronger, Gek said.

Where's the meat? I'm not a goat, only eat greens, Ben demanded.

Gek mumbled something then went back to the kitchen. I took out another cigarette, leaned back into the sofa and lit up. Another year of my life went up in smoke.

I'm eating, Pa! Ben shouted angrily at me.

I stood up, stuffed my pack of Marlboros in my shirt pocket and went to the window of the living room, stuck my head out, stared at the crescent moon and puffed away at the stick while the bright end glimmered to a dying inch of ash.

Ash. Funny enough, that's what I see sometimes when my maid thinks I'm too dumb to notice. It can't be mine. I've stopped smoking ten years ago. Right after Gek died. She passed away at sixty from lung cancer. She never smoked once. And me? Whose lungs should have hardened and blackened from abuse, whose steel heart should have conked out, whose blood should have curdled from eating lard and guzzling the malt of gold, I'm still alive twenty years after my good girl has gone, still chugging along. You're a sick bastard, God, taking the good ones and letting those who should have expired live on.

Ben said the maid is twenty-three. She looks thirty to me. Back home in Bandung, she has a son, three years old, no husband. A widow. Her parents are forty, even younger than Ben, who is forty-three or forty-four, I can't remember. These days I don't see my grandsons anymore, both growing teens who have this or that class in Chinese or Math or Music or Karate. Always something that Juliet is sending them off to. I don't see Juliet either. She has a horse face, the temper of a cornered bull, short and petite, a firecracker of a woman born in the wrong year of the Rabbit. I don't think she dislikes me. I think she doesn't care for me. But it's okay. As long as no incident is fatal, they leave me very much alone. The maid takes care of everything. She keeps me alive, and that's the best they can do. For now.

* * *

It's twenty-five degrees Celsius this morning, unusual for Singapore. Raining three nights in a row, each morning dazzling bright with damp that sticks pins into my skin. I'm thin now, didn't used to be. Not able to withstand temperature changes so much.

Oi, your sweater. Don't get sick. Sir later scold me.

My maid lifts my arms and wriggles an old smelly sweater on me. She's a sharp one. Didn't tell her where it was but she found it alright. I haven't worn this in over a year, when the last maid had stuffed it in the back of my wardrobe. It smells of mothballs and decaying mixed wool. It was a present from Ben and Juliet years ago when they had just gotten married, when Juliet was still filial and showed it. It was blue when I had it, dark Prussian blue that had gotten greyer over the years. I grumble as the sweater is put on me. I always grumble, but I still do whatever she wants me to do.

Complain always. I only help you. I don't help you who else will? You old man like baby sometimes, like my son . . .

The maid stops in her tracks. I am still grumbling. Even with the milk creeping around my irises, I can see her eyes are red, veins spiking across the whites of her eyes. They're wet around the corners. The maid, after a minute more, breaks from her bubble.

Hurry up, Oi! Morning exercise, one, two, three! Go!

She always waits for me to walk ten steps in front of her before she whips up her mobile phone. Actually, she doesn't need to pretend. It is just her and me. Ben never comes around for surprise visits. Though technically he is her employer and pays her the salary; I am her patient, her charge.

In the house, while I sleep, sometimes she watches the TV. I can hear it when it is on. To be fair, the maid is always doing something around the house. The water will run. The floor gets mopped. The laundry hung. The furniture dusted. The windows gleam so clean a bird thought it was open and flew right into it last week, banged its head and died. There was blood on the glass. The maid screeched in horror as I sat on the dining chair, staring into space as usual, and watched her muttering and shaking her head as she cleaned the blood off. Things die, you know, I wasn't that surprised. It just shocked me with the impact of the collision. The velocity of the bird's flight path was at such speed the accident would automatically kill the animal, what with the surface being as impenetrable and hard as an old man's heart.

Today it's a different man. I've only seen one other; this one is new. More handsome, darker, taller, more facial hair, bigger smile, buys her breakfast. A curry puff. I can smell the curried potatoes and chicken when she bites into it and makes that *mmm* sound.

I'm sitting on the bench at the nearby park, inhaling the morning air and the scent of the floral detergent from the neighbour's laundry. The smell of a curry puff brings me back to the time Gek always bought me breakfast on Saturday mornings from the market. Twenty cents per piece, she'll buy four; my kopi in a reused Milkmaid can on a raffia string. I'll be at home waiting, hungry, reading *The Straits Times* with a cigarette already burning on the ashtray. Gek did that for forty years. I never thanked her for it. She had always assumed I liked it and needed it. I did. I just never said anything. She never knew how much I liked and needed her; I never admitted it to myself until she was gone. Now this young girl is making me jealous through no fault of hers. Damn curry puff.

Sedap, terima kasih, the maid says to the new man who can't stop grinning.

They are conscious of me, but to be fair, he merely touches her arm once and then leaves. I feel particularly cold today. The morning breeze is whipping me in the face and nipping coolly at my sockless, sandaled feet. Old people sit like statues, bronzed by wisdom, not moving, eyes darting, knowing everything without saying a word. The maid knows I know. Yet, she can't be faulted. She is never out of my sight. Except when I nap or sleep. Then I don't know what on earth she is up to.

I want to say something to her. She looks radiant, happy, nibbling at the ends of a curry puff, the crumbs staining her blouse, greasing her fingers. I want to ask her about the man before that, who brought her soya bean milk, who smiled less, was shorter, fairer, less hairy, less handsome. I've only seen that man twice over the span of two months. Something tells me I'm going to see this new man more often.

What happened to Teng Teng? No longer together? Bring her around, Ben, what she likes to eat? Chilli crab? Assam fish? Sambal sotong? Ma can cook.

Gek said that when Ben was moping for a week while the phone rang and rang and he refused to pick it up. Even I couldn't keep up with the names. It was either Teng Teng or Wei Wei or Lina or Neela or Mila or Gila. Ben turned out fine looking by the time puberty left him and he was a strapping eighteen-year-old with intense eyes, a cleft inherited from his granddad and a chiselled profile that made everyone praise him. Kim, my daughter, on the other hand, had soft features, little eyes, button nose and a square face; a sibling no one could tell was related to Ben. Three years younger than Ben, Kim hated and rebelled against me ever since she knew the word *No!* could be empowered by action, left the house when she turned seventeen, met a middle-aged Austrian engineer, married him a year later when she became pregnant, and had been living overseas all this time. From Ben, I found out she had been back to Singapore many times, often seeing him and his family and, of course, Gek whom she adores. But me? Once when Kim's daughter was five. Another time when her other daughter was ten. And finally, at Gek's funeral. I'd lost my daughter the day she outgrew me and knew she could open a back door and never return. God knows what I did that she never forgave me for.

Thing is, Ben broke many hearts. The phone at home was always ringing. Sometimes he picked it up, and dripped down the cord with sugary sweet talk I was sure the girls on the line were being hooked on one by one. In the end, before he met Juliet and committed himself to her, he had caused one to be pregnant, forced one into abortion, driven one to become a lesbian, led one into a shotgun marriage with another man even though Ben was positive the baby was his and pushed another to be committed for six months into a mental institution. I had no idea the power my son had over women until he told me one day, while he was chain-smoking Marlboros with me, and Juliet was one of two girls he was seeing. Juliet had studied law in Cambridge. She was the plainer of the two but could outtalk Ben, outsmart him and had him on his toes. I said to Ben, You can *be* a man; and not *become* a man. The phone stopped ringing all day afterwards.

My maid's phone is now beeping. More often than not, her phone beeps rather than rings. I know who it is. She's so excited I can feel a wave of warm energy radiating from her. I'm no longer twenty, but I know men, and they are all the same: rascals.

Ben was one. I was one. Gek saved me from the wrong path I almost took. Water under the bridge, she used to say. I may not have as many notches as Ben. But Gek knew my past. Three or four girlfriends was still one too many for her in those days. It was a stained spot compared to Gek's white sheet of nothing.

The maid giggles, blushes, texts. The phone beeps again. More giggles and blushing. More texting. This goes on for several minutes. A runner jogs past us twice. A terrier sniffs my leg then runs off. A pigeon circles us three times. Finally, the maid breathes out a sigh then squirrels away her phone in her pocket. We sit in silence on the bench. I'm thinking of curry puffs now. I bet she's not.

* * *

Two times in a row, she's managed to stain my white singlet undershirt to a dirty yellow, like the colour of pee sprayed haphazardly. I grumble louder. She knows it's her fault. I don't know how she does laundry, but I see an orange rag lying around. She uses it for cleaning the walls, sometimes the ceiling fan or bamboo poles to hang the laundry clothes out in the sun. And other dirtied parts of the house I don't care to know. I doubt the cause of my shirt stain has to do with the faded yellow bolster. Gek made it herself. Used to be canary yellow but it's been washed a thousand times, so for it to suddenly stain is unusual. No, I don't think I'm paranoid. No doubt about it. She must have mixed the laundry with the orange rag and what she thinks is the rag of an old man in the washer; letting dirt and age stain each other yet say nothing about it.

First the undershirt, then the floor. These days it's stickier than usual or it's too slippery. She still cleans the floor, I know that, but what she puts in the wash pail and with what chemicals, I have no idea. One capful? Two capfuls? Half a capful? It's not rocket science. One pail of water? Half a pail? Or is there something else she's thrown into the mix? She does what she does and thinks it's good enough, as long as I don't complain. Sometimes it's because I don't dare. She's young and strong. I'm a hollow, brittle bag of bones. Better not push my luck. Young people can have a temper. They can make things difficult if they don't get their way. I remember I was once like that. Everything revolved around me. My way or the highway. If I complain too much, about the stained singlet or the unclean floor, she may show me who's boss in the household. I don't want to get into trouble. This is not Gek. I'm just a job to the maid. A monthly salary. A mortgage for the house she built back home. I'm nothing to her.

Oi! Eat dinner. You want more rice? I take this chicken, okay? You eat more ve-ge-ta-bel. More vitamin.

The maid has summoned me over to the dining area. Our tingkat meals have arrived, a delivery service Ben has found that drops off warm cooked meals twice a day for lunch and dinner in bento boxes: each section of the box filled with a portion of rice, meat and vegetables so there is a bit of everything to eat.

She takes half my chicken portion and gives me half her vegetables. The maid eats so fast and with such an appetite she's finished before I have even scooped my third spoonful of rice. Then she whisks away her box and slips away to somewhere in the house. I can hear her cackling away, nattering on the phone. Her voice goes from loud to soft to a murmur and then I can't hear anything else. It is anyway time for my nap; after lunch, it is one of my midday pleasures. I make my way to my bed, lay down, shut the mahogany door and my eyes and let nothing that doesn't matter stain an old man's peace of mind.

* * *

I dreamt of history. In two hours, my mind managed to compress four decades of my life lived with Gek into a few random short scenes one after another.

In her youth, Gek was a woman who ticked all the right boxes. Loyal, faithful, honest, diligent with a comely face and even comelier curves that suggested she would breed healthy offspring. Through the years I'd never really noticed how beautiful she was. In my dreams, it was unmistakable. Her symmetric and delicate facial features: apple cheeks, pert nose and eyes like black pearls illuminating yet kind. How could I have taken Gek's beauty for granted? Was it because she didn't highlight it with makeup the way other women did? That she didn't fuss over her frizzy hair, letting it go wiry and unmanageable like an unruly bird's nest? That she wore dowdy slacks and formless blouses to hide her womanly figure, every colour chosen in the dullest grey, black and blue? The colours of a widow?

Want to watch a movie? Lin Qing Hsia's latest. You like her right? We can go for supper afterwards. Cheng teng or prata? Gek, you choose.

Her black pearls opened so wide she looked like she had won the lottery. I had called her by her name. I didn't know why. Maybe I was softening. It was two years after Ben was born. He was finally sleeping through the night, no longer waking Gek up for feeds. I suggested she could ask her mother to sleep over while we both snuck out on a date. Two years . . . since we had been out together, by ourselves. She looked at me stunned, her eye bags evidence of her daily firefighting; I knew she was about to cry.

Put on something nice. Don't think so much. Ben will be fine. Your Ma can handle him. Better hurry. Otherwise, we will miss the movie.

That was the first time I'd seen Gek wear a pink dress. It was tucked at the bosom, cupping its roundness. Tight at the waist, curves on her hips. I didn't even know she had it in her wardrobe. Maybe she was saving it for a special occasion. It was a shade of pink-coral, pastel, delicate, so feminine she blushed when she caught me gawking at her.

Too much right? I'll go change, Gek apologized. She was embarrassed at being out of her comfort zone. I saw her reach immediately for a grey dress. I stopped her in a voice that was low, husky.

No. I like it. Suits your complexion. Pink goes with pink.

But it's a bit too short. Haven't worn it for so long I didn't realize it's above my knee. People might say something. Cannot. Must change.

I'm your husband. I say it's okay. Don't change for anyone. Unless you really don't like it. But I do. Makes you look . . . feminine.

I don't remember whether the following happened in real life or in the dream, but all the same, what happened after we came back from the movies was heading straight to the bedroom and making the baby that was Kim.

With one hand on Gek's back, I put one hand up her skirt. Her thighs were cool and quivered as my hands roamed upwards, tickling her flesh, finding goose bumps along the way. Gek's pink dress was glowing like her skin, her cheeks, her lips; moist and inviting. I pulled her body close to mine. The moment she uttered *Ah!* I closed my lips on hers, relishing everything that was soft about her, a pink, steamed huat kueh, my sweet hot dessert, and then I woke up.

And I'm back in my bed, staring at the mahogany door, hard in my pants. Old man with a wet dream, how about that? In all those years that I've taken my wife for granted, I've finally come to envision her as a sexual object. Now that she's become dust, I've finally dusted the gossamer off the matronly image my wife had been putting up as a performance for me all this time. It's true. You don't know how good you've got it until you finally lose it.

* * *

It's bound to happen. The maid's performance in her work goes downhill. Whether her forgetfulness is deliberate or not, I'll never know. Not cleaning the windows anymore? Laziness most likely. After three weeks, the glass of the window is no longer transparent; instead, a layer of dust and rain streaks cloud the windows, closing the apartment in with what appears to be extra walls.

Coming out of the shower in her towel while texting? She has forgotten she's not in her own house. The maid screams when she sees me standing there, confused, looking at her. She runs straight back to the bathroom to change, avoiding my eyes the rest of the day. I don't know what she has in mind, but I've never seen her as anything more than a caregiver or housekeeper. Old man I may be, but I do have taste. And she isn't tasteful, with her funny eyes, her uneven nose and thin lips that hide a lifetime of secrecy.

Now when a maid starts barking at you for nothing you've done, you know she's lost her will to work. At this point, she's no longer keeping her phone out of sight. No matter where she is in the house, or what she's doing, she's constantly plugged to her phone, yakking away or punching the keyboard furiously. The maid laughs as loud as she wants as if I'm not there. Everyone and everything is becoming invisible to her. Three months pass. I grumble as usual. She takes my grumbling less seriously. Sometimes it even makes her smile. Then three more months pass. One day, it happens.

Sir, I don't want work here anymore. My family need me. Must break my bond.

She doesn't call me Oi! which means she is serious. I'm not surprised. Perhaps I'm glad. But she has been good to me, as much as a maid can be. I don't have the authority to change her working arrangement. It will have to be Ben to do so. The maid knows that.

What are you going to do? Go back to Indonesia? Stay in Singapore? What about your boyfriend? I ask, curious.

The maid bristles. She doesn't expect me to ask her about her private life. She has kept that part of her quite separate from work. Since the curry puff incident, I haven't seen any men of hers in her presence. Does she only meet them on her days off? Or does she work her dates around my naptime?

No boyfriend lah. I go home, see my son, see my family. I'm only tired, want to rest, help my father, grow rice paddy.

Her lie is so bad I laugh. Seeing that we are on the same page about the truth, she relents.

I like working for you, Sir. But I need earn more money. I want get married. I fall in love. Very good man, Sir, please understand.

I do understand. I wish her all the best then call Ben and tell him the first lie she said so he doesn't give her hell. Ben arranges her papers. She will return to Indonesia in less than a month. He doesn't want her hanging around Singapore at his expense. On her last day, two hours before her flight, I ask her about her plans.

I go agent, find new employer. Come back Singapore. More pay, more off day. My boyfriend, he working construction supervisor. Very hardworking. He save money for our wedding. He say later we must have children. One girl, one boy. Also he want my boy come live with us.

Where? In Singapore? Can he do that?

Don't know, Sir. Don't matter. Singapore cannot, India also can. Indonesia also can. I'm very happy. Must work hard, save for future. Next time I come visit you, introduce you my husband.

Next time you come here I will be gone. Flying in the wind. Become dust. Forget about this old man. You be a good girl. Long life ahead of you.

The maid weeps as Ben comes round to take her to the airport. What did you do? Ben asks. I feed him a lie he will believe. Nothing matters at this point. I'll never see her again. The maid who has been taking care of me for over a year; she has been the wife and daughter by proxy in small ways. Nowhere close in quality but she's been the presence that my late wife, my distracted son and absent daughter will never be able to replicate.

* * *

It was the fall that made Ben decide a home was a better solution for me. After the maid had left, Ben engaged another, this time from Myanmar, who only spoke Myanmarese and five words of English, who didn't understand anything I said or what to do around the house. She broke the Whirlpool washing machine the first time she used it, forcing the door on our front loader open when it hadn't finished the spin. It was a sign, definitely, that whatever biodata the maid claimed she could or couldn't do regarding her domestic abilities, was suspicious.

A week later, the fool that I was, I wanted to demonstrate how the previous maid climbed up the barstool to wipe clean the ceiling fan when, for a split second, I missed my footing and fell, yelping and grabbing the air for support while plummeting, landing with such great force on my chest, I broke a rib that nearly punctured my lung. Ben panicked, dispatched the maid off back to the agency, and after my recovery in the hospital, dispatched me off too to Evergreen Sanctuary, advertised as a 'home away from home'.

It's not exactly a home, the kind we have in mind, filled with familiar creature comforts in our memory, but a final resting place for those who have lived a ripe long life with the basic necessities to see them through their expiration dates. It is a place to close the chapter on decades of history; men and women whose blood has flowed through the engines of change, a gathering of hands and heads and the fluttering hearts of the old and infirm.

The nurses here are either cranky or cold. Only the volunteers are warm and energetic, but they come and go, as always. Then there are those with an agenda, like that female doctor who comes round each day with a notepad and a fake smile, and a pen she clicks on-and-off nonstop to punctuate the silence between our conversations. I never found out who she is. A scientist? A psychologist? A palliative understudy conducting research? Who knows? I'm just a part of a numbers game for her. Maybe she knows my name. But it will be pegged to a number, and she will add and subtract me to fit her purpose. In the world of statistics and in the name of research, I serve her. She doesn't serve me.

My naptimes become longer; I sleep deeper. Each time someone like her wants to talk to me, about my physical or mental health, I think of the nap I'm about to have, and I lie. For an old man such as I, nothing matters more than the pleasures of sleep, sound and deep, a somnambulistic prescription to cure the problems of age-related aches and pains. In dreams I become young. In dreams I become me. Not a number. No one's burden. I long to sleep while the sun is still up, and awake when the sun's about to set.

Perhaps I know time is running out. It isn't long before I continue to sleep even when the sun has gone out, leaving me in the dark, and perhaps one day, not wake at all, remaining in darkness till everything around me expires.

That day finally comes. Kim is there. Ben is there, with Juliet and the kids, each one a head taller than the next. I must have fallen asleep and then awoken. I peer at them with half-closed eyes.

Pa . . . Pa . . . my children call.

I smile, seeing tears in Kim's eyes. Her hair is much greyer now. She's dressed like Gek. Long black pants, blue shirt, grey cardigan. Ben is tight-lipped. Juliet is holding the hands of her boys. Yes, I do like taking naps when it is light. For it is very bright right now.

Near the door I see her. My heart warms, expands. It is time for my final nap. I look to my children, my grandchildren. My smile tells them what they need to know. Kim bursts out crying. Even Juliet is sobbing. Ben clutches my arms tight, pleading.

I see her by the door and know my way to the dream that is all of my history, the reason for the hearts beating in this room right now. She made them more than me. Gek is smiling at me; and I smile back.

Chapter 15

The Dying of Abel

Abel simmered, his indecision so intensely torn between two opposing actions it gave him a sore throat. He gulped, his saliva lubricating the abrasive sides of his oesophagus, a globule of moisture he could almost hear travelling downwards slowly inside his ears. Now what?

Hold on, his guardian angel answered. Give it some time.

Why should I?!? his inner demon yapped.

This doesn't change anything. Be rational.

Life is irrational! Don't tell me to be rational!

This is his body. You can't tell him what to do with it.

I've watched him waste his entire life doing nothing. He SHOULD just go ahead. BE A MAN.

What good does it do? Ask yourself, what am I trying to achieve here?

Good? Who cares about being good? Please yourself! Listen to yourself! Because no one else will.

SHUT UP!!!

With an index finger stuffed in each ear, Abel tried to block out the noise. But it was coming from inside him, not outside. It was useless. He could still hear them both barking in his brain. His eyes hurt so much from their squabble, and the sting of the glint of sunlight roasted his lids. In any case, he didn't need to look. His eyes lowered till they closed. The talking continued, though what intrigued him now was how coral orange everything was in his temporary blindness.

All was aglow; he felt heady, light, transcendental, his feet no longer weighed down by what happened earlier.

One foot lifted, moved forward. Then the other. His arms were outstretched. Abel imagined himself as a bird about to soar.

But he didn't. Plummeting forty stories down the apartment block, his fall was more like a bulbous rock thrown off the precipice of a jagged cliff.

* * *

It would be an understatement to say that it was an unusual morning. Two police cars. An ambulance. The section of the ground where Abel had fallen was cordoned off. One would have to change their morning route, circumvent the scene, to make their way to work or school. All eyes were on the ground, body covered, where only tall passers-by could notice blood seeping out from under the blanket. The horror of what had happened was whispered and traded like secrets no one had the full story of. Who was it? Why did he do it? What made him do it? Why here? This block? So very unfortunate for the residents, the sweeper sighed.

Carol was one of the last to witness the scene. She was often late for work, and today, her watch read 9.20, meaning she would reach her office close to ten. She didn't care. Her boss was abroad. The other girls in the office, especially the toady-eyed admin clerks, could say whatever they wanted. Let me be fired, Carol smirked. I'll gladly take severance pay; go on a holiday with my stud muffin.

Every morning, Carol's routine was to wake up late, shower, get dressed, go to work. Her timing avoided her husband's, who was an early sleeper and an even earlier riser. Sometimes he would text her when he reached his office. She never texted back. Didn't feel the need. She would text someone else.

Morning, sexxy bunny, was her usual message.

Good morning, my Valentine, thought of me much? was the usual reply.

Today, she didn't have the time to use her phone. Carol saw that her route to the traffic lights leading to the train station was cut off by the ambulance.

Oh great! Carol cursed. She would be later than usual.

There were at least six other residents crowding her route, obstacles she would have to skirt around.

S'cuse me! Carol said.

Hello! A voice piped, and a hand gripped her arm rather firmly.

S'cuse me, I'm late, Carol repeated.

Eh, hello, wait.

Carol stopped. She looked at the woman who was in her way. Carol frowned at the sight of the woman's untamed perm, a nest of black and grey wiry curlicues and her braless pyjama top, the dark nipples of a sixty-year-old vaguely visible.

Police? This lady . . . you ask her. The woman turned to face a uniformed man, her hand and manicured nails digging into Carol's flesh.

What? What's the problem, officer? Carol asked.

Madam, there's been an accident, a fresh-faced policeman replied.

I can see that. What do you want me to do?

Police, I think she is the one, said the woman whose talons still held onto Carol.

Let me go, Carol tried to shake off the woman's grasp.

I'll handle this now. The policeman waved the woman off, taking Carol aside.

I have to get to work, officer.

Madam, that woman said you know the victim.

I do?

Can you identify him?

What?!? Carol was incredulous.

Please. I know this is difficult, but that woman said the victim is your husband.

WHAT?!? Carol half-shouted.

The policeman led Carol to the covered body. All eyes were on her. She wanted to laugh at the absurdity of the suggestion. How grotesque was the situation? For her to check out a dead person early in the morning before her Coffee Bean cappuccino? Was her mind even alert?

Then she saw the shoes. Bata. She didn't need to see the face, but the policeman had slipped the white sheet off the face for her identification. It was useless. Her eyes were blinded by tears. She was overcome before she even knew for sure. The first thing her husband had done that morning was to get away from her in his trusted shoes, as fast as he could.

* * *

Jeremiah Abraham Roberto Rodrigues Jr. looked undeniably Asian, about 70 per cent Chinese, 20 per cent Malay and 10 per cent Aryan, which was the nose, really. His name was so long the font size had to be reduced on his name card. Everyone called him Jeremy. He preferred Robert, shortened from Roberto, his paternal grandfather. Carol had always, for some reason, called him J.A.

A burdensome lineage of his Eurasian roots, Jeremiah's pompous name made him the butt of many jokes when he was growing up. Kids called him 'Jarr-head' or just 'jar', 'jam jar', 'Jimmy Junior' or 'Mr Roberto', in reference to the song, 'Mr. Roboto'.

The first time Carol saw his name on his name card, she stopped herself from laughing in front of him. Picking the two capital letters from his first two names, she decided it would be easier to skip the rest of the superfluous letters and settle on a J and A. Sounded like a hip hop star, she said.

Like who?

Oh, I don't know. The whole lot of abbreviated hip hop celebrity pseudonyms.

I only listen to metal.

That's nice. You must have deaf ears.

Jeremiah roared with laughter. Carol eyed him quizzically.

It's not *that* funny.

You are. Funny words. No one has ever shortened my name to letters. How do you know I won't be offended?

You won't. Now that I know you listen to metal.

Sometimes, just occasionally, I sleep to classical baroque music. Chopin, you know? Études?

Well, I didn't expect that one. From one spectrum of taste to the other. You surprise me, J.A. Now, where are those photos?

Jeremiah handed her the package at her desk cubicle and watched her with interest as she inserted a letter opener into the sealed flap of the envelope and sliced it open. Ten years ago, freelance photographers like him would pitch to publications such as hers with CD-ROMs of images. These days, it was mostly thumb drives and virtual photo banks. Though if photographers didn't mind making the trip, such a personal touch ensured editors continued to give them contract jobs. And with an unusual name like Jeremiah's, coupled with his charm and not unattractive physique, it wasn't easy to dismiss him just like that.

But in Carol's case, it was the specific way his very large black caviar eyes ogled at her. The way his lips curled to the side with suggestive glee.

The first time Carol met Jeremiah, he thought she was the editor of *Property Portfolio*. She was, in fact, a senior writer who oversaw most of the editorial work whenever her editor was away on business trips, which was often, or came in late to the office from attending launches or meetings, which occurred four times a week. No matter, for he wanted to sell his pictures and she needed fresh sources.

Carol took his name card and slipped it inside the breast pocket of her cotton blouse. Her heart throbbed against the length of Jeremiah's letters; she imagined them coming to life like ants animated by the heat of her chest, tickling the skin of her mammaries separated only by the thin veil of a fabric.

It was the beginning. It was the end. It was the obvious conclusion to the start of an uncertain alliance.

Carol had just gotten married. She told him that. What she didn't tell him was that Abel had been her boyfriend since she was fourteen in school, as a classmate, then schoolmate, and finally even in the same college. They had been married only for two years after having dated for over a decade; their relationship having cooled— and died—in the interim that Carol had given up on romance. They were so familiar with each other, spending their adolescence together, they were practically siblings.

Get some lunch later? Together? Jeremiah offered slyly.

I've just met you, Carol said bluntly, her pretence at indifference not convincing. Jeremiah inched closer. She leaned backwards. As he was about to speak, she picked up the phone receiver and placed her ear on it. The dial tone sounded like a warning. Doop. Doop. Doop. Doop. Doop.

I'm not an animal, Carol. I'm not going to eat you, Jeremiah said, thumping fingers on the top of the PVC partition of her cubicle. Unless you want me to.

Carol put down the phone receiver back in its base station and pretended to examine the contents of the envelope. Her heart was pounding. *Eyes watching, Carol, eyes watching.* The words repeated in Carol's head. Most days, the clerical assistants and interns floated their vulturous bodies around her desk, or the one behind hers that belonged to the editor of *Monique*, a popular women's magazine, the publishing company's crown jewel. Today, everyone seemed to have vanished into meeting rooms. It was just Jeremiah and her. And the pantry lady who was in the corner minding her own business.

Carol lifted her head and boldly locked eyes with Jeremiah. His eyes twinkled. He placed both his elbows on top of the PVC partition and leaned into her space. She didn't flinch. They stared at each other like this for mere seconds, but this short interlude was so thickly erotic she could feel the heat rise from her chest to her cheeks. She was aglow, deliciously.

So, how about it? Lunch?

The canteen is too crowded, Carol sighed, not knowing what she was sighing about.

I know a café round the corner. Come. My treat.

No. I don't accept bribes. I still need the editor's decision on the photos.

But bribe he did. On the guttural coughs of his swanky new Ducati Monster, with her legs astride, Carol was persuaded to ride five minutes to a quiet café she kept telling herself was only *round the corner*. Hands around his waist, Carol couldn't help noticing his lean, taut torso; her fingers clung onto him as her thighs spliced wide on the synthetic leather seat, her groin nudged against his butt while the silky rayon of her blouse was a useless barrier against the broadness of his warm back, ensuring her breasts were firmly meshed against his flesh—the two stood no chance against nature. As the bike trundled against the uneven road, loosening Carol's stiffened joints, she found herself bobbing up and down rhythmically. The air surrounding her was a gust of noon heat swimming past her limbs, both cool and simmering at the same time. She didn't know what to think, or what to do, only that her life depended on the swift manoeuvres of this man she had just met.

Jeremiah swerved this way and that with purpose. The sounds of the motor were too loud for them to speak. Neither of them wanted to. Strangers one minute, accomplices another. As if on cue, to ease Carol into a more comfortable position, at a red traffic light when the bike halted, Jeremiah leaned forward a little, his bottom pushed back so their bodies cupped closer. What this did, of course, was to wedge Carol's pelvis right against Jeremiah. Even with the sputter of the engine, she could hear him clear his throat twice.

Lunch that day was a blur, mostly for Carol, who was in a haze that fogged her capacity to think clearly. She ate something, steak probably, iced tea most likely, a tiramisu she might have shared with him, or not. Or that could have been another lunch she had with him. She couldn't remember the details.

They were chaste that day. They behaved themselves the next. On the third lunch date, Jeremiah boldly planted a wet kiss on her lips in public with her still straddled on his machine after he had hopped off. She was horrified, taken aback, but the sensation shot right down from her lips to her sweet cherry.

No! Carol protested weakly.

Yes.

Stop now, Carol insisted vainly.

No.

Please . . .

She reciprocated. She bit him back lightly on his ear as his tongue was travelling down her soft neck. The deal was sealed. No reason could peel these two away from their passion simulated on the minutes they spent flesh on flesh, riding pillion on the roaring grunts of his bike.

Lunch most days afterwards, for four months running, was a blur of lust. Carol became more emboldened by her need for release, and with a fast getaway vehicle, Jeremiah snatched her away from the routine of her office and into his arms.

Their first rendezvous was a quickie that happened after dark in the unused toilet of a park.

I can't see, Carol whispered.

You don't need to, Jeremiah panted.

What happens if someone comes in?

We're alone. His fingers dug in. Relax.

I'm not sure about this, she mumbled. Then she added, Tighter.

Still not sure? He sucked on her breath. This?

I said tighter. Faster.

Her moans—for she was a loud moaner—frightened Jeremiah, who, despite his eagerness, didn't want to be caught for public sex. The second day was in Hotel 61 that, while serving the purpose, made Carol feel like a hooker as she passed real-life prostitutes along the hallway who gave her knowing looks. Subsequently, she took longer lunch hours with their intimate acts in Jeremiah's rented apartment where he was a boarder in a single room in a house that belonged to a divorcee mother with one child and a maid. A complication Carol didn't have the patience for.

Hence, it was with bravado and wickedness that she took him home.

Only on the sofa. Maybe in the kitchen. Definitely in the showers, Carol told her lover.

All was obeyed until the cad gambled his luck and whisked her off to her bedroom while she was intoxicated by his kisses. In the sanctity of her marriage bed, which had long since been frozen through disuse by a couple who had abandoned matrimonial intercourse, the forbidden aroused her more, plagued her more— their act became more prolonged, intense, and louder she moaned, yelling his name at the top of her lungs.

It was this name-calling that cracked open her shelled solitude and brought her to a beatific sublime. Her sounds circulated above the bed, travelled outwards, a long, continuous wail of love not for her lover but for herself, the person she had long shed in place of a miserable spouse, a workaholic.

The same name-calling that sauntered out like a ghostly song towards the wooden main door of the HDB apartment leading to the outside world. The day Abel had been sick with stomach flu and returned early on half-day leave, the minute his key turned on the keyhole, and the sliver of an opening of his door let him hear the joy of his wife herald her freedom, as the name of JEREMIAH! stretched as long as her chords would allow, filling the air, tainting the sanctity of his home, and he knew another man was thrusting his manhood into his wife, while his own wilted.

The day the adultery was discovered was the day Abel's voices became louder in his head. He was decisive—he usually wasn't—for his manhood, and freedom, depended on the choice. To leave or not to live. Isn't that a perennial question?

* * *

No. He couldn't leave the corridor, the longitudinal bridge between the door to his home and the rest of the horrifying, unkind world. Except this time, what was unkind was an act being done to him, at that very moment, in his own bed. Maybe on his sofa. Perhaps in the kitchen. Oh god. In the chambers of his bathroom, the sanctuary of his mornings and after-work evenings. Where would they be doing it? Had they been doing it more than once? In all the places he had just imagined?

What filth. Who had seduced whom? Who removed whose clothes first? Whose tongue first penetrated whose lips? Who had reached across the divide of sin and touched skin first? His wife? Or the unknowable stranger banging her mad, making her sing with the pureness of a diaphragmatic vibrato?

Why couldn't Abel move from the spot was a question he couldn't answer. In the presence of occurring intercourse, he was, like someone addicted to porn, sucked into the role of voyeur, or in this case, eavesdropper. His heart answered what his mind couldn't decide. It was his bass leaping out of his speakers, a kind of chant that was hypnotic and chilling at the same time. Abel looked down at his pressed trousers. A discernible bump jutted out where his fly was. He wanted to cry.

It was only an hour later when the real question of whether he should leave the marriage popped up in his rational head. By then, all kinds of questions were popping up everywhere like a firework of raging energy released like tadpoles unspooled into a rushing tide. He had been trying to stem back the voices for years. He was fairly successful, as long as his life was stable; and it was; not a hair strand out of place. Now look what happened! Uncorked. Unboxed. His wife, the unsuspecting Pandora.

Close to an hour after his ears had picked up the truth—for the sounds had dissipated half an hour ago replaced by silence—Abel had retreated from waiting at the door to waiting in the corridor, heart thumping, staring at the still heads of treetops. The door to his house clicked open. Abel was so captivated by the quarrel of two pigeons on a thick branch, he hadn't heard the door swing wide open or seen a lone figure appear, closing the door gently behind him, walking in the corridor in which Abel himself stood.

It was only after Abel had felt the flow of movement as the man who had just fucked his wife then passed too close to his body that he woke from his trance. Turning his head swiftly, Abel saw it was a man not unlike himself, younger perhaps, better looking maybe, more athletic definitely.

Uh!

A sort of gasp almost came out of Abel's mouth before it was swallowed. His wife's lover hadn't recognized him. No sign of recognition, guilt or glee. Just one stranger passing another stranger. When the man turned the corner to get to the part of the building where the lifts were, his look was blank. Abel was stunned by his own lack of reaction; he was certainly no fighter. Cuckolded he had been, but his reaction was lame, even by another's standard.

And just like that, the man disappeared from sight. Abel looked down at his trousers. The discernible bump was long gone. Before, it made him want to cry. Now he felt miserable. Then he heard the voice that was not inside his head.

I've got the blues / I feel so lonely / I'll give you the world if I could . . .

The song. Radio. Bessie Smith singing their blues.

I'm gonna telephone my baby / Ask him won't you please come home . . .

He could hear his wife echoing the chorus. *Baby won't you please come home . . . Baby won't you please come home!*

Her voice, off pitch and tinny, layered brokenly over the blues classic, grated against his eardrum.

You were once my home, a voice inside Abel said. I opened my door for you, Abel heard another. I let down my walls for you, a new voice piped up. I changed my life for you, an old familiar voice resurfaced. My home, my hell, my hooker, my honey, my heathen, my high, my hate, all the voices coalesced. The song had ended, the female voices behind the door to his house had quietened, but the ones in Abel grew louder. He swooned. His head swelled, squeezing his eyeballs out.

Abel held onto the wall of the corridor, steadying himself. He gagged. Nothing came forth. Only a loud growl of his stomach from the acid and bacteria fighting it out inside his gut.

He should go into his house, lie down, rest, ask his wife for warm water or herbal tea. She was in, after all. She would take care of him if he were ill, wouldn't she?

Or would she stand there and cackle like a demonic hag? Pleasured by his suffering?

Entirely fatigued by his sudden condition, Abel sat down on the dusty concrete of his now trusty corridor. Head leaning on a wall, he breathed deeply, calming himself down. In this position, as if meditating, he somehow slipped into unconsciousness. The longer hand on his watch moved one oscillation. One hour crept past. Then he woke up, eyes bright, rested, like it was a new day for him.

He stood up briskly, feeling altogether fine. The radio was still on. His wife was still in. Perhaps she had taken the rest of the day off. Or was working from home. What should he do? He looked at his watch. Two o'clock. His embattled tummy growled with the familiar pangs of hunger. He would have lunch first. Go across the road. Then return. Think first. Then come back home. No, correction. To his house.

Bak kut teh. One person. One rice. Peanuts also.

Abel ordered his lunch and ate fast, his stomach soothed by the warmth of the tonic soup swirling inside him. They were still talking inside him, sometimes to him, sometimes to each other. When hungry, he ignored them. When sated, they became louder, but by then, he was in a state of contentment and feeling too sluggish to bother.

It was then he noticed a man sitting on the complete other side of the kopitiam. It was him, the adulterous culprit. The man finished his meal, stood up and left. Abel perked up, pushed his chair back and followed him. No, he had missed him again. Damn! Abel knew he should've cornered him earlier at the corridor. Now, Abel would miss his opportunity again.

Go back home! They are doing it again! Catch them red-handed this time! Why would you? Just leave the whore! Your angel, are you sure, not the Satan incarnate? Entrap her, make her pay alimony for your suffering! Stop confusing him now, let him think, let him decide, you're all one worse than the other! Revenge loser! Hello, anybody home? Hello?

Abel moaned painfully. He would go home. It was his prerogative to reclaim his oasis.

His wife had gone. The sheets were taut, made neat, erasing all traces of a crime. The sofa had no stains, just the usual dust he recognized, the stain from a red wine spill he remembered. The kitchen untouched, immaculate. The bottles and appliances were not shoved into corners or thrown on the floor as passion often overtook lovers. The bathroom floor was wet, like someone had showered. He saw fresh strands of long dark hair. She had washed up and shampooed. The damp smelled strongly of something sweet and floral, and the base of sandalwood.

Abel sat down on his bed, depleted. He lay down, bunched himself up, arms over his abdomen. He was no longer sleepy, but he was groggy from lunch.

Baby won't you please come home . . .

The words came out of his mouth, like a bird chirping, confused and alone. His eyes closed, his head heavy, a tear wriggled out between his tightly shut lids. Then another. Abel couldn't stop weeping for himself, a man-turned-child who just found he had lost everything important to him.

He stayed this way for many hours. Not moving, not sleeping. Singing to himself while the others jabbered on between his ears. There was a calmness to the storm that put Abel in the middle of it all—the eye in the maelstrom where the damage floated around in a large mess and he remained still, omniscient, powerless yet powerful. Since he couldn't control it, he would surrender, and in doing so, release the force that depressed him. To live, sometimes you have to leave, said the loudest voice of all. Let fall like a leaf. Leave the place, the demons, the ones that hurt. Leave it all behind. Leave yourself. Stop, rewind, restart.

Abel agreed with this voice. He appointed this one his guardian angel.

Hey, you okay? Abel?

It was Carol. She had returned. The room had darkened in the hours since he became so very still, a corpse with a beating heart.

When did you come back? Are you sick? Carol continued.

No response. Carol could see her husband was either sleeping or pretending to sleep. Either way, she was ignored. She shrugged.

At midnight, Carol crept into bed. Abel hadn't moved at all, nor spoken to her. He was breathing, so she let him be. She took the farthest side away from him, tucked under blanket, shut her guiltless eyes and soon drifted into sleep. She dreamt fitfully, a tiny moan escaping her. Carol shifted her legs, widening and closing them. One heavy arm rested on a breast. It unconsciously caressed the curve of her bosom.

Abel had fallen asleep before midnight, awoke abruptly then couldn't sleep anymore. In the dark, he lay there quietly, listening to the voices that kept him company while his body was beside an embodied person who was distant from him in every possible way. As his wife enjoyed her sensuous dream, her thighs wrapped tightly against the blanket, getting warmer, he knew what dream she was having. He was not in it; Abel was convinced. Her betrayal inside her body, inside this room, inside this house they had made home of, stabbed at him with a methodical and clinical precision. She had butchered his heart till he could feel no more.

When dawn broke, Abel gave up. He got out of bed. The voices had become stronger.

I have tried in vain / Evermore to call your name / When you left you broke my heart . . .

He found himself taking the lift to the highest floor of the apartment block. He got out, walked the rest of the way up the stairs to the top of the building, stood there while the day started, the buses burred, and lights started to bloom golden in rooms. Waited for courage to bless him. Abel surrendered himself and leapt into the sky, arms wide open, hoping a second chance would be better than the last.

His body would not survive this. His heart will.

Chapter 16

Says the Bells of the Clement

He was born on the streets of Chinatown. Well, across the road at Upper Cross Street in People's Park Complex to be exact. His delivery was performed by a midwife in KK Hospital to be precise; an impressively easy labour that lasted three hours from the start of contractions. Not a ragtag street urchin was Leonard Koh En, though he liked to tell people he was born in Chinatown just to test their reaction.

Smack in the midst of a cultural tourist spot is the private condominium he calls home and where his parents have lived since their marriage in the eighties. Since he was a child, Leonard could always count on raised eyebrows when he told his teachers where he lived. When they didn't believe him, he would show them his key, in the form of a card used for the slot of his main door where the keyhole was.

It was as if he lived perpetually in a hotel. He became the cool kid in school.

Everyone thought Leonard dined on bak kwa on a daily basis. They assumed his house was decorated with red and gold the whole year round since Chinatown was not lacking garish decoration with calligraphic knick-knacks and two-dollar souvenirs. His apartment was unusually pale in comparison.

How come your sofa is so white? Wei Loong, his best friend in primary school, had remarked when he first visited Leonard's place. Walls also white. Floor also white. Fan also white.

Dunno. Mother likes white. House small, white makes the house look big.

Years later, the apartment turned vanilla.

Eh, bro, your house not very Chinatown. Beige here, beige there. Ryan, his best friend in secondary school, said when he first entered Leonard's apartment. They were supposed to prepare for an upcoming math test but ended up sitting around playing the Xbox.

Mother likes creamy colours. Says it's cozy.

When Leonard went to national service, on one of his weekends off, he met a girl who was studying at the Nanyang Academy of Fine Arts. They started dating after he kept texting her aggressively for days, wooing her using a combination of humorous wit and sentimental one-liner quotes: *On a scale of 1 to 10, you're a 9 & I'm the 1 u need; I would offer u a cigarette but you're already smoking hot; My love for u is like diarrhoea, I just can't keep it in.*

She relented out of curiosity and a dash of exasperation.

The first time Leonard brought his girlfriend home, her critical eye picked up what she saw as flaws of the apartment's interior decor. Eh, why is your house so yellow? Yellow so boring. I want to paint this wall purple. This wall red. Keep the white floor. Change the fan to black, no, bronze better still. This other wall, make it light grey, almost sky blue with a bit of grey. In-between colours keep people guessing. Then change all the cupboards to lilac. Hip with a bit of retro, fits the Chinatown skyline nicer. Tell your mother, Leonard. I can help with the sketch, Jesseca said, painting the landscape in front of her with gesticulating hands.

The artist in her saw a challenge and became excited. She also liked to keep people guessing when she went to a lawyer and paid $50 to do a deed change for her name from Ling Ling to Jesseca. It was on purpose that she rebelled against her father's wishes to have a Western name, and a deliberate snub at the rules of grammar to misspell what was a common name meaning, 'what God beholds'. In this case, what Ling Ling beheld was a unique Jesseca, a one-off signature senorita until she discovered there was one Jesseca in the Thai restaurant where she worked during her December school break, two Jessecas in the second year of her art class and three Jessecas among her Facebook acquaintances. She almost burned the deed change in a rage.

Mind your own business. Mother doesn't like loud colours. This is her nest, not a boudoir, Leonard reminded his girlfriend.

Jesseca didn't know what a boudoir was. She refused to ask, hating Leonard for using words she didn't know to put her in her place. He was going to be a *da shue shen*, a university graduate, going to SMU right after national service having graduated from ACJC. Jesseca's 'O' Levels were never going to let her go down that path, with her Cs and Ds and that maverick A popping from out of nowhere for the Art subject she took.

Leonard could choose any of the local universities with his grades, and even colleges abroad if his parents were willing to sponsor him, but he picked the one downtown, closest to where he lived, which was SMU, a mere two kilometres down Hill Street from his address. He'd grown up surrounded by a neighbourhood of kitsch and colour and a sheltered roof of neutrals. He couldn't imagine being anywhere else.

Jesseca, on the other hand, hated everything about her three-room flat in Woodlands where none of the furniture matched and the walls hadn't been repainted since 1994 when she was born.

The walls, once baby pink, now bore a sickly fetid salmon-like shade, made worse with the ash brown curtains bursting with white chrysanthemums her father had inherited from his late mother. The shelves were overfilled with crockery and faulty electronics that once had its use but now had become dusty artefacts adding to the apartment's claustrophobia. The altar with the Guanyin statue hadn't been cleaned for years, shrouded by a thick layer of ash from fallen incense. Her late grandmother's portrait hung beside the statue, morosely looking upon the unkempt household in which junk accrued, never removed.

Her father, who worked two jobs, as a cook and an illegal 4D runner, was hardly in the house, only availing himself to an annual spring clean prior to the lunar new year. Jesseca, always alone in the apartment since she was in secondary school—her mother having remarried and relocated to Penang—now found herself spreading her wings outwards as her mature, independent self grew. She was the latchkey kid tucked up in the leafy suburban heartlands, unlike Leonard, the downtown mummy's boy, fussed over from his combed coif to his double-knotted laces.

Jesseca couldn't remember her mother combing her hair or tying her shoelaces. She couldn't, in fact, remember her mother at all.

Leonard didn't know her exact address; she would never tell him. The last time she had a boyfriend when she was sixteen, she brought him back for dinner and he called her apartment 'ang zhang'. Yes, it was dirty, but it was her residence; she dumped him not long after. No one was going to rub salt in her wound.

* * *

My mother wants you to stay for dinner, Leonard said, bringing his girlfriend the siu mais his mother had bought from the renowned dim sum eatery across the road. They were in the living room with the dull yellow walls. Each time she visited his place, Jesseca would goad Leonard into letting her paint a mural on one wall. She could use it as a showcase for her portfolio and, besides, she would do it for free. Each time, Leonard would refuse.

Jesseca took one siu mai and bit into it. The warm juices from the shrimp, pork and water chestnut pooled into her mouth; she melted with a soft sigh.

I have to finish my project, she replied, taking her second dumpling. Her stomach relaxed. I don't want to hand it in late. Again.

You can eat and leave. She's starting to cook.

The smell of cinnamon, anise and cloves filled the air, commingled with a robust smell of meat. She recognized it as bak kut teh. In the absence of her mother and the busyness of her father, Jesseca sometimes cooked the hearty dish to feed her father and herself.

Don't make excuses, Leonard warned her. You don't want to stay, you tell her yourself. Leave me out of this.

Fine.

Jesseca rose from the sofa for the kitchen. Mrs Koh was wearing an apron, leaning her face into the vapours of the pot. She closed her eyes, savouring the aroma of the comfort soup. She stirred the ladle.

Auntie, Jesseca started to speak, I . . .

Bring me that soy sauce, Ling, Mrs Koh interrupted.

Jesseca stopped and stared. Her mother used to call her that. Not Jesseca, not Ling Ling. Just Ling.

Come, bring it to me. My hand can't reach.

Her eyes sought the object Mrs Koh's finger was pointing at. It was on the other side of the kitchen counter, closest to Jesseca.

I'm cooking bak kut teh tonight. Luo han zhai too. Later I'll steam a red grouper. Bought it this morning. Very fresh! And you can try some of my neighbour's homemade kimchi. It's the best, Leonard's mother continued, her hands and eyes busy with her cooking.

Jesseca remembered she had entered the kitchen to state her refusal.

But, Auntie, I have school projects I need to finish.

Never mind, Ling, you eat quickly then you go back. Must have dinner then you have strength to work, right?

Jesseca steeled her resolve, Cannot, Auntie!

Mrs Koh put down her ladle, looked right into Jesseca's soul—or so the art student thought.

Girl, my boy only comes home once a week. Army is difficult, and I haven't seen him for a week. We would like you to have a meal together. That's not much to ask, is it?

No, Jesseca thought. What Leonard's mother doesn't know, of course, is that Jesseca has started devising ways to break up with him. The last thing she wanted was to sit and dine with the woman who adored and protected the man she was attempting to hurt.

How about next week? Jesseca offered, softening.

Next Friday his father is coming home from Tokyo.

Leonard hadn't seen his father in the last six months. He never talked about him. It was always about his mother, the woman who was a goddess in his eyes in every way. His father's work as a regional sales director took him out of his country many months in a year. Now he was in Japan. Previously he was in Korea. Before that he was in China, Thailand, Vietnam, Malaysia. From the little that Jesseca knew, Mrs Koh was a married woman who raised her son not unlike a single mother.

I suppose I could eat a little bit, Jesseca found herself caving in.

Good girl! I'll start cooking the rice now. This rice cooker takes sooo long to finish cooking. Ling, you like sambal chilli? I made some yesterday.

Yes. Yes.

Jesseca walked back to Leonard weakly and sank into the empty space beside him. She stared at the creamy curtains flitting back and forth idyllically to the incoming breeze. Her shoulders and back moulded into the leather cushions, leaving an imprint of herself on the reupholstered furniture belonging to the Koh family. She couldn't stop the sigh that escaped her. Above her, the white fan spun without sound. In her own house, the seven year old standing fan cranked gratingly with each turn of its blade. Every revolution was burdensome. Even her beaten black PVC sofa was shredded in corners and smelled of something pungent and expired.

So did you tell her? Leonard asked nonchalantly, chuckling at a repeated episode of *The Noose*.

I tried. She didn't let me. I'm staying for dinner, Jesseca sighed a second time. Then she perked up. By the way . . .

What?

Why does she call me Ling?

That's your Chinese name, isn't it?

Well, yes, but I don't use it anymore. And anyway, Jesseca said, it's Ling Ling. Not Ling.

So what if she shortened it? Leonard yawned. The credits on *The Noose* rolled; he switched the channel. She used to call me Leo.

There was a funny feeling inside her. Something that grew furry and warm in ways she had forgotten what it was called.

What time later do you want to leave? I can send you back, Leonard asked.

Home. That was the word. Her single father had tried his best to create a space she could return to, cubes of concrete that fed and housed her, roofed her, sheltered her, gave her room to grow and learn and unlearn and revolt and leave when she would finally outgrow it all. He gave her the space to become what she was today.

But why the solitariness in her heart?

Ling, no Jesseca, didn't know—had forgotten—how a home looked, felt and smelled like, until the mother of someone else had reminded her with a gesture so simple it cracked her hard-won shell.

* * *

At dinner, Jesseca was halfway into a land of comfort and conflict. The more she slurped away at the soup, the more she felt she was selling herself out for a meal ticket. *Ling, Ling, Ling* was all Jesseca heard at the table. Have more fish, Ling. You must try this kimchi, Ling. Enough rice for you, Ling?

Under the table, Jesseca curled her toes till both feet were two hermit crabs hiding in their shells. Leonard devoured his meal like a pig. Mrs Koh fussed over the twenty-year-old like he was two. She selected the choicest part of the fish for her son, picking out the bones.

Very yummy, Auntie, Jesseca paid her the obligatory compliment. Fact was, her father, a professional cook, was so skilled in the culinary arts of Chinese cooking he could make the pedestrian bean sprouts taste gourmet.

Oh, happy you like it, Ling! Mrs Koh beamed. That produced more shiitake mushrooms on Jesseca's plate.

Enough already, Auntie. I'm very full.

Only mushrooms. Your stomach is bigger than that. Look at my boy. Not a grain left in his bowl!

Mother, you're the best, man! Leonard patted his mother's back.

I'm not a man. I'm a woman. Please.

Mrs Koh waved her chopsticks at him.

Leonard, I really need to go, Jesseca whispered to her boyfriend. The experience was, strangely, making her homesick. She wondered if her father had returned from work.

Come again next time! Mrs Koh sang breezily to the young adults as they prepared to go. Jesseca called out I will! Thank you! as Leonard and she closed the door behind them and the last of Mrs Koh's *Ling* tingled in the air like a wind chime that wouldn't stop.

Not my mother, Jesseca reminded herself, the boyfriend's mother, not the mother who left me and my father for another man.

Outside the apartment building as they waited for a cab, Jesseca dug her bag for her keys. She fished them out jangling, tucked them in her pocket to save time searching for them later. Leonard opened his wallet and checked that he had his key, the rectangular card squashed next to his supplementary credit card, his EZ-Link card and his pink IC.

Found your keys? Leonard asked, adding cheekily, I've got mine. He waved his bulging wallet.

Hao lian, Jesseca scoffed at him. Calling him proud made him burst out laughing. He enjoyed teasing her just to get a reaction.

You say, to-may-to, I say, to-mah-to.

What are you talking about?

Nothing. You won't get it.

Yeah, I don't get why you are a stuck-up rich, spoilt kid.

I'm not rich. I might be spoilt. And stuck up, maybe. But I'm not a kid, Leonard suppressed a smile. He lunged towards her with a kiss. Jesseca swiftly averted. He tried again, blocking her movement with a bear hug.

You're an idiot, Jesseca growled. Move! she barked, trying to catch the attention of a passing cab with a roof sign illuminated with a green display.

Leonard moved. The cab stopped right where they were. She scrambled inside first. He followed. She gave her address to the cab driver. This time, Leonard managed to plant a quick kiss on her lips. She pushed him away lightly.

Are you going to ask me to your house? Leonard asked with a wide grin, wrapping an arm around her back.

For what?

I don't know, Leonard smiled slyly then added unconvincingly. To see your father?

Jesseca pondered over the question. The dinner with Mrs Koh had changed her heart somewhat. She wasn't so sure about Leonard or Mrs Koh or his family anymore. In fact, she wasn't so sure about herself or her father or her family now.

It was as if the soup had some transformative medicinal quality in it that treated some ailment that she didn't know she had. As if the Luo Han Zhai, a vegetarian Buddhist dish, had some secret zen ingredient that mixed all her confused feelings into a holistic, coherent whole. As if she had ingested abundant blessings from the steamed yu. Or that Mrs Koh's sambal chilli had awakened her, spiced up her dull, monotonous existence. Or even that her neighbour's kimchi, stewed for days in an earthen pot with spring onions, ginger, garlic and chilli flakes, had extracted the flavour of the domestic kitchen and sucked out the embittered marrow in Jesseca's unhappy bones.

Or that her birth name had rung like the misplaced bells of Ling Ling's childhood. It was coming back to her now. There was a bell on a bunny named Ting Ting. There was a bell on her tricycle. There were bells from the ankle bracelet she used to wear when she was a toddler. There was a baby rattle with a metallic tingle her mother used to wave in front of her face. There was her mother's silver necklace that jingled when she grabbed at it with her chubby infant fist.

And the best tingle of all, was the dulcet voice of her mother, as she cooed the loveliest sounds of *Ling, Ling, Ling, Ling* over and over again.

Hey! Dreaming, are you? Leonard's voice brought her right back. We're here. Leonard saw her eyes were red. What's wrong?

As they got out of the taxi and watched it leave, Jesseca leaned into Leonard, put her head on his chest. He drew her close, stroked her head gently.

What's wrong? he murmured.

I'm going to call my father, Jesseca said, lifting her head. Let me check if he's in and you can meet him.

Serious?

Why not. I've seen your house many times. It's time you see mine, Jessica said, as she dialled her father's number. I'm not ashamed of my home.

On the other side of the line, Jesseca's father answered her call.

Chapter 17

I Think I'm Alone Now

It could have been because I saw her naked that she thought there was something wrong with me. Her breasts full frontal, paraded without self-consciousness as she made her way from the bathroom to her single bed while I was lying on my single bed in our twin-bedded hotel room, shocked by the view. She knew I was heterosexual; I behaved like one, I admitted a love of men. But there was a certain immodesty to the way Tiffany showed off her glorious boobs in front of another woman not so well-endowed as her. Cover up! was my first instinctive thought, as my eyes roved to the ceiling in an attempt to unsee what I had seen. Was it envy speaking? Or me being conservative?

The light in our hotel room had dimmed when Tiffany was preparing for bed. She had warned me before the trip that she slept naked. Whatever, I had told her, dismissing it as a joke. But now, seeing her in the flesh, her caution was certainly substantiated. How should one react? This was a first for me. I didn't know whether to pretend not to look or to look and pretend I couldn't care less.

At least she had a thong on. A thin slip of a G-string thong that revealed the moons of her fulsome butt. It was a visual spectacle overload.

Instead of stating the obvious, I prattled along with some late-night small talk.

About that project you were talking about the other day, I blurted in as steady a voice I could muster, I'd like to do it.

I picked a random topic just to distract my mind, focus on the practical, monetary concerns.

You're still thinking about that? Tiffany responded while slathering lotion on her exposed skin, which was her entire body, really. The scent of freesia teased my nostrils, making me want to sneeze. Marks & Spencer—I recognized the make of her moisturizer.

Sure. Extra income, who wouldn't want it?

Tiffany was settling into bed, pulling her duvet over her till it stopped at her waist. She put out an arm, rested an elbow on the pillow. Her breasts stared blankly at me like the black eyes of an alert lioness. My own eyes panned away from her and landed on a blank wall as I continued to converse. I didn't know who was ruder here.

You're fine with the amount I suggested? she asked breezily.

It's alright, I answered in an almost detached tone then decided that now was a good time to renegotiate, since she was exposed in a blatant way and there were only two of us here in the dimmed and darkened room. We were not back home in Singapore. I felt emboldened by the distance of who I was in my own turf and here, as an itinerant in a foreign city. I could pretend to be whoever I wanted to be. Say whatever I wanted to say.

I turned towards Tiffany with purpose, staring straight at her eyes, avoiding any misunderstanding of stealing a peek at her twinned mangoes.

I'd like you to consider raising the rate. I know I'm worth more than that.

How much more?

Tiffany could barely conceal a bemused expression. I couldn't tell whether it was because of my sudden change from the civil niceties I performed on other occasions; or that I was trying not to be intimidated by her brazen nudity. It was odd that someone's nakedness was not necessarily a sign of vulnerability; rather a weapon against decorum, even if it was within the confines of a private space. It was as much her hotel room as it was mine. It was an unspoken rule that roomies, cohabiting the same space with their own ships of rest, had to negotiate their rights over a shared bathroom, study table, chair, mini fridge, cans of Coke, miniature bottles of liquor, kettle, sachets of tea and coffee, and what not. Back home, she might be accustomed to doing whatever the hell she liked, as I was, for we have ownership of our own rooms. Even if technically our rooms were in our parents' homes. But here, we were not in our own homes. This was no man's land.

Double, I said without missing a beat. My heart thumped loud enough for me to feel embarrassed for myself. It was bad enough to corner a friend when she was unprepared, nude and about to retire for the night. It was worse to lie through hustling.

Mmm.

Think about it.

I turned and examined the shadows on the ceiling. They looked eerie. This room was much darker than my room back home; here I caught glimpses of uneven shadows splattered erratically like black blood. I tried not to think about stories of hauntings in hotels from the oft-repeated urban legends always retold by some friend of a friend. Floating heads and nightmarish visitations. Strange noises in stilled and solitary rooms. Tiffany with her long black hair reminded me of a spurned Pontianak. I said nothing of my paranoia. She yawned, I'm very tired. Long day today, all that shopping and running around.

You know, I have an idea about who can write the articles, I said, trying to keep the momentum going, Susanna would be great for that beer story. Also Ricky emailed me the other day and told me he lived in Italy for four years, so he can write a three-page spread about it. We will need to get a few more freelancers, maybe a few of them from my ex-company. You know Mina Teo? Sharifah from the lifestyle magazine? Viknesh has a lot of contacts for the food section. He can write, he can farm out the assignments, and he shoots occasionally. Very useful. He can give us the text and the pictures, no problem. Funny guy, witty writing.

Mmm.

You need to tell me when the models can shoot. And where? Have you chosen the models yet? Or do I need to do this too? How tight is our budget? Also, since I will be running from place to place, will you provide a transport allowance? Entertainment expenses? Petty cash? The layout and design of the issue, who will be doing it? Shall I find a graphic designer, or have you got someone in mind? If you don't mind, since I like to write, can I also write certain articles? Like the interview of the CEO of the spa resort, I can cover that. I have the exact idea on how to angle that story.

I'm going to sleep, Tiffany murmured. Her eyes were closed. Her arms huddled around her nakedness like a shield from the cold air-conditioning. Or from me.

Okay, let's talk tomorrow then. I'm really excited about how to make this travel edition as snazzy as possible. I've got so many ideas. I'm so psyched up.

Goodnight.

The door of opportunity was closing. I stopped pitching and covered myself up to my neck with the soft, warm duvet. I forgot about the day's travelling madness, about the editorial project Tiffany had commissioned me to do, about my life back home writing regurgitated news about the newest property launches, the success of the highest earning realtors, the trends of buying or selling property, and other news nuggets I have had to distil from copious research. Journalism was a top-down hierarchy where the reporter, at the lowest rung of the editorial staff, was forever aspiring to the editor's seat, or even better, the managing editor's post. I forgot about my life an ocean away as said reporter, being trusted with a full-fledged magazine to helm as editor for a few months while earning some extra cash. Like a dream come true.

By the time I had finished up my thoughts, and before I could say goodnight to Tiffany, she had let out a genteel, feminine snore so delicate it could have been a ghost clearing its throat.

* * *

When Tiffany woke up the next day, she was in a foul mood. She scowled, skulking around the carpeted floor in her heels saying nothing to me. I woke up later than her, but it being a rest-and-relax day, I didn't think waking up at 9 a.m. was a big deal.

Half an hour of avoiding any conversation with me—I had asked her if I could use the bathroom, the hairdryer, the kettle to boil water, turn on the TV, to which she merely grunted indifference— she finally blurted, Let's go!

I wasn't fully dressed yet. I had just made a weak greyish English breakfast tea and hadn't touched it yet.

Now? was my rather annoyed response.

Yes, she commanded.

She was fully covered, in skinny jeans and a black blouse with cap sleeves, while the neckline plunged two buttons below where she was supposed to have kept them closed. Her glory was unexposed, while a valley of a shadow hinted at them. Each time she moved, her blouse revealed while concealing some cleavage. I had enough of seeing her exposed. She sounded like she'd had enough of me.

The girls are waiting downstairs, Tiffany relayed the information without looking at me and strutted her heeled feet out of the door. I heard the click of the door clutch. Something inside me clicked too.

It was then I realized why she had such contempt for me. Why she had commissioned me for a project at a rate that no other 'real' professional editor would accept.

I wasn't good enough in her opinion. I was not her equal.

I made my way down to the hotel lobby where I was greeted by the rest of our entourage: two other travelling Singaporean ladies, Darlene and Yen. They were fresh, perky, excited about today's exploring. Tiffany had on a pair of enormous black sunglasses that were so large half her cheeks were covered, as were her eyebrows, with her lips painted scarlet. No smiles, no small talk. As the three of us made plans for breakfast, Tiffany disappeared behind her mask like a trailing spectre following us, a noir femme fatale, with her own devious agenda.

It was my first time in Bangkok. Yesterday had been an eye-opening gastronomic experience. Gastronomic, not culinary, for as we sat dining on a gorgeous spread of green and red curries, pineapple rice, tom yum goong, mango salad, basil stir-fried chicken, pandan wrapped chicken and skewers of moo ping, my gut was so overwhelmed with the incursion of foreign ingredients, jam-packed most notably with killer Thai chillis, that I had to visit the bathroom in the restaurant twice in the midst of lunch, my intestines overwrought and overcome before I had even finished my meal.

Today being the second day, I wanted to give my stomach a rest. I had no idea what the Thais ate for breakfast. Surely it couldn't be curries?

On the advice of the concierge, we headed to Pratunam where we saw food stall after stall along the thoroughfare peddling noodles of the soup and dry variation. There was plenty to choose from. I was hungry, didn't care what I picked. I didn't spend a lot of time discriminating against food, as was my usual practice.

Tiffany dragged Darlene wordlessly to a stall selling pad thai. Yen followed me, not wanting to be left alone in a crowded marketplace where she didn't speak the language of the locals. I didn't either, though I was always the more resourceful and confident of the two of us. Yen, being a rookie reporter, having just joined the company five months ago after graduation, was a natural unquestioning follower—acquiescent and cooperative.

Porridge! I quipped, pointing to a stall where a few women and a child had parked themselves, slurping on spoons of steaming bowls of congee.

This was a surprise to me. I hadn't expected the Chinese influence to infiltrate daily Thai cuisine, the result of diaspora, the migration of the Chinese, especially from southeast China. I heard a spattering of Chinese dialects, one of which I was familiar with, Teochew, the language of my father. At once, I felt less alone, connected to biological lineage and the kind of breakfast I was familiar with. Porridge is comfort soup; a detoxicant. The Teochews believe it is responsible for the clear and beautiful complexion of their women.

As my ears followed the voices, I spotted two other stalls selling congee metres away. The one I had picked seemed to have a larger crowd, bigger buzz. I followed my Singaporean foodie instinct: where there is a queue, the food is likely to be better.

The queue was less painful than I thought. We were able to make our orders in ten minutes, and as Yen and I settled ourselves on a rickety wooden bench with a square table that didn't leave any room for our elbows to rest, I saw Tiffany and Darlene in the distance.

Tiffany's sunglasses were atop her head, holding up her fringe like a hairband. She looked relaxed and chatty. Something Darlene said made her laugh uproariously. Yen followed the direction of my gaze.

Are they finished? Yen asked.

How am I supposed to know? I answered, rankled by a general vibe I had no idea where it emanated from.

I hope they don't go off without us. Later we can't find them.

Good, I responded vehemently.

What happened yesterday?

The remark surprised me. I hadn't anticipated that Yen would be so sensitive to the change in dynamics of the group.

What do you mean? I answered the question with another question. Now, I was the one who felt naked.

I noticed Tiffany was behaving strangely towards you this morning.

Was she? I pretended to be surprised.

You two shared a room. You didn't notice?

She was fine last night.

And this morning? Was she behaving normally?

Yen's investigative journalism was coming to the fore. She grilled me the way she grilled her subjects. I was beginning to have a newfound respect for this pipsqueak.

Fine, I guess, I lied as my heart thrummed aloud.

At moments like these, and many other times in my life when I had to utter a half-truth, or a half-lie, I knew my heart would expose me. If I had been given a lie detector, I would fail miserably, not being able to synch my physiological response to my psychological machinery. What my mind wanted my heart couldn't give. Much of the success of Edgar Allan Poe's short story 'The Tell-Tale Heart' was attributed not only to the horror of the narrative as the lure of the grotesque speaks to many readers' fear of the unknown, but also to the most human psychology of guilt.

The congee had arrived. I buried my face in the hot steam, my enlarged facial pores opened wider, and my mouth held a spoonful of hot congee that smarted my tongue with the first scoop. In that instant, I deliberated whether I should swallow or spit, either option being unpalatable. The former would send a stream of hot gunk all the way down my throat, burning like volcanic lava all the way into my gut. The latter was disgusting to look at, no matter where the expulsion ended up.

Yen waited for her congee to cool down. She was in no hurry.

You know what she said this morning?

This was a teaser for something I wasn't sure I wanted to hear. Yen knew how to build a suspenseful narrative. Darlene once mentioned Yen had won first prize in her school's writing competition. There was, indeed, merit to this apparently meek meerkat.

No, what? I said impatiently. I opened my mouth wide and huffed, trying to blow the steam out of the congee in my mouth. I had decided to swallow. I was that hungry.

Yen scooped her first spoonful of congee slowly, barely skimming the surface of her breakfast. That way, she got the most exposed part of the congee that had the widest area, likely to be more cooled than the rest beneath the surface, which was a cauldron of fire. Rice grains burning in watery hell, that was how I would describe them.

She tasted the congee at the tip of her plastic spoon. Satisfied, she slurped slowly, bit by bit, till the pond of porridge was ingested with no problem.

What? I repeated, getting increasingly irritated. I could see in the distance; Tiffany checking her handphone with Darlene doing the same. Darlene saw us and waved. Yen waved back. I nudged my head to acknowledge her.

She said . . . Yen drawled, that you are weird.

I nearly choked on my third and very hot spoonful. The rice grains rushed down my larynx like a free-falling silk aerial acrobat.

I'm weird?!? I half-yelled. *She* is weird!

Why would you say that? Yen said. Her face was pretentiously sagacious. This girl, five years younger than me, was now trying to be full of wisdom.

She sleeps naked!

Does she? Did you know that or did you see it?

I couldn't *not* see it if I wanted to. She just shows off her boobs like she's on her own nudist beach. My god! I sputtered, finally able to let off steam. The words were coming out faster than I could censor or edit them.

So, what's the problem? Did you like seeing them?

My spoon dropped into the bowl and some congee splashed out. I was stumped. What was Yen trying to get at? Was she messing with me?

I don't understand what you are talking about, I said and stared at her, anger rising. From a low murmuring thrum, my heart was now furiously trying to beat itself out of its caged room.

Maybe she felt uncomfortable with you looking at her.

I wasn't looking at her! Not in that way, if you know what I mean. Besides, when two people share a space, each person has to honour the other person's presence. Don't you think? I rebutted.

Darlene and I didn't have a problem, Yen said blithely.

I could see Darlene and Tiffany standing up from their seats. They were headed towards us.

What makes you think we had a problem?

Tiffany said she felt uneasy around you.

So now I'm the weird one? I hissed. The two other girls were metres away. Yen was halfway through her porridge. I was almost done with mine. During this short dialogue, I attacked my bowl with a ferocious appetite. I was mad, spurred by the convoluted contrivance of matters beyond my control.

She can go fuck herself, I spat out the words vehemently. There was only so much heat I could swallow. I couldn't control what lay dormant inside me. This mountain of myself, with its complex matrix of riverine nerves and cells that formed this beastly personality, this oft-misunderstood creature, so solitary yet so maligned.

They had reached us, our travelling companions. I could smell fish sauce from their clothes and hair. Two mermaids out of their depths, looking to lure unsuspecting sailors to their doom. I could feel the MSG in my congee working its way to my brain. I felt heady.

How's your food? Darlene said cheerfully.

Tiffany put her sunglasses back on, masking her eyes. Her expression was stolidly blank, a shopfront mannequin with a resting bitch face. She finally spoke.

I'm going to look at some bags. That shop over there. See you there.

She careened off with Darlene trotting along in tow, like the faithful mare to its rider.

Yen was almost done with her bowl.

Want to follow them? I could buy a bag too. They're so expensive in Singapore, the leather ones, Yen said.

I agreed reluctantly, not knowing what else to do or where to go. Bangkok was a shopping paradise, and that was what these girls were here to do. That, and food bingeing.

The shop was situated in a row of shop houses that sold designer apparel, handbags, costume jewellery, wigs and eclectic merchandise to attract the deep pockets of tourists such as us. Everything shone with bling, glimmering from the reflected morning sun. Like a school of herded rodents, the chattering crowd filled one shop after another, attracted by the shiny baubles on display.

Tiffany was holding on to two leather bags. They looked plush, exquisitely stitched, one red as her Chanel lip colour, the other one black, studded with metallic spikes. She saw me and suddenly broke into a smile, as if her spell from last night had broken and she would magnanimously forgive me for whatever it was I had done.

Nice? she asked me.

Our two travelling companions were examining purses in a corner. I lingered around the shoes section, disinterested in the merchandise. I responded to her question with a shrug.

Super cheap, Tiffany said. You can't even tell they're not real.

In my mind, I thought, I can't even tell if *you* are real. She shoved a hobo bag in my hands. It was a weathered tan. This suits you, she offered, a girlish, cheeky laugh escaped her lips.

I was distracted by how bright red her choice of bag was. It even matched her rouged lips and looked like a knockoff of something very posh. Which brought to mind the movie *The Devil Wears Prada*. Tiffany certainly fit the bill of the wicked.

I scanned the merchandise nearest to me and spotted a duffle bag in crocodile leather, immaculately crafted and textured with undulating ridges, dyed in a stylish gun-metal grey. I shoved it into her arms. You'll like this, I said.

Her face instantly lit up with glee. The slow curl of her lips turned into a grin. I love it! she enthused, returning the red bag to the salesgirl then turned to me and said, You do know this is real leather?

Is it? I was surprised. I didn't know. I only knew the brand from the logo and the bag design was modelled exactly like that of a couture product in a magazine. But there was no capacity in me to determine or differentiate the skins of something authentic from imitative.

Sexy, I've always loved crocodile, Tiffany cooed. At that, there was a look of something appreciative in Tiffany's eyes. Under the gleaming crystal lamp and surrounded by golden damask wallpaper, I thought I saw a softening of her demeanour towards me—this person who had earlier dismissed me and branded me a freak among friends. In this clique, I was the one who didn't click.

It could have been clumpy mascara that made Tiffany rub her eyes as she was queuing up at the cashier. A line had formed, and she was midway through. She fiddled with her lashes, blinked her eyes repeatedly. Darlene and Yen were still picking their purses, calculating exchange rates. I watched them all, wondering why I felt so tired suddenly. Going home felt like an attractive option. But I wasn't a cab or bus ride away from the familiar. There would be a vast ocean to cross, aboard an aerodynamic vehicle piloted by strange men with foreign accents who would deliver me safely all the way

from the Thai monarchy to my island state. I was the baggage the
airline industry couldn't afford to lose. Human cargo numbered like
all the rest; a homogenous statistic so normative it was preferred I
didn't stand out.

Tiffany kept on rubbing her eyes till they were bloodshot and
teary. She gestured towards me. I went to her.

Do you have a tissue? she asked.

I looked at her eyes, which seemed to burn as angry red as my
annoyance with this entire, wasted trip. Did the others feel the same
way? Or was I blowing things out of proportion? I would never know.

Leaning forward, I caught sight of Tiffany hugging the leather
bag she was about to purchase. Her infected eye glistened. I smiled,
in spite of myself.

Crocodile tears huh? I couldn't help saying.

Tiffany had a puzzled look, What?

No, I have no tissue, I answered and walked away, calling out to
Yen, I'll see you back at the hotel.

Following cues from the local crowd, who were hailing cabs
from a side street filled with taxis, I caught one and gave the driver
the name of my hotel.

Once back in my room, I boiled some water, fished out the
chamomile tea sachet I had brought along from home, dunked
it in the hot water and let the soothing scent linger up my nose.
I propped up some pillows on my bed, grabbed two from Tiffany's
bed and made a nest of duck-feathered pillows where I lay inert for
hours, watching television and surfing channels one after another till
my eyes hurt and it was time for a late lunch.

I forgot about being the ugly duckling in the group. I forgot
about the lemming crowd of the marketplace. In here, by myself,
I enjoyed the privacy of my own fully clothed presence, swallowing
no one's insults or suggestive innuendos of what could possibly be
wrong with me.

Previously Published

'The Elephantine Apple' was originally published in *Quarterly Literary Review of Singapore* (Oct 2014)

'Says the Bells of the Clement' was originally published in *The Brooklyn Rail* (2016)

'The Cuckoo Conundrum' was originally published in *The Cuckoo Conundrum* as part of the NAC-NTU Writer-in-Residence box set series by Ethos Books (2016)

'Fresh Blood' was originally published in *The Brooklyn Rail* (2018)

'Underneath the Ruins' was originally published in *The Brooklyn Rail* (2018)

Acknowledgements

I am indebted to Nora Nazerene Abu Bakar for giving these stories a home, each of them having lived and breathed and been frozen by time, where fiction and nonfiction become indistinguishable. I also wish to thank Thatchaayanie Renganathan for her eagle-eyed editing; Kenny Leck for giving me that pivotal push to my literary legacy; my late Pa and Mommy for giving me the freedom to write and imagine; the generosity of Junot, Sebastian and Felix for their words; and most of all, my family—*kisses to I and K!*—who grounds me and gives me wings with their unconditional love.